Crash

By

Stacey Brandon

&

Karen Bell

Crash

Book One in The Crash Series

Cover Designer/Photography
Stacey Brandon Photography

Editing
Donnie Bell

Design and Formatting
Tyler Bell

Copyright © 2015
by
Stacey L. Brandon and Karen L. Bell

All rights reserved.

First Printing, 2015

ISBN 978-0-9967928-0-6

www.BrandonBellAuthors.com

First Edition

Dedications

This book is dedicated to our husbands, Calvin and Donnie. They love us, believe in us, and want us to succeed... mostly in hopes that we earn enough to buy them new boats. We dedicate this to our children: Shawn & Tyler and Kayla, Steven, & Hannah. Being Moms taught us to take the good with the bad and enjoy every minute. Finally, we dedicate this to our "book girls." Without the encouragement, laughter, and endless beta reads... this would never have happened. We love you Amber, DeAnna & Carol.

Contents

Chapter One: Charli
What's With The Shoes?

"Get your ass in gear, Charli. You've got drinks up for two tables."

"I got it. And, quit looking at my ass," I throw back flippantly. Ronan may be my boss, and the head bartender at The Crash but his barked orders don't bother me in the slightest.

"I've got no use for a smart-mouthed girl that's half my age," he responds gruffly, before shaking his head and turning away. Rubbing an imaginary spot on the bar with enough force to remove the varnish, I suspect it's to hide his amusement. Aware that I'm not intimidated by his demanding tone, he loves to give me a hard time. However, he doesn't love it when I pretend to hit on him since he thinks of his staff as family... but it's so hard to resist.

"You know you love me," I insist, with a smile.

"I know I love to see my employees doing their job," he responds.

Ronan is an ex-marine who's forgotten he's retired. Sometimes working for him makes me feel like I'm going through basic training. Initially, the stern commands and rigid posture had panicked me, but after working at his bar for almost a year, I've got him pegged. He's a total marshmallow.

Holding my heavy tray high, I wind my way through the maze of tables with precision. My orders are always correct and delivered swiftly, and I can't remember the last time I spilled a drop. A job well done is important to me and I believe in giving everything one hundred percent.

I deposit the chilled bottles onto the round table in front of two women who are completely absorbed in their own conversation. Shifting my weight from one foot to the other, I clear my throat. I get nothing and think I might as well be invisible. Deciding to bail and check back later, I see Liv near the bar and go to join her.

"Okay, take a guess," Liv says when I reach her side. As best friends, roommates, and fellow waitresses, we can pick up a conversation at any point and completely understand each other.

"This one is easy," I reply confidently while looking back at the table I just left. "The brunette's face is puffy and her eyes are red. She's also shredding her napkin like it deserves the death penalty. I'd bet good money she's been dumped."

Liv and I might get a paycheck for waitressing, but our favorite thing to pass the time at work is making assumptions about our customers. I've been accused on multiple occasions of having an overactive imagination, so I sometimes have a hard time reigning myself in. It's not unusual for me to become convinced a bar patron is actually an international spy or a hired assassin. These suspicions have never been confirmed, but I hold out hope.

"You're probably right," she concedes, pretending to straighten the napkins on her tray in order to steal a quick peek at the table in question.

"Of course I am. What about you? Anything good tonight?"

"Not really. Just a few regulars mostly."

"What about them?" I nod my head in the direction of one of her tables. Two young guys, barely out of their teens, are slamming back beers and brazenly scoping out every female in their vicinity.

"Tweedle Dickhead and Tweedle Dumbass?" she asks. "They are barely twenty-one and if the freckled one doesn't quit staring at my tits, I'm going to put him in timeout and call his Mommy."

"Liv, we're only a couple years older than they are," I remind her.

"Age is irrelevant. They act like toddlers, so they deserve to be treated like toddlers."

I notice the freckled one she mentioned is now making obscene hand gestures behind the back one of the other waitresses. "You may have a point."

"Hey, I think the dumped girl is trying to get your attention," Liv tells me while tipping her head in the direction of my table.

"Okay. I better go check."

Making my way back to them, I catch the tail end of their conversation and it takes everything I have to keep from laughing. I literally have to cough to cover the suspicious noise that does manage to escape. The allegedly dumped girl is telling her friend, "He was a total douche canoe anyway."

Douche canoe? Did she really just refer to someone as a douche canoe? I'll have to remember to share this one with Liv. Having her as a best friend means I've learned to appreciate the humor found in a variety of profanities.

Between their colorful descriptions of the douche canoe's underwhelming "package" and a detailed account of his poor

3

bedroom skills, I throw in, "Can I get you anything else?"

"Can we settle our tab now?" the friend asks, finally realizing I'm standing there.

"Of course."

"Thanks, you've been great." She looks up at me and smiles.

Pleasantly surprised by her appreciation, I briefly pause my removal of their empty glasses to smile back. "You're very welcome," I tell her. Most people are pretty decent, but it's rare to receive thanks from the ones in the midst of a personal drama.

Moving away to check on my next table, my attention is drawn to a new group that's just entered the bar. Three men and two women, all very attractive and in business attire that screams they are several pay grades above most people I know, are heading my way. I paste on my most accommodating smile and meet them as they take their seats at table four.

Slipping my hand into my apron's pocket to grab my order pad and pencil, I look to the guy closest to me. "Hello. Welcome to The Crash. What can I get for you this evening?"

"What do you recommend?" He asks, with an overconfident smirk and a raised eyebrow.

He's slender with an athletic build and meticulously styled, dark blonde hair. His words are polite, but the tone is setting off my warning alarms. I'm getting the impression he is that particular breed of man that thinks a woman is lucky if she gets his attention.

"We have some great IPA's? Or would you prefer a cocktail or wine?"

"Beer is fine. You pick for me." He leans back in his chair slightly and takes a long, lazy look at me. "You look like you know what you're doing."

My night is shaping up to be a disaster. This guy appears to be settling in for a nice long stay and as much as I like my job, quitting time can't come soon enough. I don't mind guys that flirt and confidence is sexy, but he oozes arrogance. I've had a few too many experiences with guys that think too highly of themselves and it's hard to remain polite when hit with a barrage of innuendos all evening.

"The lady's choice okay for everyone else?" he asks his companions, without taking his eyes off me. The two other guys nod in agreement.

"I'm not drinking beer," says one of the two women. She has a platinum blonde bob that barely grazes her angular jawline and a body that could model swimsuits though she's wearing a conservative, designer outfit. "I'll have a Martini." Her order sounds like a command.

"Same," adds the brunette next to her.

"Got it," I say as I force myself to smile. I know my job well and experience has proven time and again that smiles increase tips. On a side note, so does red lipstick for some reason. It's a universally acknowledged mystery among waitresses. Liv is happy to apply her "Cherries in the Snow" or "Wicked Scarlett", but I'm more reluctant, being a neutral lip balm kind of girl.

Turning to walk away, my progress is halted by the light pressure of a hand on my forearm. I tense slightly. Not a fan of my customers invading my personal space, I clench my teeth to remain calm. It's no surprise to discover the owner of the hand is the self-appointed spokesperson with the belief he is someone important.

"Yes?" I ask, not bothering with the smile anymore.

"I was just wondering..." He pauses, leans far too close to my chest and pretends he is studying my nametag. When he raises both eyebrows in mock surprise, it's obvious he is putting on a show. "Charli? Your name is Charli?"

I look pointedly at his hand and then back at his face, but he chooses to ignore my hint. He keeps his hand resting right below my elbow as he smiles predatorily. This guy is definitely playing with me, and when he tosses back his blonde hair with a practiced flick of his head, I snort. *What an attention whore!*

"Yes, that's right. I'm Charli," I answer with deliberate slowness. "Can I get you anything else or answer any more questions?"

Hearing my saccharin sweetness, he narrows his eyes in challenge. "It's so nice to meet you, Charli. I'm Matt."

We stare silently at each other for several more heartbeats. He finally relents and removes his hand, but I doubt he's done with me quite yet. Crossing his arms over his chest and tilting his head to one side, he inspects me from the top of my ponytail to the soles of my shoes. I feel like I went through the full-body scan at the airport.

"Are you even old enough to work here, Charli?" he asks. At this point, his gaze has stopped its roaming and is fixed on my shoes. His two female companions laugh as though he's being ridiculously funny. I hate it when women play up to a man's ego.

I think back to the conversation at my previous table and their assurances that the ex-boyfriend was a douche canoe. It seems a fitting name for this guy too.

"Matt, just leave her alone," the man seated directly across from where Matt and I are locked in our battle of wills, whispers loudly. "Let her do her job."

This guy might honestly be trying to help me out, but I'm doubtful. He's probably as bad as his friend Matt. What sounds like taking my side could actually be a ploy to get me moving along so I can hustle back with his drink.

I take a minute to look at him a little closer. I'd been so distracted by Matt's grab for attention that I hadn't really given him much notice… but I'm noticing now. His thick hair is a warm golden brown interspersed with strands of honey. Deeply tanned skin, without a hint of that Oompa Loompa orange that accompanies spray tans, suggests a good amount of time outdoors and contrasts dramatically with the idea of an office-bound job. He is also broad across his shoulders and torso, but slim through his waist and hips and I'm convinced there is a drool worthy body under that expensive suit. After looking him over quite thoroughly, we lock eyes. Deep mossy green and gold-flecked with the hint of laugh lines at the outer corners, his eyes are beautiful. I can't look away.

"See something you like?" Matt asks, breaking the spell. He's smiling but not hiding his aggravation. "Would you like an introduction? This is my friend Logan." Matt isn't happy about losing my attention and I decide my best option is to act as though I didn't hear him.

"Do you need anything else?" I'm trying to regain control of the situation.

"No, we're good. Thanks," Matt's friend, Logan, assures me with a mischievous smile that hints he noticed my stalker stare too. *Great. He probably thinks I'm hot for him. Am I?* I'm scared to answer, even to myself.

"Oh, okay," I say directly to Logan, trying hard not to get caught up in his eyes again. "I'll just go get those…ummm…drinks."

"Not so fast," Matt says. "You still haven't answered my question. I need to make sure you're old enough for…well, we'll just say, old *enough*."

"Matt…" The warning in Logan's voice is clear.

Tired of being excluding from the conversation, the blonde woman takes this opportunity to back Matt. "Well for fuck's sake

Logan, look at her. Matt's question is legitimate. She no bigger than my kid sister and dresses like a teenage boy."

Oh, hell no.

She might look like a guy's wet dream and wearing an outfit that cost a month of my income, but I'm not intimidated. I've been down that dark path before and learned that I like who I am and to hell with anyone that sees me as less. Never again will I waste my time with someone that believes certain people are more deserving than others.

"Well, we don't all have to make an appointment with a needle to look youthful, Botox Barbie." I smile wickedly when her glossy lips pinch in fury. She starts to stand but Logan stops her by placing his hand gently on her shoulder. She calms immediately and it causes me to wonder about their relationship. Her chair is pushed close to his and her body is leaned so far in his direction they're practically one silhouette. My best course of action becomes perfectly clear.

I turn slightly to look directly at the green eyed, incredibly hot Logan and flash him my best, dimpled smile. To finish her off, I wink at him. His returning smile is instant and the blonde bitch's mouth falls open. It's the least attractive I've seen her. My pride in her reaction is childish and petty, but I'm not going to lose any sleep over it.

Mission accomplished, I pivot and saunter back to the bar with enough swing in my backyard to set my ponytail bobbing with each step. I can hear the appreciative laughter from the guys and imagine the bitch's sneer, but no way in hell am I turning around to confirm it. I know how to play the game too.

Liv catches up with me back at the bar as I slam my tray down with enough force to cause the empties to rattle.

"I'm guessing that table four pissed you off?"

"You mean, the douche canoes?"

"Douche canoes? Well, that's a new one."

"Yeah, I picked it up from the dumped girl's table. What do you think? Should we add it to the list?" I ask.

She takes the time to seriously contemplate its worthiness. "It works for me. I can see its usefulness in our lives." She nods her head in approval and continues, "Now, tell me what they did to ruin your evening."

"Nothing too heinous, I suppose... but enough that I may have showed my ass a little bit," I answer.

"You're usually pretty good at letting things roll off of you."

"I know, but they figured out which buttons to push."

"Which buttons exactly?" Liv asks.

"The arrogant prick with the floppy hair is giving me shit about looking too young as if I *never* hear that one. The lumberjack has no patience and just wants me to hurry up and get his drink. You know his type, if we're waiting on them then they think they own us. And then to top it off, the blonde goddess of perfection thinks that by comparing me to a young boy she'll impress her friends, especially the aforementioned lumberjack."

"Lumberjack?" Liv looks over at the table in confusion, then dawning awareness slides over her face and she starts laughing.

"Charli, are you picturing that hot guy in flannel and hiking boots instead of a suit and tie? You are so messed up. Why do you always do this?"

Damn, I've been so busy complaining, I didn't even notice my slip. "I'll admit it, I pictured him in a nice plaid shirt with jeans... maybe even with a nicely trimmed beard?" Liv is right about how often I do this. It's my "go to" fantasy. Maybe my past mistakes with a certain man I'd rather not think about has made me leery of men that are a little too polished. I'll take rugged and casual from here on out.

"You have serious issues," Liv tells me with a grin.

"Really? I have issues? Who gets off to fantasizing about Thor or Captain America?"

She smirks, "Thor AND Captain America actually. I could totally handle them both."

God, I love her. She's probably the only person more twisted than I am.

"Well, if I can get you to move on from your ménage a trois plans... I really wish you had this table, Liv. You're gorgeous and the minute Logan saw you, the blonde wouldn't have a chance."

One perfect, auburn eyebrow arches and I know I'm done for. I've said something else to pique her curiosity. "So you know your fantasy lumberjack's name? Interesting."

Shit. What is wrong with me tonight? "Don't change the subject," I demand with an embarrassed scowl. Again, she laughs at my expense but I'm generous and don't hold it against her. It's not like I'd have reacted any differently if our roles were reversed.

Leaning in close, she whispers into my ear while keeping her eyes locked on table four. "I think you underestimate yourself, Charli. Your hot lumberjack Logan can't keep his eyes off of you. I actually noticed him watching you the whole way over here and I don't think he's looked away since. Maybe you should give him a go. He's fucking hot."

I scoff at her suggestion. "He probably thinks I'm an easy lay. Isn't that what guys think of waitresses in bars that wink at them?"

"Stop that shit. Every hot guy in a business suit isn't going to be like Nick."

"I'm not talking about Nick!" I shut her down quickly. She knows better than drag up my past. Nick is ancient history and

I'm done with him. At least she has the decency to look remorseful.

"Any problems, Charli?" Ronan asks, once I leave Liv's side and come over to pick up my drink orders. I know he's trying to keep the question light but must have noticed my tension.

"Nope. I'm all good, handsome."

"Cut that out," he barks, with a menacing scowl and amused twinkle in his eyes.

"When are you going to marry me, Ronan?" I lay it on thick and even bat my eyelashes a little for good measure.

"You're not much older than my daughter."

"That doesn't stop most men," I counter.

Finishing off the martinis with a couple of olives, he stops and looks directly at me. "I'm not most men. You need to find someone your own age, and some poor guy willing to put up with that attitude." A small smile breaks his stern demeanor. "Good luck."

"I just can't find anyone as great as you. You need to wake up and realize how awesome I am." Ronan really is amazing and if he were a few years younger and didn't feel like my dad, he could be a real contender.

"Speaking of waking up… When are you going to wake up and put poor Kyle out of his misery?" he throws back.

"I don't know what you are talking about." I evade his eyes. "Just give me the drinks. I'm trying to work."

"Uh huh." Looking rather smug, he slides the glasses toward me.

Liv won't let up about Kyle either. Kyle's been helping Ronan out with the bartending at The Crash since before Liv and I were hired and I like working with him. He's funny, sweet and major eye candy. Watching the girls that fight over his attention is like

11

getting a free show. For the past several months, he's been letting me know that he's interested in becoming more than just friends. I'm tempted to give in, let him be more to me, but if I take that leap and it fails then I run the risk of losing his friendship. It could also cause a shit storm of problems at work. *Why can't everyone else see that?*

Loading the drinks on my tray and steeling my spine in preparation, I head back into battle. I refuse to let this table get the best of me.

With no hesitancy, I walk right up next to Matt, lay down five paper coasters with the bar's logo, and top them off with the drinks. "Here you go. Would you like me to run a tab?"

"Charli!" Matt grins and I brace myself. "Just the girl I was waiting for. Definitely start us a tab." Lifting his glass to me, he takes a deep drink.

"Okay, just let me know if I can get you anything else." Speaking quickly, I try to make a hasty retreat. I have other tables to deal with and the less time I spend at this one, the better I'll feel.

"What's the rush?" Matt asks before I can escape. "I'd really like to talk to you."

"She's working, Matt. Let her go." The dark haired woman has decided to speak up.

"Thanks, Mari... but surely she can spare a few minutes to talk? I promise I tip well, little Charli. It's all about the tip, right?"

His lascivious smirk turns my stomach. This pretentious shit really thinks he's something. I smile back at him with slightly narrowed eyes. Several replies about what he can do with his "tip" curl across my tongue and I work hard to bite them back.

"So, Charli," Matt starts up again. "We were wondering..."

"Shut the fuck up, Matt," Logan insists, with a hard stare at his friend.

"No. I *need* to know." Matt takes another hit off his drink. "What's with the shoes?"

"The shoes?" This questions derails me and I'm totally confused. It was the last thing I expected to be asked. I look down at my faded black Converse. They're my favorite, beyond comfortable, and way cute in my opinion.

"Yeah. The shoes. A girl named Charli and she wears Chucks. Seeing as how that's the nickname for your name, you can see the humor in it, right?" His question seems to imply perhaps I'm not bright enough to catch on to the correlation.

"Wow, thanks for explaining. It never even occurred to me before," I say with false appreciation. "Thankfully you came along to point out my oblivion to this humorous coincidence. Do you have any other wisdom to share?"

"Oh, I've had about all I can take of her," the blonde woman hisses. "There are plenty of other bars. Let's just leave."

Logan stalls this idea. "We're already here, Victoria, and I happen to like this bar. Besides, we haven't exactly been nice to Chuck anyway, so we kind of deserve her giving us some shit back. Why don't we just play pool. Who's up for a game?"

"What did you call me?" I ask quietly through my clenched teeth.

The table goes silent and then explodes in laughter while I watch Logan's face redden in embarrassment. He is realizing what he's done.

"Oh shit, I'm sorry, Chu... CHARLI! Maybe I've already had a few too many." We both know I just served his first drink and with my job I've seen my fair share of drunks. This guy is totally sober.

"It was an accident. Honest." He looks miserable as he pleads for forgiveness and I try to decide if it's been a sincere mistake or if he thinks the humor of it will diffuse the tension.

Matt, standing up and still laughing, walks over to where Logan is sitting. He pounds him on his back with amusement. "That was priceless, my friend," he proclaims, before turning to the pool tables behind him. "Let's play pool."

I watch as the blonde he called Victoria leans even closer to Logan, trying to reclaim his attention. Abandoning even the pretense of "just friends", she wraps her arms around his thick bicep. She's very determined, but I'm not sure she is very successful. As Liv had said, Logan is looking at me and his friends are starting to notice. They cut their eyes between us speculatively, and one of them clears their throat loudly. Continuing to look at one other, we ignore everyone else.

The sound of a chair being pushed back with extreme force startles me and I break our eye contact. Victoria stands up and places a possessive hand on Logan's shoulder while glaring at me.

"Logan?" she says loudly. I notice her fingers tightening and the fabric of his jacket puckering beneath her grip.

"Huh?" Reluctantly, Logan looks up at her. Smiling down like she isn't completely pissed off, I'm impressed by Victoria's acting skills.

"You wanted to play pool, right? Let's play teams. You can play with me," she tells him and I snicker.

Does she think she's being subtle? She's about as subtle as being hit by a Mack truck. Seizing the opportunity, I use her distraction to escape.

I wonder briefly if I can bribe Liv into covering this table? No, that would make them think they've won. I guess I'm in for the long haul, but I'll be so glad for this night to be over.

Chapter Two: Logan
Chuck... I Mean Charli

What the hell is her deal? I apologized for screwing up her name. She should have understood it was just an accident.

I know Matt can get carried away sometimes, his comments were a little rude, but he was just screwing around. He's not a total dick, but I guess if you don't know him well it can seem that way when he's trying to get someone's attention.

My guess is that he's into this little waitress and he thought his shit would impress her. That had backfired miserably and it just looked childish. I was actually rooting for her until I called her Chuck by mistake and she'd lashed out.

Damn, did she have to get so bent out of shape over something so minor? And why am I stressing over what the waitress thinks of me anyway? It isn't like I'm interested in her. Chuck... shit... I mean, CHARLI... is not my type.

Taking a drink of my beer and turning to look around the bar, I try to sneak a better look at our waitress. Matt is about to take his shot in our pool game, so I have a few minutes. As

Victoria has pointed out, Charli is short in the extreme but no one could call her a child. Thin and small chested, she doesn't have the curves I usually prefer, but her ass is a total work of art. Thick, dark waves of hair, pulled up into a high ponytail, bounce when she flits around between her tables.

Wait, is her hair blue? I swear when her ponytail moves I can see strands of blue and maybe even teal peeking through. *Is that a thing?* It makes me feel old, even though I'm only twenty-six. I've always been into a more classic, sophisticated style but on Charli, the edgy thing works.

When she pissed Victoria off by winking at me, I wasn't able to stop my smile. Thinking about it, makes me smile again. Charli obviously read the situation correctly and it was extremely hard for me not to wink back at her. *Why exactly had I decided this waitress isn't my type?*

"Logan, get your head out of your ass." Looking up, I see Matt waiting expectantly at the edge of the pool table. It's obviously my turn and I wonder how long I've been unaware.

Chalking my pool stick, lining it up, and thoroughly missing what should have been an easy shot, I groan. Matt looks pissed. He loves to win, but I doubt it feels like a victory when I'm just going through the motions.

Flashing me a sneer trying to disguise itself as a smile, Matt looks down at the pool table and shakes his head. He has one remaining stripe before he can go for the eight ball, and my solids are still scattered everywhere. "So... are you thinking about our little Chuck? Surely you don't want a piece of that?"

I'm not fooled. He wants me to back off. Victoria isn't happy about my interest in the waitress either and stiffens, waiting for my response.

"Hell, no. You know me better than that." Frowning, I slam

16

my now empty beer bottle down on our table with a little too much force and watch as Matt sinks his last ball in the corner pocket. There's no point in letting them get the wrong idea about my curiosity in Chuck.

Shit, I mean Charli. I passed the bar exam, remembering this girl's name shouldn't be so damn difficult.

Matt and Victoria share a look of satisfaction. I said exactly what they wanted to hear... but I regret it. I made Matt's suggestion seem ludicrous. Implying Charli is below my standards had been cowardly and it makes me sick. Spending a good portion of my childhood around people that assumed they were better than me because of where they lived or the things they could afford should have taught me better. I hated those assholes for treating me as less and now I'm acting just like them.

Having lost the pool game, I join Victoria and Mari at the table, as Scott gets up to join Matt for the next game. Scott has been pretty quiet, but he's one of my closest friends and I'm sure he will have a few things to say about this evening.

Watching Victoria tell Mari about an incident from the office, I wonder, as I have in the past, why I haven't taken Victoria out. She's beautiful, sophisticated and has an amazing body. For the last several weeks, she has been making it very clear we should team up outside of work and I have no doubt her dedication to a job well done would be to my benefit. I should be jumping at the chance to be with her. Let's face it, I can't even remember the last time I got laid. *That's damn depressing.* My career has consumed me since finishing law school, but maybe it's time I make some changes.

"Don't you agree, Logan?" Both women turn to look at me expectantly and I realize Victoria is asking me something.

Feeling like an idiot and not wanting to admit I'd zoned out again, I nod my head. "Absolutely." *Shit, I hope I didn't just agree to something I'm going to regret.*

Scott joins us, fresh from his victory over Matt. "Victoria, you're up! Ready to lose?"

"I'm not scared of a challenge," she says while looking at me. Slowly leaving her chair, she chooses a stick and steps up to the end of the pool table.

"Now there's a visual worth appreciating." Matt lowers himself into the chair Victoria just vacated and whistles under his breath. He has reminded me often that she's not just incredibly bang-worthy but also a great choice for all the social events required by our firm. "You've worked hard and earned your new position, Logan. I think you deserve a reward. Victoria would make a hell of a reward."

"It's kind of shitty to think of her as a prize earned, Matt."

"Not if she wants to be that prize," he assures me.

"Logan?" Victoria interrupts us. "I can't seem to figure out my best shot. Help me out?" Considering I've never seen anyone more capable when she is determined to have something, I assume she's faking helplessness for my benefit. She can be damn scary when she puts her mind to a new project. *Am I willing to be her new project?*

"Let's see what you've got to work with," I tell her.

"Just for tonight," she warns, "I'll let you be in charge."

I have a feeling that letting me be in charge will last only as long as the pool game. It might be interesting to take her home and surrender some control to her. "Gladly," I agree, with a smile.

Coming up behind her, I lean down to survey the table from her perspective. *Damn, is she pushing her ass back into me?* She's never been shy about her intentions, but I'm guessing our winking waitress had upped the stakes.

After a quick glance, her best shot is obvious, and I move her arms into position while whispering directions to her. She turns her head slightly toward me and my mouth almost grazes her ear. *Okay, maybe Matt has the right idea.*

I press in a little closer to her, enjoying the feeling of her toned curves against the front of my body. Then I make the mistake of looking up from the game and away from the willing woman planted firmly against me. Involuntarily, my eyes are drawn past our game of pool and the table where my friends sit watching me.

Still intimately nestled against Victoria, I find myself the object of Charli's penetrating stare and when she sees me notice her, her smile speaks volumes. Blowing me off with a roll of her eyes and a quick smirk, Charli turns her attention back to the table where she's now delivering drinks.

I jerk away from Victoria like I've been slapped and she raises her eyebrows in hurt confusion. I try to think of something to say, but I don't know how to excuse my involuntary reaction. There is no excuse. *What the hell just happened?* Charli and I aren't even acquaintances and her opinion shouldn't bother me.

When Scott makes a pronounced show of looking between the waitress and I, before asking if I'm okay, I can't find a way to explain what doesn't even make sense to me.

"I'm fine," I mumble as I walk back to our table and grab my beer to cover my embarrassment. I'm pissed when I remember it's empty. My chance with Victoria is probably screwed now and that should be what's really bothering me, but it isn't. *I don't think I even care.*

We continue to play, with Victoria acting like nothing happened, but I can see her aggravation simmering right below the surface. I don't blame her. Everyone takes their cue from her and acts as though I didn't just behave like a complete fucking tool and the effort is appreciated.

A few games later, all of which I lost spectacularly, I finally feel safe enough to try and steal one more glance at Charli. I wish I didn't want to, but I've fought the urge for most of the evening and I need to look at her again. Allowing myself this secret glance gives me a sense of relief that scares the shit out of me.

I just wanted to go out after work, have a few drinks, and forget about all the stress I've been under. Instead, I've been obsessing all night over this tiny little waitress. *Why?* She's admittedly easy on the eyes, but it's more than that. Quirky and different, she stands out in a sea of sameness. Everything about her is a contradiction. She may be tiny, but her energy makes her fill the room. A funky, casual sense of style is paired with a wholesome beauty and I want to stare at her for hours. Her curves may be subtle, but her body rocks and I'd love to get a taste of it. Like it or not, I want her.

Watching her gracefully balance a tray so full of beer bottles, napkins, and liquor filled glasses that it's damn impressive, I acknowledge to myself that she's good at her job. Well, at least the mechanics of her job but maybe her people skills could use a little work.

I need to get her out of my head. "Okay, Scott…let's go again." Grabbing Matt's stick from him after he's lost to Scott again, I make my mind up to quit embarrassing myself.

"You're a loser, dude," he laughs. "You totally suck tonight. We should have put some money on this."

"Don't get used to it. It was a momentary setback. I'm ready now."

"Feeling a little out of it tonight, Logan?" he teases quietly while returning his stick to the rack on the wall.

"I'm good. It was just a shit day at work. I'll take your ass in the next game." I grin at him with confidence I don't feel.

"Well, not tonight," he responds loudly to our group while finishing off the last of his beer. "Kelly was cool with me coming and hanging out for a drink or two, but if I don't show up at home soon and give her a break with the twins, I'll be hiring one of you worthless guys to represent me in divorce court."

"We don't practice family law, but for you..." Matt trails off and tips the neck of his beer bottle in Scott's direction.

"Thanks. I knew I stayed friends with you for a reason. Even when you douchebags decided to go to law school instead of being smart and going into finance like I did..." Scott trails off and Matt and I laugh. It's been a running joke since were in college that he's doing us a big favor by still hanging out with the blood-sucking lawyers.

When push comes to shove, I know Scott and Matt have my back. A lot of people think Matt is an arrogant ass, but I probably wouldn't have my job if he hadn't managed to get me that interview. Scott is fucking brilliant at math and had forfeited numerous hours to ensure I understood Calculus. Now that Scott is married and a father, I love to give him shit about being old and boring, but I might be a little jealous. His wife, Kelly, is great and they seem really happy.

Right now, though, I'd settle for a night of hot sex to break my dry spell.

Victoria stands up and grabs her purse. "Maybe it's time we all move on to a new location anyway?" She's still feeling rejected and it eats at me. I hadn't meant to be cruel.

"I'll get the tab," Matt offers.

"I suggest heading up to the bar to pay it," Scott says. "Charli doesn't seem in any big hurry to come help us out. Not that I blame her. You were kind of a dick, Matt."

"She just needs to get a sense of humor. Waitressing can't be that difficult. She needs to lighten up."

Matt, Scott and the girls head off, so I grab my jacket off the back of my chair and plan on following them, but a sound stops me. *Is that Charli?*

Despite her being several tables away, I hear her laugh. It is deep, throaty and sensuous, and the huskiness jolts me. If I had to imagine Charli's laughter, I would have conjured something light and energetic, or even snarky if the occasion called for it, but not this. This sound evokes passion and carnal images that I'd be best leaving alone when thinking of the waitress. It isn't helping me leave.

Trying to avoid watching her has been impossible. I'm fascinated as she zips around the bar, waits on tables with a smile, and talks to everyone like a little Energizer Bunny. Then she has to go and top it off with this laugh that makes me want to find a secluded spot to become familiar with every inch of her.

I look at the two guys sitting at the table she's now serving. *What had they said to make her lower her chin and laugh so seductively?*

Unable to tear my eyes away, Charli must have sensed my stare, because she glances toward me. When her eyes widen and her lips part slightly, I catch my breath and feel off balance. Tentatively smiling, I hope she realizes I'm not an asshole despite our earlier misunderstanding. But as her eyes dart from me to Victoria and then back again, her scowl convinces me she isn't ready to forgive and forget.

It's a shame she doesn't smile and laugh more. Her dimples are cute. And that laugh is… Okay, I need to let this go. Maybe I've had a few too many and need to get laid. I'm just reacting to the excitement of something unknown.

Knowing it's time I go, I'm still struggling to leave her. I want her, it's that's simple. *What can I do to make her laugh like that again? Is she aware of my interest in her?*

I want to tell her that I don't make a habit of staring at women that are virtual strangers, but there's something that compels me to watch her. *Yeah, that's not creepy at all. You might as well tell her "it puts the lotion in the basket." Keep this up and a restraining order will be in my future.*

My friends and I have made her job harder than it should have been this evening. With Matt's jackass sense of humor and Victoria's jealousy bringing out her bitchy side, I feel ashamed that I also played a part in this clusterfuck. Turning back to the table, I leave a generous tip for her. I don't come from money like my friends. Working hard to put myself through school, I'm now going to have to work harder to pay off the student loans. I understand the shit we have to put up with sometimes to get what we want.

Chapter Three: Charli
Methinks Thou Doth Protest Too Much

"Why me?"

My exaggerated sigh falls heavily on the side of melodrama, but still gets no response. Trying again, I throw an arm up over my face and fall backward onto our lumpy and frayed, but incredibly comfortable couch, right next to Liv.

She chooses to ignore me, as usual. Eyes barely open, she hasn't made a sound since coming out of her room. Never fully functioning until she's had her breakfast, checked her email and looked over the social media updates, she will sit quietly for at least thirty minutes.

Reaching past my prone, pajama-clad body to the small trunk we use as a coffee table, she grabs for her bowl of half eaten cereal.

"I will never understand how you can eat cereal without milk," I tell her. "Even worse, you won't eat the good cereal!" No cartoon characters grace her boxes. She likes cereals aimed toward the uber health conscious hipsters and the geriatric scene.

"Whole Grain," "No GMO's", and "Fiber Rich" are emblazoned across the environmentally friendly packaging. *Gross.*

I'm used to carrying on one-sided conversations when our day begins, so I'm not at all deterred. "I hope those asshats from last night find a new bar to frequent. I'm not up to the challenge of having them as regulars."

"Hmmmm" is all I get from Liv. It's a start.

"And I know Logan thought that just because he's hot he could make fun of my name and impress that Victoria woman." I frown at the memory of the laughter that came at my expense.

Looking toward Liv, I'm surprised to see I now have her full attention. "What?" I ask nervously. This sudden alertness makes me cautious.

Slowly her lack of expression is replaced by a delighted smile. Her first spoken words of the day tumble out in the light, musical manner usually relegated to playground rhymes about "K-I-S-S-I-N-G" in a tree.

"You think he's hot... You like him. You want to fu..."

I cut her off quickly and loudly. "Hell, no! Shut up!" Trying to express my level of disgust and shock at such a suggestion, I have to punch her arm to let her know my denial is serious business.

Her laughter rolls and she has to set the cereal bowl back on the table or risk spilling the flakes everywhere. "Charli," she begins, after catching her breath, "the guy was shit hot. And he totally checked you out. I'm not telling you to stalk him and try to have his babies or anything, but he's very pretty to look at. Normally you would admit this, so what is it about this guy that has you so keyed up that you're babbling non-stop about how awful he is? Methinks, thou doth protest too much."

"Don't throw the Shakespearean quotes at me, Olivia! That's my area of expertise. You aren't the one with a degree in British

Literature." *What's wrong with her? Isn't my best friend supposed to take my side?*

Hotness aside, Logan is a douchebag. Well, maybe not as much as his friend. Matt had been the really awful one. *So why is Logan the one I'm thinking about?*

Still laughing, she stands up, stretches all the way up onto her tiptoes and yawns loudly. Her wake-up ritual complete, she starts to walk off toward her bedroom.

"Hey!" I scold at her departing form. "Aren't you going to put this dirty bowl in the sink at least?" I won't claim to be the neatest person on the planet, but this girl drives me bat shit crazy with her clutter and endless messes.

Swaying her hips in exaggeration, she pretends she doesn't hear me. Then, when she reaches her door, she looks back and smiles sweetly as she shoots me the finger and gently closes the door behind her. Typical. Liv would take a bullet for me, but asking her to clean up anything is an exercise in futility.

Groaning loudly, to hammer home exactly how much I have to put up with in order to be her friend, I pick up the bowl and walk to the small kitchen at the far corner of the room. The single basin sink is in the center of our small "L" shaped counter and is already full, even though it only has a couple of dishes in it. *Damn Liv.*

It takes me only a few minutes to wash and dry the few dishes, but when I try to put them away on the floating shelves above the counter, I can't find my stepstool. "Liv! Did you move my stool again?" I yell in the direction of her room. "You know I can't reach anything in this damn apartment!"

Her muffled voice filters through the door. "Check the studio. I think I used it to clamp up a backdrop yesterday."

Sure enough, the stool is in the large open space Liv uses as her photography studio. Our whole apartment is actually one big open space, except for the two bedrooms and one bathroom that give us the little privacy we need.

Coming out of her bedroom, she's now dressed in white shorts, a black cami top, and a bright yellow cardigan, with her brilliant red hair in a thick braid over one shoulder. Liv looks ready to tackle the day.

"How do you always look so put together?" I ask her. "If I didn't already love you, I'd have to hate you. It isn't fair."

"If you'd let me do your makeup or maybe wear something other than jeans and a T-shirt, you might look as good as I do. Maybe. I'm pretty fucking amazing to behold."

"Nothing will ever give me curves like you have. Even a boob job wouldn't help me achieve what you got naturally."

Crossing her arms and narrowing her eyes, she taps a foot while scolding me. "Stop your whining, hooker. Clothes were made for stick thin bodies like yours."

Using the ponytail holder on my wrist to twist my hair up, I then start straightening up the cushions on the floor, the stacks of photography magazines and the random piles of crap Liv has deposited all over the apartment.

"Have you booked any more photo sessions?" I ask.

She sits down at the desk we made from a vintage door topped with glass and laid across two short wooden filing cabinets. "I just finished editing the images for the Johnson family, and I'm doing an engagement shoot next week, but right now I need to really concentrate on the show."

Liv and I waitress at the The Crash most nights, but we have big dreams. She's been doing photography on the side for the last couple of years and she'd just been offered the chance to exhibit a series of images in a local gallery near the end of the year. This could be her big break. My plans involve writing and publishing a real novel.

"How's the book going? You plan on writing today?" she asks me.

"Yeah, after I clean up your shit and take a shower." She just smiles, knowing I don't really mind the cleaning. I find it kind of relaxing, but I love to harass her about being so messy. *Liv's right, Charli. You have issues.*

Liv swivels her chair around to face me. "So have you written the sex scene yet? It's been so long since you got laid, I'm not sure you can accurately describe it."

"Thanks a lot!" She isn't lying, though. Ever since my monumental mistake with Nick, I've been skittish about relationships and I'm not the type to go for one night stands. "I'm still a few chapters away from my characters doing the deed. I'm sure my memory will suffice."

I've always wanted to be a writer. I've written a lot of short stories and small things for myself, and I've taken several jobs writing for our local paper, but I'm determined to complete this novel and see it in print. Liv likes to tease me, but she's behind me one hundred percent.

"You know, Kyle would be happy to refresh your memory," she teases.

"Ugh...Kyle is my friend, Liv. I love him, but I think making it more would be a mistake."

"He isn't Nick," Liv says, "In fact, he's the exact opposite of Nick."

"No more talking about this!" I demand.

"Fine," she huffs while throwing her arms up in defeat.

"Are we still having dinner with Carol and Dana tomorrow night?" I ask to change the subject. Carol and Dana are Liv's moms, but they've been surrogate parents to me too since I was thirteen, when I lost my own mom and dad.

"Yeah, Mom says we should come over around five to make sure we have time to visit before eating. She knows we have to be on shift by eight. And Momma D said don't forget the bottle of wine. She seems to think that just because we work in a bar, the alcohol is our duty."

"What is Carol cooking?" I straighten the last cushion on the couch and try to act like the answer isn't that important, but Liv knows better.

"Relax, Charli. She knows how you eat so it won't be anything weird. I will never understand how you can eat all the junk food and crap that you do, without being the size of a house."

"Yes, I'm currently having a love affair with Hostess cupcakes and I only have a couple left. Can we stop and pick up another box on our way to your moms' house tomorrow?" I put my hands together in prayer and look toward her with a look of pleading.

"Fine." It sounds like a major concession, but she doesn't really mind.

"Oh, and don't forget, we need to pay Ronan the rent tonight too. He gives us a hell of a deal on this place so we shouldn't be late with the payment." We love our apartment above the bar and I worry that one day Ronan will decide he could get a lot more money for such a cool space.

"Jeez, I feel like I have another mom, Charli. Isn't two enough?"

I laugh, but she's right. She doesn't need me reminding of her of everything. "Okay, sorry!"

I have a great apartment, a great job, I'm following my dreams and I have the best friend anyone could ask for. My life is just about perfect.

Chapter Four: Charli
Winner Takes All

"Hey! Liv? Charli?"

The banging on the apartment door brings both Liv and I out of our rooms simultaneously, but without confusion. Showing up before shift is Kyle's trademark.

"You get it," I command and head back to my room to finish getting dressed.

"Chicken!" Liv whispers, but she grins and she goes to open the door.

Hearing her talking with Kyle in the living room, I pull my hair up into a messy bun and add a quick swipe of lip gloss. It may take Liv hours, but I can be ready to go anywhere in about fifteen minutes. According to her, this skill reinforces her belief I'm practically a dude sometimes.

I think about her accusation when I insisted she answer the door. *Am I really being a chicken where Kyle is concerned?*

Kyle and I are already friends, he's decent and honest, and as if those reasons aren't compelling enough, he's extremely hot.

Liv tells me I'm crazy for not jumping him and she's probably right. I see the girls that come in and check him out constantly. They go up to Kyle's end of the long bar and order their drinks while praying he'll notice them. And when he does flash that killer smile and flirt with them, he knows just the right balance to strike. He makes them feel special without the false hope that it will go farther than a little innuendo and fun. His skill prevents them from feeling rejected. It's a gift.

Have I mentioned that he's hot? Shit hot?

With eyes that look almost black in the dim lighting of the bar and his long, dark hair, he's enough to catch the eye of even the most faithfully committed woman. Then there is that body. Lean, ripped and made for sinful activities, Kyle is a prime example of why women have an obsession with the bad boy. *Why exactly have I been so hell bent on resisting him?*

I bend down next to the bed to grab my Chucks. Seeing them makes me think of last night. They make me think of the green eyed, broad shouldered Logan. *Why? I have a guy in the next room that is gorgeous and he shows me all the time he wants me. Shit. I'm smarter than this.*

I'll probably never see Logan again anyway, so it's a colossal waste of time to dwell on him. Slipping the shoes on, I walk out of my room and up to the man I should be dwelling on.

"Hey, you." I smile at Kyle with real affection, and he responds in kind.

"Up for a game of pool before shift starts?" he asks. I like that he makes it clear he hopes we do, but there isn't any desperation or neediness in the offer.

"Sure. Sounds good to me." I respond, and Liv agrees, even though she isn't the best pool player.

Locking up, we head down the metal stairs outside our apartment door that end in the backroom of the bar. There's another set of stairs on the far side of the hall that leads to an outside entrance, but this one is convenient for getting to work. We're blessed that Ronan trusts us like he does and gives us access to the bar, even when it's closed.

"Hey Kyle, can you flip on the lights while I grab our sticks?" I ask, after pushing open the heavy door that connects the stairwell to the small stockroom.

"Sure thing," he responds.

Entering the main bar, he heads for the switches on the far wall while Liv and I walk assuredly to where the pool tables are located. We can navigate the bar with our eyes closed.

"You two start and I'll play the winner," Liv says as she pulls out a quarter and hands it to me. "Flip to see who breaks."

After several games, Kyle and I have an equal number of wins, but poor Liv hasn't won once. She's used to this inequality in pool, but never lets it bother her since she knows she can kill us in darts. She also excels at archery and at the gun range. She can be a scary bitch when she wants to be and I want her on my side during the zombie apocalypse.

"Okay, this will have to be our last game, and then back to the real world," I sigh. Our jobs are great, as far as jobs go, but this afternoon has been fun and I'm sad to see it end.

"Well, it needs to be the tie-breaker between you and Kyle then," Liv says. "Winner takes all."

I laugh. "Takes all of what? We don't bet, Liv."

A mischievous glint enters Kyle's eyes as he looks at me. Sitting on the edge of the pool table, playing with the frayed edge of his black T-shirt, I can tell he's about to propose a wager. "Okay, let's say... If I win, you have to get my name tattooed on your ass." He grins and knows that making a crazy demand to start with will give him bargaining power for something less outrageous.

"Absolutely," I declare with a completely serious face. His instant shock is genuine, but then the skepticism takes over.

"Really?" he asks hesitantly.

Managing to keep a straight face during my offer isn't easy. "But, only if you agree that when you lose, you have to spend a girls' day with Liv and me that will include a facial, a mani/pedi, and a massage. And shopping. Lots and lots of shopping."

"Fuck no," he says slowly and emphatically, but with a huge grin. Liv and I crack up with laughter. I hadn't held out any hope of him agreeing.

"How about the loser buys lunch next weekend?" I offer up. I can tell he likes this idea a lot more. And when he saunters closer to me, in that way he has that makes every female in a ten-mile radius confirm her belief in a benevolent God, he's now so close I stop breathing. Smiling lazily, he thrusts his hand forward to seal the deal.

"Agreed."

And when I beat him, he doesn't even look disappointed.

Chapter Five: Charli
The Crash

I can't believe it. I cannot fucking believe it. He's back. I've never seen him at the bar before last night, but here he is again less than twenty-four hours later.

"Here you go." I put a drink down on a table in front of an older couple while not even looking at them. My eyes are riveted to another table.

"Excuse me? What is this?" the woman asks politely.

"Huh?" I look down to see I have placed a new bottle of beer in front of her. It is sitting right next to the full glass of wine I had delivered just a few minutes ago.

Shit.

"We didn't order this, little girl," the balding man across from her says irritably. "I'm not paying for this."

Picking the bottle back up hastily, I look around, trying to remember which table had ordered it. "No, of course not. I'm so sorry. Wrong table!" I'm backing away in confusion when I bump into Liv.

"Charli, that's mine," Liv says as she neatly swipes it off my tray. "What the hell is wrong with you tonight? Distracted, much?" She's laughing at my embarrassment and I feel heat crawling up my neck and cheeks. "Could that be a contributing factor?" She points to the table where she just left Logan. He's watching us.

"I'm fine. I just grabbed the wrong drink. Lay off."

Liv can't keep the smirk off her face. Logan is here with his friend from last night. It's not Matt, but the other one that hadn't said much. He's not as tall as Logan, has light brown hair and is a little soft around the middle, but still attractive. They're in Liv's section and she's spent more time than normal with them.

What on earth have they been talking about? Why do they keep laughing and smiling? I guess he isn't rudely suggesting Liv get back to work! Her feminine wiles have won over another guy. *That's great. Maybe they can get married and have babies and buy one of those minivans and...*

"Charli?" Kyle's voice breaks into my ridiculous mental rant.

Looking behind me, I see he has my order ready and is waiting for me to notice. I'm also pretty sure he's been trying to talk to me and I've not heard a word.

"What?" I try harder to pay attention, but my success is limited.

He leans forward on the bar and nods in the direction of Logan's table. "Do you know those guys?" There is an unpleasant edge to his voice.

"What guys?" I feign innocence, but he isn't stupid. Raising one eyebrow, he looks at me like, try again.

Sighing heavily, I attempt to find an explanation that doesn't make me sound insane. "Okay, I don't actually know them. They came in last night and gave me shit. Nothing too bad, and you know I can handle myself, but I can't help but wonder why Liv seems to be having a grand time waiting on the assholes."

Kyle frowns at the table but looks a little relieved. Looking back that same way again, I see Logan is staring right at us. He even smiles at me, and Kyle's relief dissolves.

Coming around the bar, I reach my hand up to rest it lightly on Kyle's shoulder. This immediately gets his attention and he slides his arm around my waist and gives me a gentle squeeze. Kyle's scowl is long gone, but out of the corner of my eye, I discover Logan is now wearing it.

"Thanks for the concern, Kyle. It's no big deal. Really." I carefully pull away from him. I use the pretense of arranging things behind the bar so I don't hurt his feelings. "They probably had too much to drink last night, but now they're sober and behaving fine for Liv. I'm glad. So just let me get the drinks to my table before they decide I don't deserve a tip tonight."

"Yes, ma'am. Whatever you need, I'm here to accommodate." I narrow my eyes slightly and he grins. We both know he's offering more than drinks.

"You know I might think of something if I put my mind to it." He looks pleased at my first attempt at mild flirting. It's more than I usually offer.

Just then, Liv slides herself up next to me at the bar. "Hey, hooker, quit flirting with the hot bartender," she teases.

"Okay, whore, but only if you quit flirting with the hot customer."

It was just meant as a joke, and I hadn't thought about it at all before it popped out of my mouth, but I instantly regret it. Kyle's face becomes stone and he walks away to the other end of the bar.

Shit.

Liv looks at me with surprise and then glances between Kyle

and Logan. "What are you playing at, Charli?" she asks.

I close my eyes and exhale. "I don't know. I need a filter for my mouth apparently. It was just a joke. And Kyle and I aren't dating so I can say or think whatever I want about any other guy." Even I can hear the lame justification in my voice. "But, I did just try out a little flirting with him, and then I go and ruin it by saying that stupid shit. Ugh... Just shoot me now, Liv."

"Probably not a good plan." She smiles at me. "I have good aim, remember?"

I laugh. "Yes, I know."

"Charli, if you like Kyle, then I'm all for it. He's great for you in my opinion, but if you aren't really into him, don't string him along. That's cruel and he deserves better. Just be honest. Even if you haven't decided what you want yet, that is still okay. Explain it to him and he'll understand."

"Yeah, I know." I load the drinks Kyle made before leaving us and start back to my section. After looking to make sure both Kyle and Liv are occupied with something besides watching me, I risk another look at Logan's table, but he isn't there. *Has he left?*

It's probably better for me if he has, but I feel disappointed nonetheless. Turning my head back toward my destination, I feel the bone wrenching shock of crashing into what must be a cement wall.

"Ugh!" I always thought it was funny when cartoon characters hit their head and literally saw stars, but for the first time I realize that it can be a real phenomenon.

Feeling myself going down, I'm soon flat on my ass and surrounded by the broken glass of several beer bottles. I'm also covered in the liquid that was previously contained in those broken bottles. Now I'll have to leave work to shower, or risk spending all night smelling like a drunk on a major bender.

"Damn! Chuck, are you okay?"

Looking up, I realize my cement wall is tanned, muscled, and in possession of amazing gold-flecked, green eyes. "What did you call me?" I croak as I try to figure out how to get up without embedding glass into my hands. The image, of Frankenstein-style stitches covering my palms, is enough to make me take this seriously.

Running his hand through his hair, Logan sighs. Then he bends down and scoops me up into his arms like it's nothing at all. I know I'm not heavy, but it really looks like it took absolutely no effort on his part.

"Charli, I'm so sorry. I really am." He whispers near my ear as he continues to hold onto me and the warmth of his breath makes me shiver lightly.

"Are you sorry for calling me that stupid name again? Or for making me bust my ass?"

It's a legitimate question and I feel the chuckle reverberate through his chest. Maybe I should be upset that I'll have a bruised backside by tomorrow, maybe I should be upset that I now have a mess of glass and beer to clean up, and maybe I shouldn't feel this excitement at being held tightly against the rock hard body of a shit hot guy that pissed me off so recently, but...

"Both, I guess," he says, and when he smiles down at me, I find it hard to remember what I'd even asked him.

This man has a beautiful smile.

Chapter Six: Logan

She Reeks

She doesn't weigh anything at all. And her eyes, are they blue or green? A unique color somewhere between, they're so startling with her dark hair and lashes that I wonder how I ever thought she wasn't my type. *She really is beautiful.*

Then her smell hits me and I wrinkle my nose in disgust. Thanks to me she smells like a brewery and her clothes are wet enough that some of the dampness is seeping through my shirt to my chest. I'm probably going to reek now too, but I don't care enough to put her down.

"Logan?" she clears her throat and looks up at me.

I startle at her calling me by name. *Had I introduced myself? I didn't think I did. Had she just heard my friends use it and had remembered it?* I find that I kind of like that idea.

"Logan?" This time, she pokes my chest with her index finger and I realize I was just grinning stupidly at her and not responding.

Looking directly at her, I smile even bigger. "Yeah." I must look like some kind of toothpaste ad. *Why can't I quit smiling?*

"You can put me down now. This is getting a little embarrassing." I look around and notice Liv - my waitress from tonight - and both bartenders heading our way, fast. I'd also estimate that over half of the bar's patrons are watching us like we're tonight's entertainment.

Reluctantly, I set her down. "Sorry," I mumble. Standing upright, and very close, I notice she still barely reaches my shoulder.

Liv reaches us and asks if Charli is okay. After reassuring herself that her friend is fine, Liv turns toward me and I can tell she wants to ask me a few things. I'm not sure I have any answers for her.

Next, we are interrupted by the imposing, older bartender as he comes over to talk to Charli and glare at me. "You okay?" he asks her and I'm surprised at the gentle question coming from the stern face.

Charli smiles at him sweetly and answers without hesitation. I feel a strange tightening in my stomach as I watch her. It's obvious she cares about this man.

"I'm fine, Ronan. Really. Sorry about the mess. I'll clean it up." She swings her hand out to encompass the disaster on the wooden floors.

"You will not." Taking an authoritative stance that allows no argument, the intimidating man points a thick finger at a door near the back of the bar. "Get upstairs and clean yourself up. We'll get this taken care of. Liv, can you cover her tables for a bit?"

"Sure. No problem," Liv smiles encouragingly.

"Thanks," Charli says with appreciation.

My little Chuck looks so embarrassed to be the center of attention. I move closer, even though I was already right next to her, and try to shield her from the view of the rest of the bar. "Do you need me to help you?" I ask. "I feel sort of responsible for running into you." We both know she ran into me, I hadn't moved, but she's willing to let me accept the blame.

"Well, since you…"

But before she can finish her answer, the younger, long-haired bartender comes up between us. He has that edgy rocker thing going on, and his cool factor is way higher than mine. His possessiveness is clear too and he's been following every step my Chuck has made tonight. Even though I've never been the violent type, I feel the urge to shove him away when he drapes his arm around her like he has the right to. *Hell, maybe he does have the right to. I know nothing about these people.*

"I got her," he says, "Look, I'm sure you're a real nice guy and all, but I'm not letting a stranger take her up to her apartment. I can take care of Charli."

I feel like I'm in a damn pissing contest. *Are they dating?* My blood pressure elevates and a lead weight hammers in my chest just thinking about it.

"Thanks, guys," Charli cuts in and maneuvers out from under his arm. He doesn't look too happy about it either, but I feel the weight lighten a little. "I can take care of myself. I'm not even hurt, just embarrassed and stinky at the moment. So, Kyle, you can get back to work… thanks anyway. And Logan, you can go back to whatever you were doing before becoming my personal impediment to walking." She smiles at me and it takes the sting out of her words.

I watch as she turns away from all us and heads toward a door at the back of the bar. I think I could watch that ass all day. The guy she referred to as Kyle said her apartment was upstairs. *Does she live above the bar?*

Feeling a hand on my shoulder, I turn around to see Scott standing next to me. "So..." he begins with a smirk.

"Yeah..." I add.

"I'm going to assume you would rather this little incident not be offered up to Matt? It might be worth telling him just to see how many creative ways he can give you shit. But then again, I could hold on to this gem for a little blackmail too. The possibilities are endless."

Scott loves to mess with me, but I know he'll keep it between us. "You just need to forget this happened. I'm not sure why I even came here tonight."

He just smiles even more and shakes his head like I'm a lost cause. Maybe I am. I'm not in the habit of self-delusion and I do know why I came here tonight.

I'd like to think I'm here because it's a cool bar. I want to pretend that I'm ready to get back in the game and a bar is a good place to meet women. I'm also sure that the damn little waitress is like getting a song stuck in your head.

Scott walks back to our table, laughing. "You are fucking pathetic, my friend."

"I'm aware. Thanks." I'd hoped seeing her again would prove the other night had just been too many beers and too little sex, but instead she's gotten ever further under my skin. I need to find a way to see her without hanging out here at The Crash every night like some raging alcoholic.

"You know," Scott says as he pulls out some cash to pay our bill, "Kelly wasn't thrilled about me coming out to a bar again and leaving her home alone with the babies. She's losing her mind without adult interactions all day, but she agreed because you've finally shown some real interest in someone. She worries that you work too much and I told her I think you really like this girl."

Well, that's embarrassing. Since when are my friends feeling sorry for me? "It's that obvious?" I ask.

His loud laughter is all the answer I need.

Chapter Seven: Charli
I Vote For Tacos!

The next few days pass in a blur of activity. The minor bruising on my tailbone has faded significantly and work has been busy enough to make it go by quickly. I've written several pages of my book, and I have finished an article for the paper about an upcoming charity event. Logan hasn't been back to the bar and I decide that's a good thing.

He's a distraction I don't need. My job is much simpler without his presence, but I do catch myself thinking of him more often than I'd like.

"The show is about to start! Grab the popcorn and get your skinny ass in here!" Liv yells from where she's planted herself on our couch.

Pulling the bag out of the microwave, I smell the buttery goodness as I rip it open and pour the popped kernels into a large red bowl. "I'm coming! You know it's on the DVR and you can pause it, right?"

"Hell, no. There will be no pausing, only fast forwarding

through the commercials."

Liv grabs the bowl out of my hands as soon as I sit next to her on the couch and stuffs a handful of the popcorn into her mouth as the opening music starts to play. We love all the crime drama shows on television and we might need an intervention soon.

"So," Liv says as she zips through the first set of commercials, "did you know Logan is a lawyer?"

What the hell? Where did this line of conversation come from? "Oh, so he's a greedy, soulless ambulance chaser?"

"Nope." She pops another piece of popcorn into her mouth.

"Does he put bad guys in jail or get them out?" I ask, trying not to sound too curious.

"Neither."

"Just spit it out, Liv. I know you want to tell me."

"He practices corporate law. You know, the type of lawyer that makes lots and lots of money?" She grins at me.

I narrow my eyes. "Since when does money impress you?"

"I didn't say I was impressed." She looks back at the TV screen.

"Are you implying I should be? Because you know I'm not. I know we all need cash to survive, and I'm not above wanting a little extra for books and things, but extreme wealth corrupts." I'm getting aggravated. She knows how I feel about people that place too much value on the pursuit of the almighty dollar.

She steals the blanket I have across my lap. "It doesn't have to. Momma D inherited a small fortune and she's the least corrupt person on the planet."

I pull the blanket back and relax my posture. "You're right. I shouldn't judge everyone by my bad experience. Dana uses her money for good and helps so many people. I'm being a bitch. Sorry."

"I'll forgive you as long as you shut up now. The shows back on." She smiles and we turn our attention back to TV. I'm even feeling guilty enough to share the blanket with her. We watch together as the cops figure out, and bring to justice, the evil scoundrel that killed the teenage prostitute.

The next day, while stacking clean glasses behind the bar, Liv decides to share some more. "Logan drives a truck."

"Huh?" I set down the last glass and turn toward her.

She turns toward me with a grin. "Logan? Remember the hot guy you tried to mow down?"

"I know who you're talking about, Liv." *She can be so infuriating.*

"He drives a truck. Kind of an odd choice for a lawyer in my opinion," she says, before resuming her duties with a renewed enthusiasm that's unlike her.

"Why do you even know this?" I can't imagine how that could have come up in conversation while she'd been delivering drinks to his table.

"I just thought it was useful information." She takes a damp rag and cleans the nozzles on the soda taps.

"How is that useful?" I ask, with my hand on my hip and no desire to help her clean until I get some answers. Her cryptic responses are pissing me off.

"He also asked me if I knew the short little waitress named Charli. He and his friend Scott were very interested in my information about you."

What the hell? "You better not have told him anything personal, Liv!"

"Don't worry about it. I know what I'm doing." She checks the mini fridge to see if any of the fruit juices need to be restocked.

"He's probably one of those psycho stalkers and I'll end up

having to change my name or something!" I rant. "Can you see me as a Sally?"

Liv just laughs and walks out from behind the bar. In all fairness, maybe Logan is having trouble getting me out of his head. It's a struggle I can relate to, and I'm flustered to realize I kind of like the idea.

"Liv..." my tone becomes menacing.

"Quit worrying, Charli," she calls over her shoulder as she walks away from me. "I'd never give out information that could put you in danger. I want what's best for you." The last word is spoken as she disappears into Ronan's office. Now, I'm really worried. Sometimes her ideas of what's best for me, are nowhere near my own.

And now, a few days later, I sprawl across my bed, trying to convince myself to get my lazy butt in gear and get ready. Kyle will be showing up soon for our lunch date and even though I'm not into a high maintenance beauty regime, I'm guessing sweatpants and my "Book Boyfriends are Better" T-shirt might not be my best outfit choice. Liv pokes her head around the doorway and studies me intently.

"What?" I ask.

"Nothing..." She continues to stand there.

"What, Liv?" My exasperation is showing.

"Do you want any help with your makeup for your date?"

"It's Kyle. He knows what I look like, and he sees me almost every day. It's only lunch. Want to join us?"

She makes the "you're stupid and I'm trying to remember why we're friends" face. "I'm sure Kyle would love for me to tag along. It's the first date he's convinced you to go out on."

No one would ever accuse Liv of beating around the bush, or even being tactful in a lot of situations, and her sarcasm now lives up to that reputation. She may know how to behave, but she decided a long time ago that anything less than brutal honesty is a waste of her time.

"He didn't convince me. He lost the pool game. It was my suggestion if you recall, that lunch be the trophy." My words are true, but I also know she's right. He fully intends it to be just the two of us.

I expect another smartass comment from her, but instead she narrows her eyes and looks at me in a calculating way, as though she's sizing up my behavior. "Do you have any plans yet for tomorrow?" She taps one, perfectly polished, tangerine fingernail against the side of my doorframe.

"Why? Do you need me to do something?" *What is she up to now?* Does she want me to go shopping for photo props, carry cameras out to some weird location for test shots, or does she just want to convince me to deep clean the apartment before a potential client comes over?

"Now, why do you think I need something from you?" Her innocent smile puts my danger warnings on high alert. When Liv tries to look innocent, you should be very concerned. "I was just curious..." Her voice trails off as she turns around and leaves me alone in my room.

I wonder just how nervous I should be. Knowing Liv, a healthy dose of nerves is completely justified.

A half an hour later, I'm dressed in my favorite black shorts with the band of satin down the side, a gray shirt with thin straps and a baby doll hemline and simple black sandals. It may not be a dress and heels, but it's more than my usual jeans and T-shirt. Liv made me feel guilty for mentally blowing off this lunch and Kyle deserves better.

When I hear him knocking a few minutes later, I'm ready but

48

feeling a little apprehensive. I'm not used to Kyle making me nervous and I try to decide if it's a good sign. I open the door with a smile, determined to give this a real try.

"Hey, come on in." *Damn, he looks good, but he always does.*

Dark jeans are fitted and slouch over the tops of his black motorcycle boots. His black T-shirt is thin and tight, and he has pulled back his long hair. I smile inwardly at our matching sense of style. You can never go wrong with black. He looks like the quintessential bad boy. *Doesn't every girl dream of the rebel with the heart of gold?*

Shoving his hands into his pockets, he rocks forward slightly. "I'm here to pay up." He lowers his voice. "I think you cheated just so I'd have to feed you. We all know you eat like a damn truck driver."

I laugh. It's a pretty accurate comparison actually. "I like to eat real food. If Liv tries one more time to convince me that kale chips taste good, I might try to smother her in her sleep. I'll take chicken nuggets and pizza any day of the week."

"I'll bet all your boyfriends in high school loved a girl that preferred fast food to salads. Please tell me you didn't have your date take you to McDonalds after prom, though."

"Boyfriends? I didn't have boyfriends in high school unless you count all the guys in my books that I was madly in love with."

"I find that hard to believe. How could anyone resist you?" He winks and I laugh. *If he only knew.*

"Kyle, I was a total nerd. I had braces, wore glasses, and was so skinny my teachers suspected I had an eating disorder. No one wanted a prom date that looked like a little boy."

"Well time has done right by you," he says as he takes my hand and spins me around to check me out. I notice his eyes linger on my ass.

49

"Whatever…" The intense attention is embarrassing.

"So…" he says in mock seriousness, where should we go eat?" He is still holding my hand, and I decide to let him.

Narrowing one eye, I purse my lips and look at Kyle as if weighing a heavy decision. "I vote for tacos. They taste great and they are cheap. Plus that new Tex-Mex place, a couple of blocks over has the best chips and salsa. Filling me up on that first will definitely save you some cash."

"Tacos…" He considers my suggestion. "Yep, that works for me. Thanks for taking my bartender salary into account while collecting on our bet."

"What are friends for?" I smile broadly at him, but his face falls and he drops my hand.

"Right," he says stiffly. "And we're definitely friends."

Heading out the door, I realize that, once again, my carelessly chosen words have hurt him. I don't know if I should be mad at myself for not thinking before I speak, or mad at him that I can't just relax and be myself.

Chapter Eight: Charli
Zombie Apocalypse

I open my eyes and close them back quickly to remedy my mistake. *Crap, I forgot to close the curtains again when I fell into bed last night!*

I'm sure the intense light falling across my bed is the cause of my waking up before noon on a Sunday. My bar shifts make a normal human schedule next to impossible. As I lie in bed, willing myself to fall back asleep, I hear Liv's laughter from the living room. *That can't be right.*

Looking over at my clock on the bedside table, and seeing it reads only 8:00 a.m., I bolt up with alarm, truly and completely awake. Liv doesn't do mornings. *Has the zombie apocalypse started?*

Liv can't manage getting out of bed at a decent hour even after a night off, much less one where we didn't leave the bar until three o'clock in the morning. I realize that not only is she awake at this unusual hour, but she sounds chipper. *Is she excited at the prospect of taking out the undead?*

Yawning, I rub my eyes and shove my glasses onto my face. Then twisting my long hair into a messy knot on the top of my head as usual, I secure it with one of the ponytail bands I always have around my wrist for emergencies.

Dodging piles of books, and last night's discarded work clothes, I lumber toward the unprecedented noises. I have my bedroom door halfway open, and another big yawn stretching out my mouth, when I realize that deep, male laughter is now accompanying Liv's. *What the hell?*

Peeking out into our overly bright living space, I squeak. I fucking squeak, and it's not cute.

It's too late to back out now, though. They've both heard me and whip around to look directly at my open doorway. I register Liv's calculating grin and she looks rather proud of herself. *She's dead to me now.*

With my heart thundering hard and heavy, I feel warmth flood my face and I stand in shocked silence as I identify her morning guest. *Logan is here. Logan is here in my apartment.*

Logan is sitting on my couch, so low to the ground he looks like he could lick his own knees if he wanted to. *Not that he wants to, of course. Who would lick their own knees? I mean there are better things to lick anyway, right? Oh shit...* I'm rambling. *Please don't let me actually share aloud any of this crazy! I'll sound certifiable.* I clamp my lips down in order to reinforce my commitment to silence.

"Good morning, Sunshine!" Liv chirps.

I have serious doubts as to whether or not this really is Liv. Maybe she's one of those Stepford Wives or a Stepford Friend, I guess? My best friend would never be up and already adorably dressed, by the way, this early. She would not call me Sunshine in a cheerful voice, and surely she would never neglect to mention she's entertaining my hot, fantasy lumberjack from the bar.

Here in my living room, sits the man that had crashed into me, physically and mentally, last week. "Hey," I croak out in my most unsexy voice ever. And wow, my conversation skills are outstanding.

"I like your shirt," Logan says, and I melt.

The twinkle in his deep green eyes and the adorably mischievous grin he directs at me are those of the little boy that pulled pigtails on the playground. *How can he be so cute and so unbelievably sexy at the same time?* I want to ruffle his hair and attach myself to his body in equal measure.

I look down at the T-shirt I'd slept in last night. It's one of my favorites. Originally black, after a few hundred washings, it's a now a perfectly broken in gray. The front reads "Book Whore" in a nice bold font.

Yep, I am definitely shit hot this morning. I send up a little prayer of thanks that it's at least one of my longer shirts that I sleep in regularly. Several of my T-shirt/gowns are short enough they don't even cover my butt and if he gets a look at today's panties... I'll die on the spot.

Liv's idea of a perfect gift for me, for every occasion, in fact, is a pair of panties with the most embarrassing design she can find. After our many years of friendship, I have quite a collection. Today's are black, with hot pink telephones all over them and the words "Booty Call" in lime green, right across my ass. Her sense of humor is rather unique.

"Thanks," I mumble back at him, embarrassed by my utter lack of style.

He, on the other hand, is wearing a suit, a really expensive suit. He looks perfectly groomed too. *What in the hell is going on?*

Finally entering the room fully, I go over to perch on the edge of our teal and yellow, damask print, upholstered chair that faces the beloved couch. Logan never takes his eyes off of me.

"So. You look very, uh… professional? Are we being sued or something? You know it wasn't my fault what happened in the bar, right? You totally came out of nowhere. Maybe I should sue you."

He laughs at my feeble attempt at humor. "No. I'm not suing you, nor am I representing anyone who wishes to sue you." Leaning forward, halfway across our trunk/coffee table, he whispers conspiratorially, "It may seem odd, but even though I'm a lawyer, I wouldn't consider myself to be an overly litigious person. And besides, I work in corporate law. I deal with boring financial contracts predominantly."

He sits back up and looks a little ashamed at this revelation. I know it means he is well educated and probably bringing in a very impressive salary, but I can't help but wonder if he actually enjoys his job. It sounds horribly boring to me, but I guess someone has to do it.

"Okay, that clears up what you are NOT doing here, so why are you here?" I say, very matter of fact.

"Damn, Charli. Rude, much?" Liv turns an accusing eye at me, and I know I deserve it. I have the grace to look embarrassed, but Logan doesn't seem bothered by my question, thankfully.

"Liv is going to take some business headshots for me. We have to provide our own for the website and personnel files." He explains as he takes a cautious sip out of my favorite, black striped mug.

Wait a minute! Had Liv even made him coffee? She hates coffee and won't bother to make it for me. She says even the smell is vile.

"Okay. Got it. No suing will ensue." I want to groan, just like

Liv currently is, at my awful word vomit. This is so her fault! She's the one making me talk to this hot guy so early in the morning! When he chuckles, I figure it's a "pity laugh" and appreciate the gesture.

"We negotiated a trade." Liv looks a little too pleased with herself when she offers this new information.

"A trade?" I have to wonder which of them suggested this idea.

"Remember me mentioning that Logan has a truck?"

"Maybe..." I drawl out slowly. She knows perfectly well I remember every detail she's sparingly doled out over the course of the week.

"Well, you might also recall that you already promised me you would model for the upcoming Ophelia shoot?" I'm getting a really bad feeling about this, and I'd love to discuss this more privately, but she continues. "The location is pretty remote and there's no way I can haul all my equipment out to the middle of nowhere in our little car. Plus, once there, I need muscle to get the equipment from the parking area to the river's edge. Logan is willing to provide transportation and muscle in lieu of payment for a copyright released image that'll be way better than any of the other ones at his firm."

She and I both look at the muscles he is offering. They seem perfectly capable. They seem well defined and downright impressive. Our inspection might have gone on indefinitely if he hadn't interrupted our admiration by clearing his throat.

"Seems fair to me," he states. I narrow my eyes at him and he shifts his weight a little. I seriously doubt an hour long drive, hauling heavy light boxes and stands through the woods, waiting while Liv gets her perfect shot, reloading the equipment, and THEN driving another hour back into the city is a fair trade for a headshot. He must know it too, and I wonder at his motivation.

"Well then, let's get started with my end of the bargain, shall we?" Jumping up, Liv pulls him over to her studio setup near the wall of windows. She busies herself setting up a neutral gray backdrop, metering the lights, and making camera adjustments. I try to ignore them both and eat a banana nut muffin left over from yesterday's breakfast run.

Ignoring them proves to be rather difficult, though. Every time I look up, Logan seems to be looking my way.

"Logan, you know you actually need to look at the camera for this right?" Liv reprimands and I laugh.

"Oh, yeah...sorry," he says, but he doesn't look too sorry. He looks like he thinks it's funny too.

"Hey, Charli, can you come help me out for a minute?" Liv asks. Her innocent request isn't fooling me, though. She doesn't need my help for a simple headshot, but a convenient excuse to look at her subject isn't something I'm going to complain about.

"Can I at least go and get dressed?" I should've changed already, but I'd been extremely busy pretending to do things around the apartment.

Liv frowns and looks in my direction. "Why bother? This won't take long and he's already seen your craptastic sleep shirt." Well now instead of a quick and honorable death, she will suffer slowly and painfully.

"Yes! Much better, Logan! If I'd known insulting Charli was the way to get a decent smile out of you, I'd have done it a lot sooner." Liv seems excited about his new expression but has no qualms about continuing to issue her commands. "Hey! You still need to look at me. Not her!"

She hands me a large reflector panel and directs me to stand across from the window at Logan's side and tilt it toward his face. "Just watch his face to make sure it is reflecting back onto this side," she instructs me, but I don't think it will be a problem. Watching his face sounds like an awesome way to spend my early morning.

Why am I so attracted to this guy? I've seen and flirted with plenty of other hot guys at the bar. I don't know Logan well enough to say if he has a great personality or not, and it seems doubtful we have much in common when you compare our jobs or friends, but there just seems to be some kind of magnetic pull whenever he's around.

So I stand here, looking tired and disheveled, and holding what looks like a circle of aluminum foil, trying to puzzle out the tension coiling its way through me just by being near him.

"Okay, I got it!" Liv announces. "Go away. I'm done with both of you." She dismisses us both with a wave of her hand and walks over to her MacBook to unload the card and start editing the files. Logan and I just look at each other, wondering what we're supposed to do now.

Chapter Nine: Logan
Is It Hot In Here?

Do they have air conditioning in this place? I'd been perfectly comfortable in my suit earlier while sitting on that awful couch and talking with Liv. As soon as Charli appeared in her bedroom door, adorably rumpled with crazy hair and wearing an old T-shirt, the room started getting warmer.

Now that she's staring at me and shifting her weight from one bare foot to the next, I sort of feel like I'm suffocating. *Surely I can take my jacket and tie off, right?* It's like a sauna and I'm seriously overdressed now that the pictures are complete. Charli and Liv look perfectly comfortable, though. *Is it just me?*

Never taking my eyes from her face, I remove the constricting garments. I watch as her eyes dip down a little lower to watch my movements. *Does she realize she's just opened her mouth slightly?*

Fuck me.

It feels like I'm doing some sort of striptease for her, even though I'm only removing the jacket and tie. I swallow the tight lump in my dry throat and try to get my shit under control before

I really embarrass myself. I need her eyes to head north pretty soon or any pretense of me being cool will be completely ruined.

"So..." I begin, dragging the word out and hoping a brilliant and witty conversation starter will come to me. It doesn't.

"So..." She counters, and then she does that little smile. It's THE smile. It's the smile she flashed me at the bar to piss Victoria off, and I have to wonder if she knows what it does to me. My core temperature ratchets up even more and my body aches with the strain of pretending she's like any other girl I've met.

I need to sit down. Walking over to the couch I start to lower myself down onto it but that's when I remember how awful it is. I want to change my mind and sit on the chair instead, but it's too late. I'm too far down and have to commit.

What the hell kind of couch is this? I feel like a sultan in a harem or something on this crazy thing. It's so low that I can't really lower myself down the whole way and instead have to sort of fall onto it for the last foot or so. And it has so many cushions I feel like I'm an intruder. *Why in the hell hadn't I sat on the chair?*

She follows me, but her lithe, little body slides gracefully down onto the offending piece of furniture. When she curls her legs up under her and sits sideways, facing me, she looks perfectly comfortable... and so adorable... and so hot. *Is she even wearing a bra? I swear her headlights are on.*

Fuck me.

"Liv is awesome," she begins, "I'm sure you'll love the picture."

"I'm sure I will. She showed me some of her work earlier this morning. It's incredible. She deserves a better job than a business headshot." I really mean it. The girl has major talent. Liv's also gorgeous and normally I would appreciate that more, but when Charli is around, she's all I see.

I keep thinking this is going to wear off, or at least lessen, but no luck so far. My mind wanders to just how far those legs would be able to wrap around my waist. *What it would feel like to cup that perfect ass? What it will take to convince her I should find out?*

Charli smiles at me, and it takes several seconds to realize it is because of my praise of her friend. If she were able to read my mind, would she still be smiling, or pissed?

Twirling one of the long blue strands of hair that has escaped and fallen across her cheek, she looks into my eyes before speaking and I notice her glasses have slipped a little way down her nose. "Liv loves working with people, so she never minds the portrait jobs, but she's working on a new project now. She's creating her take on scenes from iconic pieces of literature. It's probably my fault. My book nerd influence has brought her over to the dark side, but the force is strong with this one."

"Amazing photographer, she is. Lucky to have her, I am." *Good God, I've just reverted to my nerdy teenage self. Will she appreciate that I caught her Star Wars reference or think I'm a total loser?* I, on the other hand, am hopelessly turned on that she obviously knows about the greatest movies ever... minus those three prequel disasters they foisted on us later, of course.

Biting her bottom lip, she rolls her eyes and grins. "That's a terrible Yoda impression." I'm fascinated by the way she crinkles her nose when she finally gives into a full blown laugh. I'm also relieved that her laughter is in amusement and not in dismissal of me.

"Well, it must not be too awful. You recognized it."

"I suppose," she admits. "I guess you already know about Liv's new project since you offered to help out with the Ophelia shoot?"

"Actually, I'm not sure what an Ophelia shoot is. She just asked for some manual labor and transportation one afternoon."

"So you'd rather give up an entire afternoon and possibly endure real work to get out of just paying for a headshot?"

Busted. "She might've mentioned you were her model for the shoot," I tell her. *Was it too much to admit this?*

"Hmmm..." is all she responds with and I'm not sure how to take it.

"You mentioned that I might have to endure 'real work' for the shoot? Are you implying my job isn't real work?" I'm just teasing her, but she stiffens.

"No. I'm sorry. I shouldn't have said that. I know nothing about what you do."

Great job, Logan. You just made her feel like shit. "It's fine. Really. I know what you meant. Sitting in an office all day isn't easy, but it isn't physically taxing."

We sit quietly together for several minutes, unsure what to say next. She grabs one of the millions of little pillows that surround her and hugs it close. Now I'm jealous of the pillow.

What is it about Charli? I know it's more than just her beauty. It's even more than her perfect little body, her smartass comebacks, and unending energy. All I want to do right now is touch her. *Okay, I'm claiming honesty right?* I want to do a lot more than just touch her. Touching would never be enough. I need her naked underneath me, or on top of me, or...

Fuck me.

She isn't like anyone I've previously dated, or even known, for that matter. I know Matt will be pissed that I've decided I have to have her. I know he was interested in her the other night and chose the wrong approach when dealing with someone like her. She made it clear he doesn't have a chance. I also know Victoria will be angry and hurt that I've blown off her advances but have let myself become fixated on the waitress she is still bitching about. None of this matters to me, at the moment, though. *I really want to ask Charli out.* I want to spend more time with her and figure out what's going on between us.

"So, Charli..." I'm not cocky, but I'm not usually nervous to ask someone out either. This time I am.

"Finally figure my name out?" she teases.

Not able to help it, I laugh and it releases some tension. I like her sense of humor and how she doesn't take herself too seriously. She's just fun, and my life hasn't had enough of that lately.

"Maybe... but I won't be held responsible for future slips of the tongue." Her gaze moves toward my mouth and she sighs softly. I consider grabbing a pillow for my lap. A tent pole might not be helpful at this point.

"Are ya'll discussing tongue?" Liv's unexpected interruption and subsequent laughter startles us both. *Damn, when had she snuck up on us?*

"Don't let me hold you back. But just so you know, using your tongue is way better than talking about your tongue." She thinks she's so damn funny. *Okay, maybe it's a little funny.*

"Olivia Marie Garrett!" Charli explodes at her friend, but Liv takes it all in stride and just laughs harder.

"Yes, Charlotte Layne Herrington?"

"Charlotte? Your name is Charlotte?" I ask. It's a pretty name, but I prefer thinking of her as Charli, or my little Chuck, and I hear her groan in exasperation.

I stick out my hand toward her. "It is nice to meet you, Charlotte. I'm Logan Mitchell." I can tell she wants to be pissed at Liv, but she plays along and shakes my hand.

My hand looks like a baseball mitt as it surrounds hers, and her hand is cold. *Or maybe my hand is just too hot?* I hope my palms aren't sweating all over hers, but she seems as reluctant as I am to pull her hand away.

Liv is laughing again and we let go of one another. It's probably time for me to go. I know I shouldn't take up their day off, even though leaving right now is the last thing I want to do.

It takes me three tries to get up off that pile of cushions on the floor they refer to as their couch. *I hate this thing.*

"I'll have your image ready and email it over to you with the copyright release by the end of the week," Liv says as she walks me to the door.

"Perfect. Thanks." I turn and look back at Charli one last time.

"Bye, Logan," she says, flashing that dimple again.

That dimple is so damn sexy. "Bye, Chuck," I answer and then hurry out before she has time for a comeback.

Chapter Ten: Charli

Bitchtoria

"Earth to Charli."

"What?" I look at Liv in confusion.

Shaking her head in disgust, she joins me at the end of the bar. "Quit watching the door. The man probably works long hours and doesn't have the time to hang out in a bar in the middle of the week. And that's a good thing. No one wants a guy with a drinking problem."

"I'm pathetic, aren't I?"

"Why, yes. Yes, you most certainly are. But I still love you. Just get your ass going so I don't have to listen to Ronan complaining about your slacking, okay?"

I grab my tray of drinks and get back to work. I haven't seen Logan in four days. Four days seems like forever. Four days isn't that long in actuality, so my pathetic factor has just elevated in my own eyes.

Why didn't he at least ask for my number? He seemed to be interested in me. I can always get his number from Liv. I know she has it and I could just text him. *Wow, I think I just hit the pathetic threshold.* I'm done. I refuse to waste any more time thinking about him.

It's pretty slow tonight, so I grabbed a bar towel and started wiping all the prep counters and shelves. I need to do something to make this evening go by a little faster.

"You guys have any plans this weekend?" Kyle asks when he and Liv join me near the sink.

Liv answers for us. "I have that shoot this Sunday for my art exhibit. It's the one Charli is helping me with."

"Oh, that's right! Need any help with your stuff? I might be able to use my neighbors van," Kyle offers.

Liv and I cut a look at each other. "Thanks. That's really cool of you, but I already have some help. I appreciate the offer, though." Liv smiles at him, but he frowns.

He sets the bottle he'd been holding down on the bar and crosses his arms in front of his chest. "Who's helping?" He is asking Liv but looking at me.

I can't even make eye contact. I'm sure I've cleaned this same shelf for far too long, but it allows me to keep my back to Kyle. "You don't know him."

"Okay, fine. But who is it?"

Damn, he's like a little terrier refusing to give up a bone!

Liv takes pity on me. She walks closer to Kyle and crosses her arms too, mimicking his stance. "His name is Logan. He's doing me a favor in trade for some photos for his job. No big deal." She heavily stresses the last sentence, but this just confirms his suspicions that there is more to this, and maybe it is a big deal.

"Isn't Logan the name of the asshole that knocked Charli down that night?"

Shit. Why can't he be like most guys and never remember

65

names? Finally turning back around, I toss the bar towel toward him. He catches it easily and sets it down behind him on the bar. "He didn't knock me down. I ran into him. It wasn't his fault."

"Okay, but you also told me he'd been an asshole to you the night before when he came in with his friends. So why do you think it's a good idea to spend the day with an asshole?"

I glare at him. "Well you're being an asshole now, but for some reason I still spend time with you, don't I?" I regret it as soon as I say it. It hadn't been fair and I know it.

"Let me fix that for you." His words are spoken softly, but his boots make heavy steps as he walks away.

Shit.

"Wow," Liv whispers in shock, "That was intense."

"That sucked," I respond. Putting my arms on the bar in front of me, I lay my head down on them and close my eyes.

Then my night starts to suck even harder. Walking up to the bar, looking like she stepped off the cover of Vogue, is that blonde bitch Victoria. *She said she didn't even like this bar!*

"Excuse me," she says, trying to get Ronan's attention. "Can we please get a waitress to our table? We haven't seen her once."

Since she has decided to sit at table four, the exact same table as before, she probably assumes that waitress will be me. That assumption is correct, but I haven't been ignoring the table. She's obviously just arrived because I'd wiped it down less than five minutes ago.

"I got it, Ronan," I tell him and he nods when I follow her back to her table.

In a black and white patterned wrap dress, and an amazing pair of black designer heels with red soles and laces up the front, her long legs make impressive strides and I feel like I am scurrying to keep up.

At the table, I see she's with the brunette from her last visit. The female friend hadn't said much that first night, but she had certainly laughed along with everyone else when Matt and Victoria had tried to ridicule me.

"What can I get you?" I ask, but my smile is unusually weak. I'm not much of an actress.

Victoria gracefully lowers herself into the nearest chair and looks up at me with self-satisfaction. I wouldn't call her expression a smile, but there is the slightest upturn of her mouth and I feel like she's weighing her options. "Just a couple of glasses of white wine. We need to unwind."

I wait a few seconds in case she has something more to add, but when she raising one eyebrow and rolls her eye toward the bar, I take the hint. "Okay. I'll be right back with that." *If she took the time to walk all the way up to the bar, why hadn't she just told Ronan what they wanted? I still would have delivered it.*

"Two white wines," I call over the bar as I pass by to go check on my other tables. Once my customers are taken care of, I stop back at the bar to slide the two wine glasses carefully onto my tray and head back to "Bitchtoria" and her sidekick. I'm almost to the table when I overhear what Victoria is saying.

"This is the first night all week I haven't been with Logan. Is it bad that I already miss him? Maybe I shouldn't wait all the way until tomorrow to see him again." I feel my stomach clench a little at her words. *Was he really with her all week?*

I set the drinks down in front of them and turn to leave, but she isn't done yet.

"Thanks." She takes a small sip before smiling directly at me. "Sometimes we just need to get out and have a girl's night and leave our men to their own devices, don't we? But it can be hard when being with them is so amazing." Sighing she relaxes back against the chair.

I see right through her. She's staked her claim and wants to make sure I'm damn well aware of it. I want to tell her she has nothing to worry about. *If this is the type of woman Logan wants to spend his evenings with, then he definitely isn't the guy for me.*

Chapter Eleven: Charli
Well, This Is Awkward.

"Quit bitching and sit still."

"I'm never doing this for you again," I gripe for the umpteenth time.

Liv knows it's an idle threat, but she'd be disappointed if I didn't grumble when she covers my face in ten pounds of waterproof foundation, glues down pale blue fake lashes, and then tops me off with a generous dusting of iridescent powder. I try not to sneeze, but it's impossible.

Liv jumps back in disgust. "You are as a bad as a two-year-old! Sit still!"

"I'm trying!" I whine, grabbing a tissue off her vanity table.

After touching up the areas I disturbed by my inconsiderate sneeze, she mists my face with a fixative spray. "Okay, once we're on location I will touch it up if necessary and you can put the dress on. No way I'm going to let you wrinkle that gown on the way over there."

"Yes, Mommy," I tease.

She ignores me and steps back to survey her work. "Check it out, Charli." I can see she's pleased with the results as she turns me toward the mirror.

Wow. I don't even recognize myself. Frigidly pale, my face shimmers in the light. My long hair has been curled into soft, messy ringlets and she has nestled bits of seaweed and leaves in it. Her vision of Ophelia is kick ass.

"It's perfect," I tell her. She knows her shit.

"I know," she replies with pleasure. Liv doesn't brag, but she doesn't suffer from false modesty either.

Slipping off my robe, I take the white shift dress Liv hands me and try to figure out the best way to put it on. It's small and I can tell it will fit closely to my body.

"It has a zipper up the back so you can step into it, but you still need to be careful," she advises. I know she's calculating the damage I can do to her masterpiece between now and the actual shoot.

Finding the tiny white zipper, I manage to dress myself. "I got it. What next?"

"Once we are at the river's edge, I'll help you put the Ophelia gown over this." I watch Liv take the dress she has spent the last month constructing out of her closet and carefully zip it into a black garment bag.

"I'm wearing this dress under the other one?" At least this answers my question of how I was going to change in the woods in front of Logan.

"Yeah, unless you want this to be a Playboy centerfold shoot?" she asks, laughing in my direction.

"No thanks. Explain."

"The dress has multiple layers of fabric but it's very sheer and light, so when you get in the water it will probably be somewhat transparent. The white cotton dress will double as a slip."

"Oh, thanks. I appreciate that you aren't turning me into a nude model."

"It was tempting to leave off the slip, but I figured if you came to my gallery show and saw a giant canvas with your nipples the size of grapes you'd get pissed at me. I do still have to live with you." Without waiting for my response, she leaves the bedroom.

We have all the photography equipment in the travel cases by the door and I've packed a small backpack with a change of clothes and some towels for afterward. All that's left is for me to grab my flip flops on the way out.

"Hey, Liv..." I hesitate in the bedroom doorway, unsure if I should continue.

"Yeah?" She is still running around double checking everything and I can tell she is in full "photographer mode."

"Nevermind." I still haven't told Liv about what I'd overheard Victoria saying. We usually share everything, but I feel silly admitting her words bothered me.

Logan is nothing to me. Hell, we just met and aren't even friends really, so I have no right to care who he's messing around with. I'll just be polite today and get through this shoot like a professional, and then I won't ever see him again. *Why would I?*

When there is a knock a few minutes later, I let Liv answer it. I'm putting off seeing him until the last possible moment, even though I know it's ridiculous. We will be together most of the day and my heart keeps betraying me by performing little flips of anticipation when I think about it.

Leaving my room and walking to our entryway, my stomach drops when I finally see Logan near the door. Lifting the larger of the two light boxes, muscles clearly visible through his T-shirt, I want to look away, but there's no way I can.

71

This is the first time I've seen him in casual clothing and he wears it well. His dark, well-worn jeans are low on his hips and his navy blue T-shirt is like a second skin molding itself to the tight muscles of his chest and abdomen. When I'd thought I could picture the body underneath his business suit, I'd been woefully wrong. The reality far surpasses any of my imaginings. He's even wearing a tattered hat with the brim rolled tight like a ball player. *And, oh my God, is that stubble on his jaw?*

He is holding the box in front of him when he notices my arrival and he stops to smile at me. It's a smile that lights up his entire face and it hurts me to give him nothing more than a polite nod. His look of confusion is hard to watch and I feel awful. Liv is studying us and I know she'll be questioning me later.

"Hey." His voice is hesitant.

How long is he going to stand there holding that damn box? It's heavy and the muscles of his arms are bulging slightly, but he doesn't even shift its weight as he waits for my response.

"Hi, Logan. It's nice to see you again." I try to keep some distance, not trusting myself near him. I'm far too attracted to this guy. The silent strain stretches out between us and I'm not sure I've ever fought so hard to keep my cool.

Liv claps her hands to get our attention. "Okay... Logan, if you can get these boxes loaded, then Charli and I will grab my makeup box and camera bag and follow you down to your truck."

"Sure." He's still watching me, but he doesn't seem excited to be helping out anymore, and I'm afraid it's my fault. I feel like I should apologize, but what for? I'm doing what's best for both of us. He can't have anything more than friendship from me if he's with Victoria.

Grabbing my arm on our way out, Liv hisses near my ear, "What's the problem, Charli?"

"Nothing. No problem at all." I pull out of her grasp.

"Really?" Her sarcasm drips heavily. "I know Ophelia was suicidal and all, but you don't have to be quite so Method. Lighten up. I thought you were looking forward to seeing him again? You two practically eye-fucked each other last Sunday!"

"Oh, we did not! Stop exaggerating, Liv!" I stomp loudly down the stairs, several steps in front of her, and she snorts.

The brightness of the day temporarily blinds me as we exit the building. When my sight returns, I'm surprised to see an older model, single cab, blue, Chevrolet pickup truck. I'd assumed he would own a brand new one with every upgrade offered. He sees me looking it over and walks closer.

"It was my Grandpa's truck," he explains. "When he died I couldn't stand the thought of getting rid of it. My friends laugh at it, but I love it." He places a proud hand protectively on the tailgate.

"It's great," I tell him, but I won't make eye contact.

Damn you, Logan, for making this so hard. He's sweet and sentimental and I love that about him. And the truck really is cool in my opinion. If things were different, I'd be all over him, but I don't mess around with attached guys.

He opens the passenger side door for me, but I hesitate. If I crawl in first, I'll spend the entire trip pressed between him and Liv. I decide that is a particular brand of torture I can live without. Just looking at his perfect body makes me want to moan, and if my body is actually touching his, the physical contact might make me throw my morals out the window and jump him.

"Liv can get in first. I get really carsick if I'm not next to the window." *Ugh. He looks so disappointed!*

"Since when?" Liv says, and it figures she would call me on my bullshit.

73

"Since ALWAYS." Obviously she knows I'm lying, but thankfully lets it go and decides to go ahead and climb into the cab first.

After checking all the straps that are securing the boxes, Logan slides into the driver's seat and starts the engine. "So where to?" he asks Liv.

"Do you know the state park right outside the city? Right before you get to Springfield?"

"The one that's on the interstate?"

"Yeah. It should take us about an hour to get there."

"Okay. Buckle up, ladies." He smiles and starts the engine. It roars to life and we pull out into traffic.

"So, once we arrive I'll show you where I have the shoot planned. You will carry the equipment boxes, but I'll handle unpacking and setting up. You'll be free until I'm done and have everything packed back up." Liv loves being in charge.

"You weren't kidding when you said I was just the manual labor." He doesn't look upset by this news and I'm struck by how good-natured he is.

"No offense, but I'm very particular about who handles my equipment." Liv winks at him and he chuckles lightly. "If you knew me better, Logan, you would know that normally a line like that would be my cue to add a beautifully crafted sexual innuendo to our conversation. It's begging for it! But I'm showing amazing restraint so I don't step on any toes."

Damn it, Liv. Shut up! Does he get what's she's saying?

"I'm not worthy of your innuendos?" he asks with a smirk.

"Oh, don't get me wrong, you're shit hot, Logan but not exactly my type. And besides, I don't go after guys my friends want."

"Liv!" I jab her hard with my elbow.

Logan tensed and his lips form a tight, thin line. "I don't think

74

that's really an issue." We're all silent for the next several miles.

After a while, Liv and Logan pick up their conversation again and she tells him about the photography exhibit she'll be in. I just stay quiet. I'm not trying to be rude, but I can feel myself being lured by the sound of his voice and I know I need to keep my distance. *Why do I always want the guys I can't have?*

I try to let my mind wander away and just think about the tons of laundry I need to do, my next chapter for my book, and not forgetting to pick up tampons since Liv stole the rest of my box last week.

"Charli?" His voice is soft, and it pulls me back to the present. The truck seems really quiet and I wonder if it's the first time he's called my name.

"Yes?"

"Are you okay?" His concern seems genuine and I feel even worse. He isn't doing anything wrong. He can date anyone he wants and doesn't have to answer to me just because I have the hots for him.

"Sure. I'm fine. Just really tired. Work last night kind of sucked." I close my eyes and lean against the window. Maybe if I pretend I'm napping he won't think I'm avoiding him.

The silence in the truck gets heavier and the stress feels unbearable. When I open my eyes a few minutes later, I notice he's gripping the steering wheel so tightly his knuckles are losing all color.

Liv sighs in frustration. "This is awkward. I really don't know what the fuck is going on, but it's messing with my creative process and I can't take it."

She reaches out her hand and turns the old-fashioned knob on the radio. Flipping through the stations, she finally stops on a classic rock song and sings along. Liv isn't shy and carries a tune well enough that she feels comfortable singing anywhere and anytime. Grocery shopping can be mortifying when she has a song stuck in her head.

The rest of our journey is a mini concert from the middle passenger while Logan and I sit and silently stare forward.

Chapter Twelve: Logan
Am I Supposed To Be Seeing This?

It's obvious she's upset, but I can't figure out why.

Thinking back to last Sunday, I know I didn't imagine our mutual attraction. I couldn't keep my eyes away from her and she'd seemed fine with it. I miss her smile. She hasn't given it to me once today.

Any other time I would be laughing and singing right along with Liv. She's funny and I like hanging out with her, but Charli's cold silence has me feeling like I was sucker punched. I'm relieved when I see the state park sign and know I'll be able to escape the claustrophobic truck cab soon.

"Okay, we're here," I say, stating the obvious because I don't know what else to say. My tires crunch over the gravel as I turn into the park. I stop at the first crossroad and look to Liv. "Where should I go now?"

Liv looks around and then points to a packed dirt path to the right. "Take that one until we come to a clearing bordered by landscape timbers. It should be about half a mile."

I find the clearing, pull up until the truck's front tires lightly tap one of the timbers, and then kill the engine. We're surrounded on all sides by dense, green wilderness and when I push open my door, I can hear water running somewhere nearby.

"The river is narrow and shallow and only about fifty feet from us in that direction," Liv says as she points a little past my right shoulder. "There's a trail between those two trees that'll take us right down to it." Liv reaches down and grabs her camera bag out of the floorboard. "Let's go," she says as she pushes Charli to get her to open the truck's door.

"How did you even find this place?" I ask in amazement, once both girls had piled out of the cab.

"I love to scout new locations. Every chance I get, I roam around and take notes for future shoots. I found this place years ago when my moms decided that a camping trip would be a wonderful bonding experience for all of us." She starts laughing and I notice that even Charli is grinning a little. "It was not! That weekend is still a taboo subject in my family."

"Your moms? Plural?" I can't help but ask.

"Yep. My moms are smart, chic, over protective, and lesbians. Pretty cool, right?" She winks at me and I feel that even though her family is probably hard to explain sometimes, she's entirely proud of it.

I smile back at her. "Definitely. I love my parents, but no one would accuse them of being cool."

The girls disappear down the trail Liv indicated as I pull the straps off the boxes. I grab the first one and follow them. Not long after that, I'm delivering the last box to the river's edge.

Once I have a minute to take a breath and look around, I notice Liv has already unpacked the first two boxes, set up some kind of lights with fabric paneled cubes covering them, and is now touching up Charli's makeup.

"This weather is great!" I enthuse, but they ignore me. The weather really is phenomenal. It's warm and sunny but not hot enough to be uncomfortable. There are also lots of thickly branched trees for shade. "I love being outdoors," I say to no one in particular. "I went camping a lot as a kid and I was even a boy scout."

"What?" Liv asks as she fiddles with the dials on the back of a camera with a lens on it that must be a foot long.

"Nevermind."

"Can you hand me that last soft box?" Liv asks while pointing to one of the fabric cubes I'd noticed earlier.

"This thing?" I ask, holding it up.

"Yeah, bring it here so I can put it on this strobe."

"You don't waste any time do you? I can't believe how quickly you got this all up." I look around at all the complicated stands, reflectors, lights, and a huge battery pack. It makes no sense to me.

"Too much to do before I lose the sunlight!" Liv yells over her shoulder.

It's obvious she knows exactly what she wants and exactly how to get it. This is what's important to her and she loves it. That must be a great feeling.

"If you like the sunlight, then why did I haul these big lamp light things out here?" I'm obviously teasing her, but she doesn't rise to the bait.

"Oh, those are just for fill light." She waves her hand dismissively.

Am I supposed to know what the hell "fill light" is? But she looks so busy that I hate to keep pestering her with amateur questions.

The girls are now standing close and facing each other. Liv puts a finger under Charli's chin and lifts it toward the sunlight for a careful inspection. "Perfect," she proclaims. *I agree.*

Next, Liv pulls a bundle of blue and green fabric out of a garment bag and helps Charli step into it. The layers completely cover the shapeless little sundress thing she'd been wearing and when Liv starts wrapping thin laces around and around Charli's tiny waist, my mouth falls open.

Liv is a genius. The strange garment perfectly matches the odd color of Charli's eyes. Clingy fabric shows off all the perfect curves of her tiny little body and when my chest starts to ache, I realize I've been holding my breath. *She already looks like a piece of art.*

"Looks good," Liv says, "Now get into the water."

Wait, what? I stare at them in shock. Has she just spent all that time tweaking makeup, hair, and dress for Charli to go swimming in it and ruin the whole thing? Charli must've known what to expect, though because she doesn't even hesitate.

She shivers, but confidently walks right to the middle of the small river. The water is at her waist when she relaxes into a back float. Managing to keep her face above the water, her dress and hair float out around her and ripple with the soft current.

The more the water saturates the dress, the more transparent and clingy it becomes. Now a second skin, I can see the outline of her legs and the damp fabric embraces the indention where her inner thighs meet. Though she's fully clothed, I feel like I'm not supposed to be seeing this. *God, thank you for letting me see this!*

"Okay, relax your legs and let them separate just a little," Liv tells her. "Yeah, now take your right arm and lift it so it rests above your head with your wrist up."

"Like this?" Charli yells.

"Yes, but relax your fingers more. You look like you're ready to claw someone."

"Maybe I am! If you don't hurry up, that someone will be you!" Liv is moving her arms around and trying to show Charli what she means, but, of course, Charli can't see her from her position in the water. Lifting her head would make her body sink.

"Raise your chin a little higher," Liv yells. "No! Not that much! I don't want to take a picture of the inside of your nose."

"I'm going to kill you, Liv!" Charli promises through clenched teeth.

Liv lifts her camera to her face. "Shut up now! That's perfect! Stay just like that!"

When the camera's shutter begins to click, I know this is the single most beautiful thing I've ever witnessed.

Chapter Thirteen: Charli
Hallelujah!

"We got the shot!"

I smile at Liv's joy and exhale as I tighten my muscles and push my feet down toward the river's bottom. After Liv had finished giving orders, I had been able to just float and let everything go. The day is warm, but being soaked all the way down to my skin has me chilled and I'm glad I can finally get out of the water and dry off.

Trying to walk toward the shore, I notice the formerly light fabric has become heavy and I feel it tangling around my legs as I lose my footing. The current is mild, and I'm a good swimmer, but still I struggle.

"Shit. Liv, can you help me please?" She needs to put her camera away and realize her best friend isn't willing to actually drown for her art.

Liv looks down at her black leggings, heeled boots, and off the shoulder, plum purple sweater before shaking her head. "I didn't dress for getting in the water. Are you drowning, or just being a pussy?"

"Really? Is this how you repay me for my help?" I screech at the redhead I used to be proud to call my best friend.

"I'm coming, Charli. Hold on," Logan's already heading toward me, kicking off his boots and pulling his shirt over his head, but his choice of words is rather unfortunate.

"Yeah, Charli...wait for him! He's *coming!*" Liv's peals of laughter carry well over the water.

Of course, she is laughing. She has the dirty mind of a teenage boy. I can tell from his eye rolling that Logan gets her sophomoric humor, but it doesn't deter him. He takes a few steps into the water and reaches for me.

I'm reluctant to accept his help, but decide that sharing Ophelia's fate isn't a good idea. *No drowning for me today, thanks.* Trying to step forward, I put out my arms, but several layers of the dress catch between my legs and I feel myself going under. Logan jumps for me and I manage to grab both of his arms, but instead of being saved, my dress now decides to wrap around his legs too and we fall to the side together. *Shit. We're going to drown and Liv is still laughing!*

I feel his arms tighten briefly around me in a supporting band of heavenly warmth, but our instability pulls us apart only a few seconds later and my chill becomes a freezing hell when my head slips beneath the water.

"Charli!" I can hear Logan yelling my name from above the water's surface and I'm trying to get back to him. He manages to regain his balance first and swoops me, and the fifty pounds of wet gown, up into his arms like you would hold a baby.

"You okay?" he whispers close to my ear and I nod.

I snuggle in as tight as possible. I'm totally taking advantage of all his body heat and trying to ignore the perfection of his chiseled bare chest pressed against me. Strong arms under my back and the bend of my knees give me a sense of security I've never felt before.

"Oh for fuck's sake!" Logan and I both turn our heads to look at Liv where she stands on dry land with both hands firmly planted on her hips. "You two look like the cover of a cheesy romance novel! Just lay one on her, Logan. I'll snap a picture. You could be the next Fabio, Logan!"

Have I mentioned her sense of humor is sick and twisted? Logan obviously finds her hilarious, though, and I feel his body shake as he laughs.

"Shut up, Liv!" we both yell at her.

I become even more aware of the body that is holding me as we emerge from the river, dripping water by the gallons. *Does he have any fat on him at all?* The solid muscles of his body are completely unyielding. And hot. Very, very hot. Like, maybe, Fuck Hawt...

Aren't lawyers usually pale and flabby from spending all their time in the office? Logan is the opposite of pale and flabby. He is tanned and strong and warm. I don't think I've ever wanted to do naughty but delicious things with someone more than I do right now.

I need to stop this line of thought, now. I'm not going to do this! I'm just too tempted to tell Liv to take a hike for awhile, and I don't want to become that girl. "Can you put me down, please?" I ask even though it kills me to do it.

"Are you sure?" His warm breath tickles as he whispers in my ear and I groan.

Shit. Did he hear me? This is so embarrassing! "Logan..." I close my eyes and try to figure out how to shut him down.

"Charli, I don't know what changed since last week but..."

"I'm not a cheater," I blurt out.

He suddenly looks pale and a little sick. I guess he isn't happy that I found out about him. "I'm really sorry. I had no idea," he says.

What is he talking about? Is he saying he had no idea I'd have a problem being the other woman?

"Is it that bartender?" he asks. "The younger one with the long hair? I didn't know, honestly. I don't expect you to cheat on him."

Did he hit his head underwater? "Kyle? Are you talking about Kyle? What in the hell does Kyle have to do with this? I'm talking about Victoria!"

He isn't making any sense at all and his face is completely shocked when he finally manages to answer. "Victoria? The Victoria I work with? You're dating Victoria?"

I groan at him. *Does he think this is funny... or is he really that stupid?* "Stop it! I know about the two of you! No more playing dumb. You're dating Victoria, and I won't help you cheat on her. I'm surprised she's okay with you spending the day with us, honestly. Or did you hide this from her? You seem good at keeping stuff to yourself."

He finally puts me down, runs his hand through his wet hair in frustration and stomps a few feet away. He then turns back to face me and I hear him start to laugh.

Maybe he's bipolar?

"THAT is what all today's shit is about? You think I'm dating Victoria?"

"Ummmm... Aren't you?" My conviction seems to be waning.

"NO!" he explodes. "We work together and sometimes hang out socially with our group of friends, but we're definitely not together. I don't want to start dating her either."

I wonder if he's lying to me. If so, he's really good at it. "But, she said she was with you almost every night this past week," I throw back at him.

"When did you talk to Victoria?"

"I didn't talk to her actually. I just overheard her at the bar saying she'd been with you."

"Maybe you should stop eavesdropping!" he explodes.

"Maybe you should stop avoiding telling me why you spent every evening with her, but now say you aren't dating her!" I cross my arms over my chest, shivering, and stomp my foot for emphasis.

"We're working on a major business proposal and we've had to stay late several times. It's just because of work. That's why I haven't had time to stop by the bar. We are NOT dating!" He throws his arms out wide and glares at me.

I'm relieved and I want to relax back into his warm arms, but I've worked myself into such a state of agitation, I can't calm down. My temper has gotten the best of me and my mouth won't shut the hell up. "Why not? She's hot and smart and obviously wants you. Maybe you should!" *Am I really suggesting to Logan, a guy that I'm totally lusting after, that he should consider dating someone else? Maybe I'm the one who is bipolar.*

"Because I don't want her, Charli. How can I make it any clearer?" He smiles sweetly and his voice has gone soft. It soothes me and I find I have no desire to yell at him anymore. "You are the person I want to go out with."

I swear, my heart has stopped beating. Walking back to where I stand in shock, he pulls me in tight and lowers his face to mine. Our mouths crash together and I think I hear the hallelujah chorus.

Oh, maybe it's just Liv screaming, "Hallelujah! It's about

time!"

Chapter Fourteen: Charli
Your Couch Swallows!

"Seriously? You forgot to grab your backpack?" Liv looks toward the heavens for divine help in dealing with my stupidity.

I'm seriously shivering now. As the sun goes down the temperature is dropping and I've just figured out I don't have my change of clothes. "I didn't mean to! I can't ride home in this thing." I pull one of the sodden layers away from me, but the minute I let it go, it falls back heavily. "It's soaking wet and so heavy I can barely stand upright in it."

"You can have my shirt, of course," Logan offers, "but it's not going to be very warm. Let me see if I have anything else in the truck." I watch the muscles ripple across his back as he jogs back to his truck and starts rooting around behind the bench seat. *I'll wear his shirt just to prevent him from putting it back on.*

Liv leans in close to me. "Stop moaning, Charli," she whispers. "And please don't have the big "O" while I'm standing next to you. That would be awkward."

I shove her, hard, but nothing she says is bothering me at the moment. That gorgeous hunk of muscles just kissed me. Well actually, he more than kissed me. We kind of devoured each other and I'm pretty sure his tongue became well acquainted with my tonsils.

As Logan comes back over to us, I decide that the view of his front might be even better than the view of his back. Maybe. *I might need to research this further, take some notes, snap some pictures...*

"Okay, I have some sweatpants I can throw on and this old college hoodie for you. If you want it. They've probably been hiding out in the truck for awhile." He puts the bundle of clothing to his nose and inhales. "They smell clean." He looks a little apologetic.

I reach out for the sweatshirt. "It's perfect. Thanks." I can't seem to stop smiling. Right now it feels like everything is perfect.

"So are you going commando?" Liv asks bluntly. I'd almost forgotten she is here with us.

"What?" *Damn, why does she have to be so embarrassing?* Logan is laughing at her of course, which will only encourage her further.

"If you don't have your backpack, you don't have dry panties." She spells it out slowly like I'm in Kindergarten. "But the sweatshirt looks long, so at least your bare hoo-hah won't be directly on his truck seat."

Logan starts to choke from his laughter. Liv takes it all in stride and just beats on his back enthusiastically.

"Gee, thanks for pointing that out, Liv." *I need to google methods of torture.*

"That's what friends are for." She leaves Logan and puts her hand on my shoulder before giving me innocent doe eyes.

Stepping behind a tree, I try to peel off the saturated clumps of fabric, but it's not easy. The layers fight me. The struggle is real. "Liv!" I yell in annoyance. "Come help me out of this damn thing!"

"Are you sure you don't want *Logan* to help you?" she asks, and I swear it sounds like we're in grade school and she's teasing me about my crush.

"Just get over here, hooker!"

"Fine!" She stomps over and starts trying to loosen the knots that secure the laces that wrap around my midsection. "They're leather and they've swollen from the water. I can't get them undone."

"Try harder! I'm freezing!" I complain.

"I can't do it! They won't budge!"

"Do you need my help?" Logan yells from the direction of his truck.

"Yes!" we both scream, and he laughs.

Liv pulls me out from behind the tree and shoves me in his direction. He catches hold of me and his warm hands on my bare shoulders make me shiver even harder, but not from the cold.

"Let me look at what's going on," he says as he bends down to inspect the laces. "I can fix this. Hold on." Rummaging in his truck, he pulls out a pocket knife.

"Wow, you really were a boy scout," I tell him.

"I didn't think you were paying any attention when I told that story."

Busted.

He slips the edge of the knife under the lace and quickly slices through it. The entire banding falls off, but the wet fabric is still clinging tight.

He clears his throat. "Can I help with anything else?" he offers and I love the way his eyes crinkle in amusement.

"I think I can get it from here," I tell him, but I'm reluctant to move. We continue to stand there, staring at each other silently, and my breath starts coming harder and faster. I have to swallow, and when afterward I open my mouth slightly I see him pull in a deep breath and hold it.

"Charli!" Liv yells, intruding into our moment. "Get back behind the tree and change, or strip naked right here, but I'm ready to go."

Grinning, I scoot back to the privacy of the tree, peel the gown down, and slip into the sweatshirt. It's long, as Liv had predicted, and it almost reaches my knees. It's also soft and really warm. *I'm not missing that backpack at all.*

Without any reference to my earlier lie about needing to be near the window, I slide into the truck's cab, right next to Logan. He turns on the heater and drapes his heavy, warm arm around my shoulder. Snuggling up against his body, I fit perfectly into the niche he's providing.

How had I started out my day looking great, but feeling like shit and now I'm looking like a hot mess, but I feel amazing?

The conversation on the way home is relaxed and friendly and Liv doesn't even suggest turning on the radio this time. The trip seems to take no time at all and soon Logan is pulling up into the parking lot behind the bar.

"You should come on up with us. We'll order some pizza," Liv tells him.

He looks at me before answering. "Are you sure?" I nod my head.

"It's the least we can do," Liv insists, grabbing her camera bag and opening the cab door.

"I didn't do that much today, Liv. And you paid me by taking the headshot," he reminds her.

"I didn't mean we owe you dinner because of your help. We owe you dinner because your truck seat was defiled by Charli's naked ass." She jumps out of the truck and head for our apartment stairs.

"Damn it, Liv!" I yell at her disappearing form, but Logan just laughs.

"I'd love to," he says, directly to me.

Taking my hand, we climb the wide stairs and enter the apartment as Liv is taking out her phone to order pizza. "Pepperoni okay? Charli is weird about toppings," she tells him while she waits for the call to connect.

"Sure," he answers and squeezes my hand lightly.

Reluctantly pulling away from him, I walk backward. Never taking my eyes off of his face, I reach behind me for the handle to my bedroom door. "I'm going to go take a shower," I tell Logan. "I can bring you back your sweatshirt if you want?" He's barefooted and wearing only the old sweatpants and navy blue T-shirt. I'm wishing he hadn't thought to remove the shirt before saving me since that would have rendered it unwearable too.

"You can keep it."

Yes!

The hot shower is heavenly, but I make it quick. There's an extremely hot guy in my living room, after all. Pulling on some flannel lounge pants, I consider which of my nerdy T-shirts will be the most suitable for the occasion. Then I decide to slip back into his hoodie. *I really like it and he said I could keep it.* I quickly blow dry my damp hair, but it doesn't take long since I didn't wash it yet, and opt for no makeup. He's seen me looking like a drowned mess today, a clean face shouldn't make him run in horror.

"Perfect timing!" Liv tells me when I come out of the bathroom right as the door closes behind the pizza delivery guy. "Grab the fine china!"

I join them in our small kitchen and pull three paper plates off the stack on top of our microwave. I also pull three cans of soda out of the refrigerator and plop them onto the counter. "We're really treating you to a fine dining experience, aren't we?" I tease as I hand a plate to Logan. "We live classy like this all the time," I confide.

"It's perfect," he says, looking at me with those green eyes of his and making me forget where I am and what I'm doing. Liv, of course, helps me out.

"Hand me a plate too, hooker!" She slides one piece of the hot, stringy pizza onto her plate. I grab three and watch Logan's eyes widen.

"Does she always eat like that?" he whispers to Liv while widening his eyes in mock horror.

"Always," she confirms as she blows to cool her bite. "She usually eats at least half of it by herself, and then finishes what- ever is left the next morning for breakfast. Good thing you have that big lawyer salary because dating her will get expensive."

I shoot her the finger, and Logan laughs yet again.

Logan slides onto the barstool next to mine at the end of the counter we use for meals. "Liv told me you're writing a book?"

"Did she?" I ask while cutting my eyes her way. She ignores me and just continues to read emails on her phone.

"Yeah, when we talked the morning she took my headshots."

"What else did you talk about?" I ask while fidgeting with the rim of the paper plate.

He places his hand on top of mine and stops my nervous fin- gers. "Not much. You woke up and joined us not long after I ar- rived."

I breathe a sigh of relief. I never know what Liv will decide to share.

"What kind of book are you writing?" he asks with interest.

"Fiction. It's a contemporary story, inspired by my parents."

Liv puts her phone away, drops her plate into the trash can and then leans on the counter next to Logan. "Charli is a great writer. It's going to kick ass."

"I believe you," he says with a smile and then turns back to me. "Have you always known you wanted to be a writer?" He has stopped eating to concentrate on my response.

"Yeah, for as long as I can remember. I used to write little stories about my imaginary friends when I first started school. As I got older, I wrote grand adventures for Liv and I and we even acted them out occasionally for our parents. I've always had this need to write down everything I experience. It helps me to make sense of my world. But, this is the first time I've attempted a novel. It's exciting and scary, but I have to try." Taking a deep breath, I look over to see his reaction. I get carried away when I start talking about writing and I hope he doesn't think I monopolized the conversation.

His face is intense, but he is smiling and I relax. "I'm impressed," he admits. "I don't know if I'm brave enough to do exactly what I want with my life, regardless of people's expectations."

I frown and think about what he's said. "The people in my life have always expected me to do exactly what makes me happy. They want me to decide what my life should be."

Liv pushes off from the counter and raises both hands in surrender. "This is getting too intense for me. I'm out."

"Where are you going?" I ask in surprise when she walks over to the desk to grab her laptop.

"I'm going to take this..." She holds the laptop above her head as she leaves. "...to my room and unload the memory card. I want to start working on my images. There are too many distractions in here." Turning to face us, she winks and closes her door.

Okay, maybe I won't torture her later for the naked ass comments. I smile over at Logan and he smiles back. We've both finished our pizza, so I grab his plate and mine and throw them away.

"We could watch a movie if you want," I suggest. "I know you have to work in the morning, so if you'd rather not I understand."

"I'd love to," he says, to my surprise.

I grab my drink and leave the kitchen before dropping down onto our overstuffed couch. Patting the cushion next me, I ask, "Join me?"

He groans with disgust and I frown at him. *He doesn't want to sit next to me?* "I don't bite," I tell him sarcastically.

He crosses his arms over his chest, plants his bare feet wide, and glares at me. "No? Well, your couch swallows!"

I choke and spit my drink out. "What?" *Surely I didn't hear that correctly?*

"The last time I managed to sit down on that little pile of cushions, I felt like it sucked me in and I couldn't get back up and off of it. It's evil."

He acts like my poor couch is the spawn of hell. I start laughing and think back to how he'd looked on it the last time he'd been here. It had been pretty funny!

"I'll help you. Be brave." I pat the cushion again. He sighs wearily and then joins me.

Since he sits down a lot closer to me than the first time we shared the couch, his weight makes me fall toward him. I'm almost on top of his warm, hard body and I have no plans of leaving.

"Okay," he whispers, so closely I can feel his breath on my face. "I've changed my mind. I love this couch."

"Me too." Snuggling in, feeling the heat radiating through the T-shirt, I tip my head against his broad chest. He is so much bigger than me and I feel like I'm disappearing into his embrace. *I'm totally fine with this.*

Feeling the remote under my butt, I pull it from beneath me and start flipping through channels. We settle on a new comedy that neither of us has seen and even though I've had a long and tiring day, sleep is the last thing on my mind. I'm fully alert and enjoying every second I'm wrapped in Logan's arms.

Soon, he begins to twirl long strands of my hair around his fingers. The feel of the light tugging and pulling at my scalp in sensuous and the pace of my breathing picks up slightly. When he kisses the top of my head, I close my eyes.

"I like the blue streaks," he admits, and he sounds surprised.

"Thanks. Me too."

"Think I could get away with it?"

I tilt my face up to look at him and grin. "Oh, I'm sure everyone in your office would just love it. Liv helped me do it and I might have some extra dye?"

"Maybe next time," he chuckles.

"Chicken," I accuse while shaking my head and laying it against his chest again.

"Tell me about yourself, Charli." His tone has become serious again. He is being direct and I want to be honest.

"What do you want to know?" I ask.

Placing a finger under my chin and tilting my face up so that we are looking directly into one another's eyes, he says, "Everything."

"Oh, sure. That should be easy." I pull away gently and laugh. "You know a lot already. You know my best friend, where I work, and I've even told you about the book I'm working on."

"Then tell me about your childhood."

"I'll bore you."

"You'll never bore me," he says confidently.

I sit up and turn so that I'm facing him. Tucking my legs underneath me, I place my hands in my lap and sigh. "Okay, I'm an only child. I had wonderful parents, but they died ten years ago, so Liv and her moms are really my only family now."

He reaches forward and covers my hands. "Oh, God. I'm sorry. I shouldn't have asked."

"No, it's fine. I don't mind talking about it."

"How did they die?" he asks softly.

"Plane crash."

"Really? I'm not sure what I expected, but not that. How did it happen?"

I smile, as I always do when I think of my mom and dad. "My parents were great. I'm not just saying that because I was a child and I idealized them either. They believed that everyone was equally important. They wanted to make a difference in the world."

"They sound like wonderful people." Logan smiles and I go on.

"Yeah, so my dad was an engineer and he worked with a relief organization to help design systems to get clean water to underdeveloped areas. My mom was a linguist and they met when she donated her time as a translator for the foundation. They were always heading out to far-flung locations to help anyone in need. Sometimes I got to go, but often they felt it wasn't safe and left me with Liv's parents, Carol, and Dana."

He frowns. "I'll bet you missed them a lot. It had to be hard to be left behind."

"It was," I admit. "But I understood. Well... I understood a lot better when I was older. I'll admit to a few tantrums in my earlier years."

He laughs. "I'll bet your tantrums were even cute." He releases my hands long enough to softly poke the end of my nose with his index finger, but then reclaims them, still in my lap.

"Definitely not! You may have noticed I have a little bit of a temper?" I'm afraid to admit that my little display of jealousy in the woods today was mild compared to what I'm really capable of.

"Hmmm... maybe just a bit." He grins. "How did your parents become friends with Liv's moms?"

"Dana's father was actually the founder of the charity they worked for. Anyway, when I was thirteen, Mom and Dad were somewhere in South America... I doubt you could even find it on a map... and they booked a small charter plane to get them back to a larger city so they could come home. They'd been gone for a few weeks, and I couldn't wait to see them, but there was an unexpected tropical storm. The pilot lost control and the plane went down. No one survived."

"I'm so sorry." He squeezes my hands in sympathy.

"I miss them, but I'm proud of what they were doing and know they wouldn't want me to be bitter about it. Their death was awful, but I won't let it make me forget how amazing their lives were and the things they taught me to believe in."

He's silent for a long time as he absorbs my story. When he finally speaks, his voice sounds emotional and a little hoarse. "Wow. No wonder you believe so strongly in yourself. You had great examples."

I tilt my head up toward his and he leans forward to kiss me so softly that his lips are barely touching mine. It's sweet, but being this near him is making me a little crazy, so I increase the pressure of my kiss. I hear him groan and I open my mouth a little to deepen our connection. He finally let's go of my hands and I bury them in his hair. His arms go around me and I feel the heat of his hands running up and down my back. He flicks the tip of my earlobe with his tongue and then takes one hand to widen the neck opening of his large sweatshirt I'm wearing. I feel a trail of sensual heat as he nips and kisses my neck, stopping at my collarbone. When he nuzzles on the underside of my jaw, I gasp at the mildly painful pleasure of his coarse stubble as it scrapes against my tender skin.

My breath is coming out in little gasps and in the back of my mind I worry that I sound like a panting dog or something. *God, I hope he doesn't think I sound like that! That's not sexy!*

When I crawl up into his lap and straddle him, I can tell I must be doing something right. I mean, I can really tell. I feel like I'm sitting on a lead pipe, a really big pipe. *Is it too early to check out his pipe?* We haven't even had a real first date. I'm acting like a total slut.

I break away and look at him. His eyelids look heavy and his breathing is as labored as mine. I see beads of sweat in his hairline too. *Damn. I'm a good little slut at least.*

"Is something wrong?" he whispers with concern. His hands have stopped moving, but they are still firmly wrapped around me, cradling my ass possessively.

"Nope." I take a deep and much-needed breath. "I'm just trying to convince myself that we should maybe try dating before doing all the naughty things I'd like to do right now." He closes his eyes and groans, so naturally, I giggle.

"You're right," he says in a tone that makes me think he is wishing I was very wrong. He opens his eyes and I see that mischievous glint I've come to crave. "I'm dying to hear all about these naughty things." He leans closer and kisses the base of my throat. "I'd really love to do all those naughty things." He uses his hands, still around my backside, to slam me hard against him and now I'm the one groaning. "But..." He pulls back slightly and I want to cry out from the loss of his full heat. "I'm not trying to rush you. I'm not just looking for a quick lay, little Chuck."

I cock my head to one side and give him my crooked smile. "You mean... you don't want to fuck a chuck?"

His laughter explodes so unexpectedly loud and deep that his entire body convulses and I'm thrown onto the floor. *Why does he keep knocking me on my ass?*

Then Liv's bedroom door is thrown open with a crash that could wake the dead. "What in the hell is going on out here?"

I stare up at her from my ungraceful position on the floor. "Liv, if we'd been having wild sex out here, you'd be very embarrassed right now."

"If your sex involves laughing like fucking hyenas, then you should be the one embarrassed, not me!" Marching back into her room, she slams her door closed with another crash.

Logan is still laughing and gasping for air, and I see tears streaming down his face. "You two are fucking insane."

"Well, we aren't boring at least."

"No. Never boring." He tries to push himself up and off the couch. His third attempt actually finds success. Then he grabs both of my hands and pulls me up too.

"I really need to go. This has truly been memorable, but I have to work really early tomorrow. When can I see you?" He's playing with my hair again and trailing little kisses on my face and neck between words.

"See me, as in for a date, or see me as in naked?"

He groans again. "Charli…"

"Yes, Logan…"

His hands are at the back of my neck and he leans down so that our foreheads touch. "I really do need to go."

"But going isn't nearly as much fun as coming." This sounds more like something Liv would say, but I couldn't resist. This man does crazy things to me.

He laughs and bends down to gently bite my bottom lip. "I'm pretty sure everything in my life is about to be more fun with you around."

Taking a step back reluctantly, he reaches out for one of my hands and pulls me with him me toward the door. He kisses me one more time and it's so good I can't even think of a single smartass comment to throw back at him. Liv would be so disappointed in me.

I'm still smiling after he's left and I've locked the door behind him.

Chapter Fifteen: Charli
I'm About To Show Him Adorable

"I can't believe you talked me into this," he says.

"Oh please, you're just scared I'm going to win." Logan smiles indulgently at me as I continue to taunt him. "I'm going to kick your ass. You should be scared." *He should be. I'm wicked good at this.*

"I can't believe we've finally managed to find time for a real date." He takes my hand as we walk across the nearly full parking lot. "You know, I really wanted to take you out to a nice restaurant or to see a movie at least."

"Our schedules suck. You work ridiculously long hours all week and I work every evening on weekends." I'm having to take almost three steps for his one, but luckily I'm excited and full of energy, so it's not posing a problem. I've been looking forward to this all week.

"It doesn't matter. We'll make this work," he tells me as he gives me a quick kiss and holds the entrance door open for me.

We're at the new indoor go-kart track that opened right outside the city. This place is huge and I can't wait to see if the drive has been worth it. We purchase the mandatory helmet liners, get fitted for helmets, sign our release, and line up for our turn on the course.

"Are you even going to fit in this thing, Logan?" I'm laughing as he is trying to fold his long legs into the go-kart. It's a tight squeeze, even with the seat all the way back. He gets his turn to laugh right back at me when they pull my seat all the way up, and still need to slide a cushion behind my back to make sure I can reach the pedals.

The reek of engine fumes and clouds of exhaust makes the whole building look hazy and out of focus, but I'm not concerned. *This is awesome!* We're given the okay to pull up to the starting line and I tighten my grip on the steering wheel, anticipating the flag drop.

I look over toward Logan and put on my game face. "You're going down!"

I might be a little competitive. He just smiles back like he thinks my confidence is adorable. *I'm about to show him adorable.*

After only two laps, I notice he's now really concentrating on his driving. He realizes my bragging has merit.

Five races later, we stink like serious grease monkeys. I have sweaty helmet hair, but I'm happy as I wait at the counter to receive the little plastic trophy that confirms my skill. When the lady hands it over, I grab it and run back toward Logan. He's waiting near the exit and smiling at my excitement. The closer I get to him, the more I pick up my pace, and by the time I'm almost on top of him, I jump up and wrap my arms and legs around his body.

The force pushes him back a little, but not much, and he settles his hands under my butt to keep me in position. *I like this position.* I can feel that he likes it too. I pull myself even higher and tighter against him and he brings his head forward to kiss me.

"Excuse me! This is a family friendly establishment. Can you please take your public displays of lust outside?"

I break away from Logan's face and see an exhausted looking, middle-aged woman with a really bad perm. She's staring at us in disgust. Behind her are two boys in their early teens, smirking and whispering.

"Oh, I'm so sorry. Really," I say. I mean it too. I'm sorry that we've probably given some spank bank material to her teens, but not quite sorry enough to let go of Logan. He apparently feels the same way, since he keeps holding on to me and pushes us out together through the nearby exit door. He continues to keep me locked onto him all the way to his Chevy pickup.

"I kind of like being your human shield," I tell him.

"My human shield?"

"Yep. I'm shielding frazzled mothers and hormonal teens from seeing your stick shift. It currently feels impressive enough that it would be impossible to hide if you weren't wearing me as your disguise."

"You are so weird." He removes one hand just long enough to unlock the truck's cab and open the door. "But I'm learning that I really like weird."

He lays me on the bench seat and crawls in too, right on top of me. I keep my legs around him, but let my arms unclasp. Dropping my trophy into the floorboard, I allow both hands to roam over his chest and back. Sliding my fingers under his shirt, I feel the defined ridges of his flat stomach and I notice my breathing is becoming erratic. His kisses are hot and intense and my enthusiasm matches his, even if it's not as visibly evident. Bracing himself with one arm, his other hand slips beneath the back of my shirt to unclasp my bra.

Well, hello hand. I'm happy to meet you. The release causes the girls to spring to attention and when that same brave hand slides forward to cup one of my breasts, I arch my back in sheer pleasure.

"Fuck!" Logan's voice is right near my ear.

"Well, not yet, but I think we're getting there," I say in a sultry whisper. Looking at him, I wonder why he looks so disgusted all of a sudden. *My tits aren't huge, but they're nice and perky.*

Then, as he yells "Fuck" again, I notice the banging noise. I try to look past his shoulder and I see a security guard is right outside the driver's side window, banging on the glass with his open palm.

"Fuck." My expletive might be redundant at this point, but it seems well warranted.

Logan makes sure my shirt is pulled down and nothing is exposed, before putting a hand on either side of me and pushing away. It ends up being a lot harder than either of us imaged in the small space, and I'm practically sitting in the floorboard with my trophy before he manages to get out of the truck.

The guard is red in the face with anger. Logan is red in the face with frustrated lust.

The heavyset security guard is an older man and he's breathing as hard as we were a few seconds ago. I'm worried he's going to have a heart attack. "We have families here and we don't need you two out here putting on a show like horny teenagers! For God's sake, you're old enough to get a hotel room and a little privacy. Just leave and don't let me catch you here again!" Obviously unsure how to deal with us, I feel kind of sorry for the poor guy.

Logan runs a hand through his hair and stuffs both hands into his pockets. "Yeah, sorry about this. We'll go." I want to giggle as I think about him making this apology with a huge erection, front, and center.

After his embarrassed apology to the guard, Logan gets back in the truck and puts the key in the ignition before turning toward me. He shakes his head but grins at me. "Get back up here and put your seatbelt on, Charli."

"I'm working on it," I grunt as I try to scramble back onto the truck's seat.

"Well, that was humiliating." Logan sighs and looks over at me.

"It was. But look at the bright side, since we've been banned you don't have to worry about the humiliation of the future go-kart races that you'd have lost to me."

He reaches out to slide me closer to him and then kisses the top of my head. "There is always that."

Chapter Sixteen: Charli
Keeping It Classy

"So, how was your date?" Liv asks me when we finally have a minute to talk after our shift. We'd been slammed tonight with The Crash at full capacity.

"Don't ask." I pull the wad of bills out of my apron pocket and start sorting and smoothing them behind the counter. Saturday is always my best tip night, and this one didn't disappoint. Liv sits down on the barstool across from me and waits for my explanation. Her constant nail tapping is driving me crazy and messing up my counting abilities anyway, so I give in to her impatience.

"We had a great time racing go-karts. I kicked his ass." I can't help but smile as I remember his face when he tried to pass off my wins as no big deal. I'll admit to being competitive, but I'm betting from his reaction, he is too.

"And..."

"And he's funny and sweet and hot. Really hot. Have I mentioned recently how Fuckin' Hawt he is?" I lean my back against the wall at the back of the bar.

"Recently? As in, several times in the last half hour, alone?" Liv reaches for the jar of Maraschino cherries near me and uses a toothpick to spear one from the almost full jar. She has a thing for cherries and cherry flavoring. When Ronan walks by glaring at her, she just smiles and pops another one into her mouth.

"Oh, I guess I've mentioned it." I grab the jar away from her and return it the bar prep area.

"So what went wrong on your date with Fuckin' Hawt Lumberjack Logan?"

"We may have been banned from the track after the security guard caught us making out in the parking lot. If he'd been a couple minutes later with his window banging, we might have been banging too. The real question is, am I upset that we were interrupted, or glad we didn't have sex on our first real date, in the middle of broad daylight, in his old pickup truck? It's tough to call."

She smiles and shakes her head. "Wow. Way to keep it classy, Charlotte."

"So..." I dread asking, but I need to know. "Has Kyle talked to you?"

"Has Kyle talked to me?" Liv taps her finger against the side of her jaw and looks toward the ceiling. Her overdramatic response is getting on my last, exhausted nerve. "Well, he told me when my orders were up. He told me when I dropped a pile of napkins. Is that what you meant?" She crosses her arms under her chest and waits.

"You know what I meant," I huff in exasperation.

"Oh, well if you want to know if he asked about your personal life or why you took all your drink orders down to Ronan's side of the bar tonight... then no, we didn't talk." I hate that my avoidance had been so obvious. "And don't ask me to go play interference now either. I'm too damn tired."

"Sorry," I mutter. "I didn't mean to put you in the middle of this."

She sighs. "I know. Other than work-related discussions, Kyle hasn't confided anything about how he's handling this little situation."

I look over to the open doorway of the back room and see Kyle grabbing several cases of beer to bring out and restock the bar cooler. His shirt is straining over the muscles of his back and it has come up just enough to show a strip of skin above his jeans as he lifts and turns back in our direction. I continue staring at him, and he must know it by now, but he carefully avoids my gaze.

Shit. "What do I do, Liv?"

"Just give him time. He's really into you and he's hurting... and probably a little pissed too, that you don't feel the same. But we both know how great he is and this will blow over eventually."

"You know... I really do like Kyle. I think it's possible that in time I could have felt more. I know we have a lot in common but..."

"But he doesn't make you feel the way Logan does?"

"No," I admit. *Logan makes me feel things I've never felt.*

"It's even different from how you felt for Nick, isn't it?" she asks, daring to say the name of the asshole that I try to forget.

"It is. I thought what I had with Nick was real, and maybe it was, but this..."

"I get it." I look at my best friend. Her forehead is creased and she seems miles away as she twists a cherry stem with enough agitation to make it shred. She's watching Kyle.

"Liv?" I reach forward to put a hand on top of hers.

She startles, like she's forgotten I'm here, and then looks

back toward me. Her face is smooth and worry-free again as she responds. "Yep?"

"Are you… Are you into Kyle?" This possibility had never occurred to me and I'm not sure how I feel about it.

Her shock is instantaneous and so extreme that her face looks like one of those caricatures you can buy on the boardwalk, the ones where they exaggerate your most prominent feature. "Hell no! Why would you think that?" Her voice is loud enough that Kyle, Ronan, and even our other two waitresses, Brooke and Chelsea, stop their end of shift duties to look at us. But their curiosity doesn't last long. They're used to our random outbursts.

"I don't know. You were staring at him like I ran over your puppy or something so I just wondered if maybe…" I shrug my shoulders.

"No, most definitely not. I love Kyle in that 'almost a brother, let me pester you constantly but still think you deserve the best ever,' kind of way. I could never sleep with him!"

I believe her. We don't lie to each other. "Okay, good. I couldn't stand the thought of you being hurt because he didn't feel the same." *I'm such a hypocrite. Isn't this exactly what Kyle is going through because of me?*

Standing, she looks at Kyle and then back at me. "I feel sorry for him, of course, and I know it must suck to be dealing with the unrequited love shit… but I'm also a little jealous that he knows what that feels like. I'm jealous of you too. I don't begrudge you this experience and I'm glad that you've met someone that makes you act completely idiotic, but I want to know what it's like too." She laughs lightly. "Damn. Now I'm whining. Ignore me, please."

I come around the bar and lean my head down onto her shoulder. She pats my head affectionately for a few seconds, then playfully shoves me away. "Don't feel sorry for me, Charli. You know I hate pity."

"I don't feel sorry for you. And I'm not worried for you either. You've always had a ton of guys panting after you, and you'll find one to pant over too. I've no doubt at all."

"I'm not the panting type, but finding one that I want to go out with more than a couple of times sounds good. Some guys are fun to hang out with but suck in bed. I've been with guys that make my toes curl, but I can't enjoy just talking to them. There have even been a few gorgeous, smart guys that are good in and out of bed, but they just didn't make me feel like I couldn't live without them. I'm a greedy and ungrateful bitch."

"No, you aren't. But you are a lazy bitch." I grab her arm and pull her over to join me behind the bar. "So help me finish up so we can go to bed. I'm exhausted."

"Slave driver! You're worse than Ronan!"

Ronan walks by and frowns at us. "No, she isn't." Naturally, we laugh.

Chapter Seventeen: Logan
Still Breathing

"Busy?"

I look up from the file in front of me to see the shape of a woman that almost any man on the planet would claim is perfect. The strong light from the window across from my office casts her as a dark silhouette and doesn't allow me to see her features, but I know who it is. "Hey, Victoria. What's up?"

Gliding into the room, I wonder, as I have before, how she does it in those stilts she calls shoes. She's tall enough to simply turn her shapely backside toward the corner of my desk and slide right onto it. Charli would've had to jump a little to even consider using the heavy mahogany surface as a perch.

Charli...what are you doing right now? Thinking of her, as I have done more than a million times already today, makes me smile.

Victoria raises her eyebrow and smiles at me. "Well, I'm happy to see you too." I realize she assumes my happy expression is intended for her. It's probably safer to let her keep on assuming.

We have to work together a lot.

"Are you here for the Stravos file?" I look down at my desk and shuffle the papers around. "I've finished going over it and it looks good."

"No, actually I was just coming to make sure you're still breathing." Her words try too hard to sound amusing and I know it has become obvious I'm avoiding her.

"Oh, well thanks for the concern but as you can see, I'm still alive and well." I smile, hoping she will let it go, but knowing that isn't likely.

Brushing at some imaginary dust on the corner of the massive desk, she rearranges the location of my stapler and pen holder and straightens the blotter before looking right into my eyes and holding my gaze. It's long enough that I start to feel uncomfortable.

I used to enjoy our harmless flirting, but now that I'm seeing Charli, it's like a betrayal.

"I'm glad to hear it," she says, finally lowering her gaze. "I know you're at all of the mandatory meetings, and I see you around the office throughout the day, but you never stop by my office to chat anymore. Matt says he hasn't seen you all week either and that you keep blowing off his suggestions to hang out after work. Is your caseload that overwhelming? Are you behind with anything?" She slowly slips off the desk, walks to the back of my chair and stops. Leaning down she puts her hands on my shoulders and I tense. "I'd be happy to help you. What can I do?" she whispers directly into my ear.

If a guy put his hands on a woman's shoulders at work, even if they hung out socially, it would be sexual harassment and his job would be in jeopardy. I know better than act like she's being inappropriate, though. My colleagues would think I was being ridiculous and actually get jealous that she wasn't directing that attention at them. As far as the partners are concerned...she is a legal dynamo and does no wrong.

Turning in my chair to face her, knowing this maneuver will force her to remove her hands, I straighten my spine before speaking. I don't want to hurt her feelings, but she just isn't Charli. "Thank you. Truly. But I have everything under control."

"Hmmm... if you say so."

"Do you need anything else, Victoria?" I smile and try hard to sound accommodating, but the slight narrowing of her eyes makes me suspect that she's aware I'm trying to get rid of her. She doesn't like it.

"Matt, Mari and I are planning on going to that bar again tonight and wanted to know if you'd like to join us?"

I feel my stomach drop with dread. "Which bar?"

"That bar we went to with the little rude waitress. What was her name?" She tilts her chin upward and looks toward the ceiling as if her memory has failed her, but we both know she remembers the name she's searching for. "Chuck? I think that's it." She looks right at me to gauge my reaction and I try my best to act like the name barely registers.

"I thought you didn't like that bar." I stand perfectly still, daring her to say more.

"It kind of grows on you, I guess." Walking to the file cabinets behind my desk, she lightly trails a fingertip along the top of each one. "Matt seems to think you really liked it. Did you?" She's turned to look back at me again. "Did you really like that bar, Logan?"

"It's fine," I study the papers on my desk, the clock on the wall, and the open doorway, determined not to look at her unless I have to. "But I think I'll take a raincheck if that's okay?"

As much as it's killing me to say no to the opportunity of seeing Charli again, I don't like the idea of Victoria or Matt playing witness to our interactions. I just need a little more time before I explain to them about my new relationship. They've been good friends to me in the past, but this situation is different. I should feel like a dick for keeping Charli a secret, but it's really for her benefit. Victoria is just too competitive and hurt over my lack of interest in her. Matt will feel like I went after something he has made a claim on as if Charli is a piece of property. They'll take their anger with me, out on her.

"You should try that new place over on Fourth. Remember, Scott told us about it. He said Kelly loved it. I think it's called ZuBar?" I tell her, in a last ditch effort to get them to alter their plans.

"Maybe," she says with a nonchalant shrug as if already bored with the conversation.

I need to change her focus. "So, since you offered, maybe you could look over this before it goes to the shareholders? Just to double check?" I stand up and hand her the folder. We both know she doesn't need to check anything, but she plays along anyway.

"Of course, Logan." She takes the folder with her left hand, briefly looks down at it, and then takes a step closer to me. She reaches out her right hand and lays it flat on the knot at the top of my tie and holds it there a few seconds while looking up at me through her lashes. Then she slowly lowers her hand, smoothing my tie down and doesn't stop until it is resting right above my navel. "I like this tie. Is it new?"

"Ummm, no. No, I've had it a long time, actually." I try not to move backward, even though my body is screaming to step away from her. I know she's beautiful and desirable, but whatever mild interest I may have once harbored, it's completely gone. Now I fantasize about a tiny, smart-mouthed waitress with thick dark hair, amazing eyes, and a smile that makes me embarrassingly crazy.

"Well, I can't believe I've never noticed it before. I'm certainly noticing it now." She finally removes her hand, and I exhale in relief. I used to find her aggression sexy, but now I'm just ready for her to leave my office.

"Thanks." I walk back to my desk and start to shuffle through the remaining files to give myself something to do. I can feel her still watching me.

"I guess I'll let you get back to… Well, back to whatever it is you're doing. Don't work too hard, though. Ambition is great, and I fully approve, but we all need to enjoy ourselves. We should really make time to enjoy each other soon." Her voice deepens and softens on the last suggestion, and then she finally walks out of my office and closes the door behind her.

How am I going to handle this clusterfuck?

We've always enjoyed mildly suggestive conversations and double meanings, but after I encouraged her that night at the bar, I know she's pushing harder. She's also smart and my fascination with Charli had not only been noted but had spurred on a little jealousy it seems. My work week will be total hell as soon as she figures out I'm dating Charli. *Shit.*

Chapter Eighteen: Charli

Lions, Tigers, and... Lumberjacks?

My cheeks ache. The muscles literally ache. I don't think I've ever smiled this much in my entire life. Looking at the backlit screen of my phone, I read his texts again. It feels like when I had that crush on Donnie Spencer in the sixth grade, and I just can't quit smiling.

"Jeez, Charli... You look like the Joker," Liv says from the couch. "It's creeping me out."

I smile even bigger and then stick out my tongue at her. Let's face it, if I'm going to feel like a junior high kid, I might as well act like one too. "We're making plans for later today and Logan's texts are so sweet. Want me to read them to you?"

"Absolutely not." She pretends to gag. "I'm not even finished with my cereal and I'm just not prepared for that kind of crap this early."

Liv's words might be bitchy, but every time I look in her direction, she's smiling. I know she's happy for me, but it's just not her style to admit it.

"So… What are you and Prince Lumberjack planning?" She takes a bite of her cereal and flips through a magazine. "Looking for another parking lot in a family establishment? Hoping for a public indecency charge this time, maybe?"

"We're going to the zoo," I say happily, clapping my hands a couple of times. I love the zoo.

"Ewwww… No, thanks." Liv turns up her nose in disgust. "Walking around, looking at all those animals and smelling their heat-ripened shit? I'll pass." She waves her spoon around like it's her royal scepter and she's made an official decree.

"Oh, you know all those baby animals are cute!" I bounce down onto the couch with her. She glares when she has to pick up a few dry flakes of her disgusting cereal that bounced out of the bowl because of me.

Giving up on breakfast, she puts the bowl on the coffee table. "Charli, they all grow up into adult animals that aren't nearly so cute. And they stink! That's why I wouldn't let you bring home that puppy those people were selling in front of the grocery store, or the kitten Brooke offered you from her cat's latest litter or even that damn gerbil Kyle's neighbor wanted to get rid of!"

"You are no fun!" I point out. "I should be allowed to have a pet in my own apartment if I want."

"You have your ridiculous collection of stuffed animals. It's creepy and juvenile, but hey, I don't judge!" she says, throwing both hands up in surrender and I laugh.

"You act like I'm suggesting we dance naked in public," I accuse.

She yawns and stretches. "I'd actually be down for that. Sounds fun."

An hour later I'm dressed in frayed denim shorts, a gray tank top, a cute little straw fedora - and my favorite chucks of course

- when I hear a knock. I practically skip to the door and throw it open with a huge grin on my face.

"Hey, Sexy!" My smile freezes when I see it's not Logan.

Shit. It's Kyle.

I'd give anything to take my greeting back, as he just stands there and looks at me. We haven't said more than a few words to each other in over a week, and I'm at a loss as to why he'd be here. He's made it perfectly clear that he isn't happy about me deciding to go out with Logan.

"Hey, Kyle. What's up?" I can't even make eye contact with him and instead I studiously pick at my cuticle as though the little-torn edge is of immediate importance.

"Ronan asked me to come up here and see if you knew where Brooke's at. She was supposed to come in early today and help me with inventory, but she didn't show. We've tried calling and texting, but we can't get hold of her."

"Oh. Ummm, no, I haven't talked to her. Sorry. Do you want to come in and ask Liv?" He's silent again for several seconds, so I finally look up at him, but he just stares back at me. "What, Kyle?" I hate thinking he's mad at me or that I've hurt him.

"I hope you know what you're doing, Charli."

I appreciate that he cares enough to worry about me, but damn, I'm an adult and I can make my own decisions. "Kyle..." I try not to sound angry, but it's hard. "Logan's a good guy. I really like him and I'm happy that he seems to like me too."

"Why wouldn't he like you? Please tell me you don't think he's better than you, or that you aren't good enough for him because that is total bullshit!" He puts one fist on the doorframe and leans into it. "Charli, you're more than just beautiful and he better damn well know it. You're smart and funny and you find joy in everything. And you're talented. Just because he works

119

at some fancy law firm and probably makes more than all of us combined, doesn't make him better." He reaches his free hand toward me, and then changes his mind and lets it drop to dangle at his side. "If he doesn't make you understand and believe that, then he's worse than stupid."

I feel the hot prickle of tears forming in my eyes and the back of my throat feels congested and heavy, as I fight back the tears. "Thank you. I do love you, Kyle. I hope you understand that."

"I know you love me, but you certainly aren't in love with me. And that's a bitch, but I don't guess there's anything to be done about it."

I take a step forward, fully intending to wrap my arms around this incredible man and make him realize how special he is, but he backs up enough to stop me and I falter. "Sorry," I mumble in embarrassment.

"Me too." He turns away and I know he's trying to escape as quickly as he can, but he's stopped by the sight of Logan coming through the exterior staircase door.

Logan, of course, has no idea about our awkward situation and strides forward. His smile is in place and hand thrust forward, as he's ready to introduce himself to Kyle. "Hi, I'm Logan."

Kyle must be at the breaking point because he isn't normally rude, but instead of reciprocating Logan's gesture of friendship, he just stares at the hand until it becomes uncomfortable enough for Logan to lower it back to his side. I'm completely unprepared for how to handle this.

"Is there a party in our hallway?" Liv saunters up behind me, places one hand on an extended hip, and raises one eyebrow. "Because I wasn't invited, so let's face it, it's going to suck." Salvation has arrived, in the form of my best friend. Liv is just what I needed.

"No. I was just leaving." Kyle says before walking to the metal stairs. His boots fall heavy and quick as he descends and I know he just wants to get away.

"What's his problem?" Logan says and looks toward the space Kyle disappeared into.

Liv comes forward, and putting an arm around him, steers him into our apartment. "Oh, Kyle is awesome and just waiting for you to screw it up with Charli so he can have her."

"Liv!" *What had I said about her being my salvation? I take it back!*

Logan is looking pissed and his fists are clenched at his side.

"I'm just letting Logan know the score, Charli. He should understand that you like him, but if he doesn't treat you right, you have good options." She pats his shoulder as if consoling a small child. "But don't worry...I'm rooting for you, Lumberjack."

His anger turns to confusion. "Lumberjack?"

"Oh, Charli hasn't told you about her little fetish? Let me enlighten you. She..."

"Shut up!" I grab Logan and try to manhandle him out the door. "We're leaving now, Judas. Please reflect on all your wrong-doing and we will discuss your behavior later when I get home."

She just laughs and waggles her fingers in farewell as she closes the door behind us.

"You have a lumberjack fetish?" He seems fascinated by this new kernel of knowledge that Liv has so generously shared with him, and I groan in disgust. Our second date probably isn't the best time to explain this little fantasy I harbor.

Of course, we aren't exactly following the normal path. Lewd behavior in public isn't typical of a first date, after all.

"So..." He wraps his warm heavy arm around my shoulder as we walk toward his truck. "Plaid shirts? Knit hats and an axe? Do

I need to grow a beard?" His laughter is playful and light and I'm glad we've moved past the Kyle mess.

Had this been Liv's plan all along? The girl is hugely embarrassing at times, but she's wicked smart and can manipulate a situation better than anyone I know.

"A beard?" I step back and narrow my eyes to look at him more closely. Best case scenario, maybe he gives in and I get to see him in some flannel in the near future. "Well, only a short one that's neatly trimmed," I explain. "I'm not into the full throttle, bush beard."

His laughter, as he pretends to consider this new look, is promising. "I'm not too sure how well that would go over at the office. It might not be considered very professional."

"Well, it would be *shit hot.*" I stress the last two words and try out an exaggerated huskiness. I'm just being silly, but it seems to throw him off and he stumbles a little as he reaches for the truck's door handle.

"Damn," he says, "Maybe I should use my vacation time to grow one. I have a feeling it would be worth it."

This time I'm the one thrown off my game when he presses my back against the truck, braces his feet on the outside of mine, and leans his body forward until I'm completely pinned in place. The heat from every point of contact is searing and I feel soft flutters low in my belly.

"Aren't you worried a beard would be scratchy against your soft skin?" He whispers softly into my ear and even his breath feels overheated. Slowly, he runs his chin down the side of my neck and exhales. I feel gooseflesh tingling along my arms and legs and the girls are responding once again. *I think they really like him.*

How does he do this when he's barely touching me? "Hmmmm…" I'm too muddled to even make a coherent sentence right now.

"Maybe it's time." His voice is deep and suggestive and whatever he's offering, I'm buying.

"Yep…time…maybe…" *Am I making any sense at all?*

"It's time to get into the truck so we can go to the zoo, Charli." He runs his long finger down my forehead, the bridge of my nose, my lips, and finally ends at the tip of my chin.

I let out the soft breath I'd been holding captive since his finger had started its path. "The zoo?" *What is he talking about? What zoo?*

He pulls away from me and holds out the door of the truck, waiting for me to crawl into the cab. Several confused seconds later, his words sink in.

"Oh! The zoo! Yeah, we're going to the zoo today. Animals. Lots of animals." Suddenly the appeal of our destination falls a few notches. There are so many ways we could spend our afternoon.

After several miles of him repeatedly smiling over at me, me smiling back in response, and then us both looking away, I finally feel composed enough to try and have a real conversation. "I told you about my parents, tell me about yours. Is your dad a lawyer too?" I wonder just how intimidating his past will be. I know that money doesn't make you better than anyone, but some people feel differently.

How does his family feel about it? Will they disapprove of us dating if they know I work in a bar? Will their disapproval change his opinion of our relationship?

"Hardly!" He laughs, and he seems happy to explain. "My dad is a mechanic and my mom stayed home to raise me and my younger sister, Jenna. We lived in a small, quiet neighborhood and I had a happy, if uneventful, childhood."

I look over at him in shock. "Really? That's not what I expected to hear."

"Why?" He looks puzzled.

"I guess I assumed you had a more privileged childhood. I thought maybe you were one of those kids that had everything."

"No, not at all." He shakes his head to emphasize his point. "We had the necessities and never did without anything important, but we were a paycheck to paycheck kind of family. I sometimes wonder if my parents would have been okay with me getting a job right out of high school. Neither one of them went any further, but I was always a good student and my guidance counselor convinced us I should go to college."

"Oh." I hadn't even been close to understanding Logan's past. I'd worried so much about how our different upbringings would affect us, but this new understanding is going a long way to calm those worries.

He smiles over at me briefly before going on with his story. "We really didn't have the money for college. My parents offered to refinance their house, but I just couldn't let them do it. Fortunately, I'm a pretty good baseball player and I managed to get enough of a scholarship that, in combination with working on campus, I could manage to pay for university. Of course, law school was a lot harder to manage, so I had to work and took out some hefty student loans." I can hear a note of worry in his voice. "It will take me years to pay it all back, even with the great job Matt helped me land."

This makes me sit up straighter. "Matt got you your job?" It's the last thing I expected to hear. Matt had seemed like such a dick. *Had I pegged him wrong too?*

"Well, he got me the interview..." he grins, "but I'd like to think I got myself the job."

He's smiling still, so I feel safe I haven't offended him. "Sorry. I didn't mean to imply you couldn't get your own job. I really don't know anything about your work."

"Matt's dad, Mr. Burke, is one of the partners so Matt always knew his job situation was pretty secure. Matt and I became friends in our freshman year of college, along with Scott, when we were all on the baseball team. Later, Matt told his dad about me and got me an initial meeting, which went really well, and now I even have hopes of making partner someday." I watch as he exits the highway and follows the signs that lead us toward our destination. "It's a future I never imagined for myself and I know it's a realized dream for my parents. I will be able to have so much more than anyone from my family ever has."

"That's great, Logan. I'm sure your family is very proud of you. You must have worked hard for your position." I don't say anything else, but my tone alerts him to the question I left off.

"But?" He raises his eyebrows, but thankfully, he doesn't look upset with me.

I plunge ahead. "I just wonder if you're happy?"

His brow furrows and he takes his eyes off the road for a couple of seconds to watch me. "Why wouldn't I be happy? I have a job most only dream about and a financially secure future. I'll be able to help my parents, as they get older, help my sister with college, and hopefully one day I'll have my own family to take care of too."

"I understand. That is all important and I'm not denying any of it... but I just wonder if you actually enjoy what you do?" I lower my voice. "Do you like being a lawyer?"

"Why would you ask me that?" He doesn't seem pissed, but there is certainly some confusion and maybe a little aggravation.

I slide my hand over and rest it on his thigh. I feel his warmth and the muscle underneath my fingers tightens when he presses a little harder on the gas. "You're at that law firm so many hours a day. Even when we talk after hours, it seems like you've had to take work home. Your quality of life is important too. I'm not trying to upset you or anything. If you like your job, that's awesome and I'm happy for you, but you've never acted like practicing law is something you're passionate about." There is a tightness in his jaw and I start to panic. "I could be totally wrong, of course! I'm just trying to figure you out. I want to know you, Logan."

He thinks about what I've said as he maneuvers through traffic and finally pulls into the parking lot of the zoo. After killing the engine, he twists to face me. "I don't think my job is awful and it will help me to get what I want from life, so I guess I'm pretty lucky. Not everyone is passionate about something that's a feasible career. I respect people that work hard, even at things they hate, to provide for themselves and the people they love."

"Okay." I take a deep breath and smile. "Fair enough."

Hoping he knows I didn't mean to suggest his career was a mistake, or that I don't respect someone for earning a living the best way they can, I wait to see what he'll do next. When I feel him take my much smaller hand off the top of his thigh and lace his large fingers into mine, a deep tension drains out of me.

"Ready to enjoy your day off?" he asks softly.

I lift his hand up and kiss the back of his knuckles. "Absolutely. Let's go."

We get our tickets and join the loud mob of families entering the gate single file through the turnstiles. The weather is balmy and there's the threat of rain, but it hasn't deterred anyone and the paths are clogged with people, wagons, and strollers. I grab Logan's hand and pull him along to each of the exhibits and laugh at him for trying to use the map and make a plan. The zoo is for spontaneity, not schedules!

He leans against the fence that houses the giraffe exhibit. "Do you ever get tired? I swear you must have ADHD or something!" he complains once again.

"We've only been here for about two hours and there's so much more to see." I grab his hand and try to pull him along. It's impossible for me to move him anywhere without his cooperation.

"Charli, I don't think I can keep up with you." He shakes his head in defeat.

I try a new tactic. Leaning my body against his, I reach around behind him and slide my hands in the back pockets of his jeans. "My stamina is legendary," I whisper with a wink. He groans deep enough for me to hear it rumble in his chest.

He pulls my hands out of his pockets and I pout. This just makes him laugh. Taking hold of my arm, he steers us over to a shady bench, partially hidden behind a statue of an elephant. I find myself being yanked hastily down to sit on his lap, but I'm not about to complain.

"Legendary?" he asks. "That's promising, but can I persuade you to rest with me for a minute?" His persuasion includes softly nuzzling at my neck, so I decide taking a break might not be too bad.

"Mmmm hmmm..." I close my eyes and enjoy the sensation of his lips gliding over my flesh. The heat of his breath as he exhales onto the damp path his tongue is making causes my bones to go limp. "Logan..."

His arms wrap tightly around my middle and I let my head fall back a little to give him better access. When I feel his fingertips tracing the edge of my T-shirt's low, V-neckline, I groan and slide my hands into his hair.

"Wow..." I bolt off Logan's lap when I hear a woman's voice right beside us. "You weren't kidding, Scott. He's very into her." The feminine observation is joined by male laughter, equally close.

Logan stands up slowly, adjust his clothing without embarrassment, and grins. "Guilty, as charged." I feel his arm snake around me and I'm grateful for its steadying support.

I look down and make sure my clothing isn't branding me the town harlot. Thankfully, the T-shirt is only slightly askew, but I pray the newcomers don't notice the damp, red irritations on my chest from Logan's stubble. *My neck is probably disgraceful too, but I can't see it!*

Bringing my eyes back up, I see the woman is petite with dark cinnamon hair styled in a pixie cut. She also has the brightest smile I've ever seen, and is standing with a familiar looking man on one side, and a monstrosity that looks like a stroller on steroids on her other. "Ummm...hi?" I give a hesitant little wave.

Expecting a handshake at most, I'm speechless when she steps forward, pulls me away from Logan and envelopes me in a firm, friendly hug. Before release, she gives me a quick tight squeeze and I smell strawberry shampoo with an undertone of sour milk. Next, she holds onto both of my hands and pushes me out to arm's length so she can inspect me from head to toe.

"You're so cute! No wonder you caught his eye." She lets go of one of my hands and uses the other to spin me around in a complete circle. "And Scott says you're smart and a little sassy and that's just what Logan needs. We have to keep our men from getting too full of their own importance, now don't we?" I'm finally free when she puts both hands on her own hips and looks from Logan to the man standing beside her silently. "Logan is great...

but I guess you know that! I've been telling him it is about time he finds someone and to remember he can't make his career the most important thing in his life. It took Scott some time to figure that out too." She puts her arm around him. "He knew he had to get his priorities in order before I'd marry him. And look at them now, both out enjoying this nice weekend! And now we..."

"Kelly, breathe!" Logan commands with a laugh. Turning to me, he makes the introductions. "Charli, this is Kelly. She's married to my friend, Scott. You may remember him from the bar?"

Taking a better look at the man beside Kelly, I do remember him. He'd been with Logan that first night we met, but also when Logan had returned the next night and knocked me flat on my ass.

"Oh, yes... I remember," I say. "It's nice to see you again, Scott. And Kelly..."

"Yes, yes...it's so great to meet you!" Kelly interrupts. "I've been looking forward to this! I'll bet we end up being great friends. Sometime soon we really need to... "

Scott quickly leans closer to his wife, kisses her temple, and lays a silencing finger gently over her lips. "You, my love, are an acquired taste. Let poor Charli try to acclimate, okay?"

In response she pushes her elbow back into his stomach, but not with any real force, and laughs. "Acquired taste, huh? You must have acquired it quickly since you started chasing me the minute we met."

"Absolutely the best decision I've ever made, too." Scott looks at Kelly like they are the only two people in the world. It's beautiful, and a little embarrassing, to witness.

Kelly seems to visibly soften under his gaze. "And later I plan..." The gentle words come to a screeching halt. "Stop it, Bella! That's your sister's binky!"

This abrupt change of pace causes me to look at the source of Kelly's aggravation. Noises are coming from her beast of a stroller and the two little occupants are now demanding attention. Identical, pink-cheeked girls with heads full of soft auburn curls and big brown eyes are precious... and horrifyingly loud. Their matching expressions of outrage might be funny if I didn't feel like my ears were about to bleed.

I look over at Logan and notice he is wincing in pain and trying to back away from the chaos. "Coward!" I mouth at him, but he just lifts his shoulders in apology and takes another step back.

Kelly never breaks a sweat. She swipes the stolen pacifier from baby number two and plugs it back into baby number one's mouth. Then reaching under the little thief's bottom to unearth the missing pacifier that had caused the theft, Kelly pops the recovered treasure into number two's now vacant mouth. This all happens in mere seconds and both babies are calm and quiet again.

I'm still feeling disoriented, but this amazing mom turns to me and acts like nothing has happened. "These two beautiful monsters are our daughters, Isabella, and Sophia." She softly touches the top of each baby's head and smiles proudly.

I find myself smiling back at this friendly little firecracker and thinking how much Liv would adore her. "The girls are adorable. How old are they?"

"Seven months. I can't believe how quickly they're growing up! I wasn't sure about us having kids so soon after we got married and then we found out they were twins and I really freaked out but now..."

I feel Logan press against my back and realize he has rejoined us. "It's great running into you guys..."

Scott puts his arm around his wife and winks. "I think that's our cue, Kelly."

"Shit...I didn't mean to run you off," Logan says, but Scott waves his apology away.

"I remember what it's like. Enjoy your date." Scott takes hold of the stroller and starts trying to maneuver it back around. It doesn't look easy.

Logan, still behind me, slides his arms around my waist and pulls be back against his body. "We will." The words are innocent, but his tone isn't and I feel myself blushing.

Kelly is shaking her head and rolling her eyes at Logan. "I won't cut into any more of your time, but Charli we really should get together and have lunch or something. I'm starved for adult conversation. I love my girls, but since I've decided to be a stay at home mom, I can feel my brain turning to mush. I'll get your number from Logan later."

"I'd like that. It was great meeting you." I'm being completely sincere. It might be hard to wedge a word into a conversation with her, but she seems so loving and fun that I find myself looking forward to knowing her better. "Oh," I call toward Scott when he finally has the stroller facing the right direction to leave. "It was good to see you again!"

"You too, *Chuck*." He laughs at his own joke as Kelly pokes him and Logan groans. "Have fun, but not too much fun. Try and remember it's a family place, okay?"

Oh, God! Logan has obviously told him about the go-karts.

"Dude, really?" Logan's laughing but I'm mortified.

We watch them walk away, pushing their babies and whispering to one another. I'm pretty sure it's about us. "I like your friends."

Lacing his fingers into mine, he smiles down at me. "They're great. Kelly is something to behold when she gets going, but

131

they're some of the best people I know." He kisses me lightly and my lips tingle from the soft contact. "I pray I have a marriage half as good as theirs one day."

I smile back, unsure how to respond to his comment. Marriage is something I believe in and hope for in my future too, but I feel weird discussing it so soon. I can't help but wonder if he wants kids with his future marriage. It's only our second date, and if I ask, he will think I'm one of those women obsessing over their biological clock. He'll assume I'm already drawing hearts, filling notebooks with a 'Mrs.' attached to my name and his, and ready to hire a contractor for that white picket fence. I'm a long way off from considering him, or anyone, serious enough for forever.

Maybe I need to worry more about us making it to the petting zoo before we have to leave, and less about a future that is too far away to even be on the radar yet.

"What next?" he asks and I wonder if he noticed my tension over him mentioning marriage.

"It doesn't matter. I'm just happy to be here with you," I tell him.

"Good." He kisses me again. "I feel the same."

We halt in front of the zebras and watch the mother gently nudging her colt to stand. "Logan?" I ask.

"Yeah?" He continues to watch the animals.

"I get your friendship with Scott and Kelly, but Matt and Victoria..." Those two had seemed like real pieces of work and I just can't reconcile what I'd seen of their personalities with what I'm learning about Logan.

"Look, I know they can be...difficult, I guess, at times, but they aren't bad people." He turns to face me, leaning on the rail that tops the outer perimeter fence. "Matt was raised to expect

132

he could have whatever he wants in life. I know his family's money has given him some definite advantages, but he's also been good to me. I try to forgive him when he starts acting like an ass because I believe that if I really needed him, he'd be there."

"And Victoria?" I ask. It's sort of a sore subject between us but want to know how he will justify being friends with her.

"We work together and she is one of the smartest women I know. You don't get how hard it has been for her." He looks off for a few seconds before continuing. "She had to work twice as hard as the men in our field to earn the respect she deserves, just because she is a woman. It's not fair, but instead of whining about it, she made herself tough enough to handle it. I admire that."

"She admires you too," I whisper under my breath, but he hears me.

Logan pulls me against him. "Charli, look at me." I do as he asks and find myself lost in the deep green of his eyes. "It doesn't matter. I'm with you because I want to be with you."

"I'm glad," I tell him. "I just think you try so hard to see the good in people that maybe you overlook too much of the bad."

"Maybe," he sighs. "but for someone who thinks everyone should be treated equally, it feels like you are judging my friends too harshly when you don't even know them."

"Shit..." I feel tears threatening to spill over.

"Charli, it's okay. I didn't mean to make you feel bad. My friends have a lot of faults and so do I."

"Okay." I take a deep breath and wipe my eyes. "I'm sorry if I pissed you off."

"I'm not pissed. I know they gave a shitty first impression, but you don't really know them."

"You're right." I walk a little away from him, needing the distance. His touch makes it hard for me to think rationally. "I'm sorry for judging so hastily, but you have to admit my dislike is based on the way they treated me that night. Actions speak the loudest, Logan."

"True." He walks toward me but stops before we are close enough to touch. "But sometimes if you know a person's motivation, you can understand their actions even when you don't agree with them."

I don't think we can see eye to eye on this. I cross my arms and try to remain calm. "So, is it alright that Victoria tried to ridicule me and convince me the two of you were together because she was motivated by her desire to have you? It's okay to be cruel if you are eliminating a threat?"

Logan exhales loudly and I see him clench his fists. "I didn't say that. Victoria goes after what she wants with a single-minded determination. It was what she learned to do so she wouldn't be swallowed alive in the corporate world. She is ruthless if she feels someone is encroaching on her territory."

I laugh, and it is an ugly, bitter sound. "So, you are her territory?" Now I'm pissed. If he thinks it's okay for her to lay claim to him, then I'm getting out of her way. I turn my back to him and try to remember where the exit is located.

Grabbing my arm, he swings me around. "Don't put words in my mouth, Charli!"

"Logan, if you allow her to think she has a right to be jealous, then you are the one doing her a disservice, not me."

We've stopped in the middle of the path, and the other guests are having to sidestep around us. Some look at us with annoyance, but our argument has prevented anyone from actually interrupting us to complain.

"I'm not allowing anything!" he insists.

"And what about Matt? Is he just protecting you from big, bad me, too?" I know I've let this get out of hand, but once I get going, it's hard to stop. I want to scream and stomp my feet, but even more than that, I want Logan to hold me again and convince me this argument isn't the end of what we have just begun.

"No, Matt has a thing for you, Charli! He was acting like an ass to get your attention! And when he finally finds out I am so fucking crazy for you that I value what we have over my friendship with him, he's going to hurt like hell."

This stops me cold. The impossibility of his asshole friend liking me makes no sense. I'd been sure he thought I was so far below him that I wasn't even worth his notice, except to use for entertainment.

"I doubt that, Logan. If he wanted to show he liked me, then why would he go out of his way to embarrass me?" I'm no longer yelling. I'm quiet, and thinking about all he's said.

Logan removes the distance between us and wraps his arms around me tightly. The warm embrace gives me hope. Kissing the top of my head, he sighs likes he's been through a war and come out on the other side, not the victor or the loser, but alive.

"Charli," he whispers, "you are smart and funny and the fucking hottest thing I've ever seen. Your sassy mouth and strong beliefs just make you even sexier. How could Matt resist wanting you? I certainly can't."

I don't know if we can ever agree where his friends are concerned, but right now it's not the most important thing. Right now, I'm just happy the man that I'm kind of crazy about seems to feel the same about me.

Chapter Nineteen: Logan

Survey Says...

"So what are we watching tonight?" I ask as Liv lets me into the apartment.

Liv closes her eyes and points to the couch, where I see my Chuck sitting and bouncing with agitation. "Charli has been watching a Family Feud marathon on the Game Show Network all day. It's driving me batshit crazy. Maybe you can talk some sense into her!"

"You don't like Family Feud?" I ask as I follow her further into the room.

"You know how competitive Charli is! If I figure out the correct answer before her, she starts making insane justifications for why her answer should have been on the board. I can't take much more!"

I'm laughing, but I believe every word.

Then Charli notices my arrival. "Logan!" She jumps up and runs over to hug me. I pick her up and swing her around, but as soon as she realizes the commercial break is over, she wiggles out of my grasp to plant herself right back in front of the TV.

Joining her, I settle myself into her death trap of a couch and pull her close to me so there's plenty of room for Liv.

"Come on Liv!" Charli yells, with her eyes, never leaving the screen. "It's almost time for the next survey!"

"I'll pass. You have Logan to torture now. I'm going to my room to work." She grabs her laptop and a thick folder of papers and photographs off the desk.

"You're just scared of me winning again." Charli's conviction is cute.

"Okay, sure." Liv waves a hand in our direction, refusing to argue. "Whatever you say, Charli. Goodnight, Logan." She disappears into her bedroom and closes the door behind her.

I look at Charli's glazed eyes, messy hair, and the faded jersey she's using as a sleepshirt. Next, I take in the garbage can filled with plastic soda bottles and an empty pizza box. I know Charli is a little obsessive about cleaning, so I have to assume each commercial break has been used to discard all the trash generated from her TV binge.

"How long have you been watching this?" I ask, scared to discover the answer.

"Oh, I don't know." She flaps her hand around dismissively. "Since about two o'clock maybe? What time is it now?" There is a clock on the wall opposite the couch, but she won't look at it.

"Charli, it's seven. You've been at this for five hours? I thought you planned on writing today?"

"I did write a little, but I just couldn't get into it. I had to step away for awhile," she tells me while reaching for a red plastic cup on the coffee table. She tilts it back and frowns when she realizes it's empty.

I take the cup and refill it from the two-liter bottle of root beer in the refrigerator before handing it back to her. "I can't imagine that kind of freedom," I admit with a little jealousy.

"What do you mean?" She looks over at me and waits for my answer.

"Do you realize that most people don't have the luxury of wasting five hours watching television in the middle of the day?" Sitting back down, I try to pull her back to me, but she resists.

"I don't usually spend all day watching TV. I do work, you know, Logan. I write almost every day and I work until three o'clock in the morning at the bar most nights. I pay all my own bills, so if I want to take a day to be lazy, I think I can." Her lips are pressed into a thin, firm line and even though the show is starting a new round, she is only looking at me.

"I'm not implying you can't. I just wonder if you realized how lucky you are to have that advantage." *Shit. I can tell I'm pissing her off.*

"Yes, Logan. I realize how fortunate I am. I need flexibility in my life and I'm able to do what I want with my days because I've decided this is how I want to live. Your choices are the reason you can't."

I'm so fucking tired of her acting like my job is something to be ashamed of. "So I've made bad choices?" I ask through clenched teeth.

"No. Absolutely not. You've just made different choices than I would have." I start to get up, but she grabs the hem of my shirt and pulls me back down. "I'm sorry. I didn't mean that like it sounded. Please don't go." She lays her head on my shoulder and I sigh.

"Stop picking fights with me, Charli. Our jobs are very different... and we are very different, but that doesn't have to be a bad thing."

"I know. You're right. I'm sorry." She pulls her knees under her and raises up enough to kiss me. "I'm tired and grouchy, but I shouldn't take it out on you. I get frustrated when my book stalls and I have to take a break. Forgive me?"

When she looks up and gives me my favorite smile, I think I could forgive her for almost anything. "Of course."

"Watch The Feud with me? I'll kick your butt like I did at the go-kart track," she promises and I laugh.

"We'll see about that. I'm good at this kind of stuff. I have a wealth of useless knowledge stored up." I tap a few times on my temple.

Snuggling back up into our usual position, we go back to watching the show. A few boards later Charli finally believes my boasts. I'm getting a lot more answers correct than she is, and she doesn't like it.

"I told you it was hockey!" I raise my hand for a high five, but she ignores me.

"Well, I don't follow sports," she responds with a pout.

I pull on her bottom lip. "Do you have any idea how adorable you are when you pout?"

"I'm not pouting," she says before sticking out her tongue at me.

She's totally pouting and it's fucking adorable. "Then why is that delicious bottom lip poked out?" Pulling her toward me, I softly bite down on the protruding lip. She grins.

"And why are your eyebrows low enough to cover those beautiful eyes?" I take my hand to smooth her brow and then place small kisses on each closed eyelid.

"I know how to stop your pouting," I whisper into her ear and I feel her body shiver against me.

"Really?" she asks hopefully. "What do you suggest?"

139

And that's when I attack. "Tickling!" Running my fingers up and down her ribcage, she squirms to get away. I'm not about to let her get off that easily.

"Stop!" she screeches between giggles. "I'm ticklish!"

"That's the point, my little Chuck!"

My frantic tickling has caused her nightshirt to ride up above her navel, and that's when I notice her panties. My hands stop and I stare.

Seeing a hot woman in her panties should make you want to find a way to remove them as quickly as possible. These panties made me laugh hysterically. She is frantically trying to jerk the unraveling hem down, but I capture both hands to stop her. I want to see them.

"I can explain!" she says, still gasping from all the tickling.

"Please do," I say between laughs.

The panties are bright yellow and the band around her waist has diagonal black and yellow stripes like caution tape. Right across the front, in bold black lettering, they say "Warning: Warranty Voided if Removed."

"It's Liv's fault," she says. "She looks for the most ridiculously embarrassing panties and buys them for me for every occasional. It happens so often that I don't think I've actually had to buy my own panties since high school."

I snap the elastic in the waist of the panties and she jerks. "So, all your panties are like this?" I'm completely fascinated.

"Maybe..." she trails off and looks off toward her bedroom door.

"This, I have to see!" I jump up and head for her room, with her close behind me.

"No!" She starts pummeling my back with her tiny fists. "You can't just go through my panty drawer, Logan!"

But I won't be stopped. I have to see this collection. It only takes me two tries to find the right drawer. Charli now has both of her arms wrapped around my bicep, trying to get me to release the drawer, but she doesn't stand a chance.

"Logan! This is so embarrassing!" she whines and I laugh harder.

I pull the drawer completely out of the dresser and dump the contents onto the middle of her bed. The pile is impressive. There are bikinis, thongs, boy shorts, and even a giant pair like an old lady would wear. *Granny Panties? Surely she never wears those awful things!*

Sitting on the edge of her bed, I sift through the numerous colors and styles, snorting at the designs. "This is the funniest thing I've ever seen," I admit, reverently.

She crosses her arms over her chest, plants her feet wide, and tries to look tough. "I'm so glad to have amused you, Mr. Mitchell."

Chapter Twenty: Charli
But Do They Have Chicken Nuggets?

I finally managed a Friday night off!

Logan's excitement that we can have what he considers a real and proper date is almost palpable. Our relationship, *yes I'm finally admitting it's a real relationship*, has gone so smoothly lately that it's a little scary. It's been awhile since I called anyone my boyfriend and as an adult the word sort of freaks me out, but that's what he is now. *Logan is my boyfriend.*

"You look beautiful, Charli," he says when he comes to pick me up.

"You can thank Liv," I admit. "She is the one that pulled this off." I use my hands to frame my perfectly made up face.

Logan shakes his head and grabs one of my hands. "Charli... YOU are beautiful."

"Oh," I whisper and step forward to kiss him.

Eventually, I manage to break away, but it's hard. We've had some fun over the last few weeks, but we both know tonight will be more.

"I'm excited to have an occasion to wear the dress," I tell him and he smiles.

"I'm glad to provide the occasion. It's beautiful." His eyes rake over me and as much as I love the dress, I'd be fine with it disappearing.

"I bought it last year during a shopping trip with Liv's mom, Carol. It cost me a small fortune and I've felt guilty every time I saw it hanging in my closet with the tags still attached."

"Do a spin and let me fully appreciate the dress then."

Taking a step back, I twirl for him, careful to keep my balance in the strappy high heels Liv had generously let me borrow. I know how she feels about her shoes and she has so many they almost need their own zip code, so I really appreciate them.

When I come to a stop, I curtsy and he claps. "Like?" I ask.

"Love," Logan answers and my heart hammers. He is saying he loves the dress, not me, but that word on his lips has caused a rush of emotions that almost overwhelm me.

"Me too," I whisper, wondering just what I'm honestly admitting to loving. "Let me grab my purse."

Disappearing into my room, I stop in front of my full-length mirror. This dress rocks. Midnight blue, with a soft shimmer as it moves, the little slip of a dress feels like a piece of silky heaven gliding over my skin. It has a halter style top, with several thin straps that weave together and tie behind my neck and a hemline that hits about mid-thigh. It's perfect.

Grabbing the small clutch bag from my dresser, I rejoin Logan near the door. In a dark suit and tie, he takes my breath away. His job means he wears suits every day, and it's a look I've seen a lot, but it never grows old.

When I'm close enough, he slips his fingers into the thick waves of my hair and sighs. "I love that your hair is down."

When his warm hand slides across my bare back, I'm the one sighing. "Where are we eating?" I ask in a breathy voice. I'm afraid if he keeps touching me we will never make it to the restaurant.

"It's a surprise." He winks. "Let's go."

After a short drive, we pull into a brick-paved, circular drive in front of a building of stone and glass. A valet, in all black, runs forward to help us out and park the truck.

"Logan? This looks kind of..." I'm getting nervous. We usually order pizza or grab fast food. *Have I ever fully explained my limited diet to him?*

"Beautiful girl and beautiful dress... You deserve a beautiful restaurant." He places his hand on the small of my back and guides me inside. "Reservation for two. Mitchell."

Oh shit. This place requires reservations? I had really thought a nice dinner out in a nice dress meant our local steak house. I eat steak, especially with French fries and ketchup.

Following the hostess into the dining room, I look around in awe. "This place is amazing," I tell him and he smiles down at me.

"I know. It's one of my favorites and I love the art deco design." He points out certain key elements of the design and I nod in appreciation.

The soft lighting from hundreds of candles and the jazz music filling the room are serene and inviting. I really want to love this place like he does. *Actually, I think I already do.*

When my menu is handed to me, I reconsider this opinion. It is a single, printed page in a large leather folio and I don't recognize anything. "Logan?"

"Yes?" he, asks while still looking over the selections.

"I don't speak 'foodie' and I have no idea what to order," I admit, and he finally looks up.

"I'll order for both of us," he offers with a smile.

"Fine," I grumble, sliding down a little in my chair.

He frowns. "What's wrong?"

"Nothing... but don't get used to making decisions for me." I warn with a single raised finger pointed in his direction. "I'm not that kind of girl." I like a good surprise as much as the next person, but I'll be damned if I let someone decide everything for me.

Closing his menu, he chuckles. "I'm perfectly aware of that, Charli."

He rattles off something to our waiter and then reaches across the table to hold my hand. "I loved all the movie nights on your couch, especially the Star Wars marathon." He waggles his eyebrows and I flush, remembering how much of those movies we didn't watch that night. "The late night phone calls and days of texting have all been great, but I can't tell you how excited I am about tonight."

I give his hands a quick squeeze. "You're just tired of Liv interrupting us or having to leave early because of work the next morning. For once, we will be all alone for the whole night."

He pulls my hand forward and kisses my knuckles softly. "The idea of spending the whole night with you makes me want to jump up and leave this restaurant right now."

"I'm good with that. Let's go."

His chuckle is low and deep. "No. I want to make this special. You deserve this, Charli."

We're interrupted by the arrival of our plates. *Shit. I think I'd rather eat my napkin.* I push the brown lumps around on my plate for awhile. I'm too scared to even try a sample. "Ummm, Logan?"

Hearing my distress, he looks up from the food he's obviously relishing and furrows his brow. "What's wrong? You don't like it?"

"What the hell is it?"

He grins and I'm glad my remark hasn't pissed him off. Liv would love this place, with the retro styling and gourmet food, but I'm dreaming of a burger.

"It's veal scallopini with brown butter and capers." He sets his fork down and takes a drink of his wine.

"Okay, and what is that exactly?" I lay my fork down in defeat.

"You don't like veal?" he asks.

I cross my arms and lean back. "I've never had veal."

"Why don't you try it?" He picks my fork back up and encourages me to take it.

Once again I use it to push the food around my plate. I just can't work up the nerve to bring the fork to my mouth. I'm up for any adventurous activity, normally. *Skydiving? No problem! White water rafting? Sign me up! Eating unrecognizable brown lumps pretending to be food? I'll pass.*

"I'm sorry. I thought tonight would be special for us, but I should have thought more about it. I know how you like to eat normally and it was wrong to assume you would enjoy something different." He pushes his plate away and drops his napkin.

I'm such a bitch. "Logan, I'm the one that's sorry! You're so sweet to plan this for me, and I'm the one ruining it with my need for toddler food. I know you like restaurants like this, and I'm sure your past girlfriends loved them too."

"It's fine, Charli. Don't worry about it." He smiles, but it looks sad.

Damn it! I'm not trying to make him feel bad! I don't want any special concessions, but the fact is, we live very different lives when apart from each other. Maybe we were fools to think we could merge those worlds when we're together.

"Logan, things have been so good between us, and I should've realized this was coming. I know it sounds like I'm blowing the situation out of proportion, but this…" I put my hand out to indicate the restaurant, "is just a little part of a bigger issue. I just don't fit in with your world." I look down at my lap. Scared to see his face when he agrees with me.

"Fit in? Charli that's a crock of shit, and you know it." Surprised, I raise my eyes to see a determination in his expression that lifts my heart. "We aren't teenagers with cliques and a pecking order. We're adults, capable of enjoying our similarities and accepting our differences." He's clenching his fork so tightly it may snap any minute.

"I grew up thinking McDonald's was fancy," he says, "and while I might enjoy nicer meals now, it's not that important to me. Tonight was meant to be for you. I wanted you to know how special you are to me, not make you feel like we don't belong together."

My throat tightens. "I just don't want you to miss out on things because of me!"

"Miss out on what? Expensive food?" He laughs. "I'll happily eat chicken nuggets and fries on every date we have if you understand how much you've come to mean to me."

Well, I'll give the guy points for knowing the right things to say to a girl, especially a hungry girl. "Chicken nuggets and fries? Do they have those here? Because I'm totally down for that!"

His laughter is loud enough to cause the neighboring tables to glance over disapprovingly. *I keep thinking we're doomed, and he keeps proving me wrong. Maybe I think too much.*

"Do you want to get out of here?" he asks while reaching across the small round table to grasp my hand.

"Do you mind?" I wrinkle my nose at the plate in front of me.

"Not at all. Seeing you in that dress, and picturing you out of it, has made my appetite disappear anyway. Let's head to my apartment." He pulls me up from my chair and wraps his arm around my waist.

"That sounds perfect to me," I whisper huskily as I give him the dimpled smile he loves. "But, Logan?"

"Yes?"

"Can I ask for just one more thing?" I play with the lapel of his jacket, nervously.

Running his fingers through the hair at my temple, he takes a deep breath before kissing me lightly on my forehead. "Anything you want."

"Can we drive through McDonald's and get some chicken nuggets on the way? I'm fucking starving."

This time, his laughter booms with such force that I'm sure they would've kicked us out if we weren't already leaving.

He pays the ridiculously high bill for food we didn't eat, tucks me under his arm, and we head for the valet stand to get the truck. I slide in, careful not to give the valet a peep show, and happily unfasten the straps on the heels.

Chapter Twenty-One: Logan
I Like Her Kind of Crazy

I've brought Charli home a couple of times, but this is the first time she'll be staying all night. I've had enough "almost" moments. Pulling out my keys, I unlock the front door. "After you," I say when the door opens.

"Thanks," she says, flashing me a sexy smile and sauntering past me into the apartment.

"Do you want anything to drink?" I ask as I look around the living room to make sure I didn't miss anything when I'd cleaned up this afternoon. Everything looks okay, so I take off my jacket and put it over the back of one of the dining room chairs. Then I drop my keys down into the jacket's pocket with my cell phone.

"No. I just want you," she says huskily and I remember that first night at the bar when I'd heard her deep throaty laugh. I had almost lost my shit on the spot.

"Do you know what you do to me?" I ask, loosening the knot of my tie a little. I'm finding it hard to swallow.

She looks right at me and I see the tip of her tongue dart out to moisten her lips. "I know what I want you to do to me."

Fuck. How am I going to keep my control long enough that I don't embarrass myself? "I need to explain how I feel about you," I tell her.

"No more talking, Logan." She puts her index finger over her mouth, puckers her lips and exhales to shush me. "I want touching."

No talking? I've found the girl every man dreams of, and no one believes exists.

She walks backward toward my couch and beckons me to follow with a curl of her index finger. I'm not going to argue. I stride forward to meet her and then she turns us both and she pushes me down onto the couch's leather cushions. Climbing onto my lap with her legs wide enough to rest a knee on either side of my hips, I realize this position forces the dress to ride high up her thighs and I can see the tiniest sliver of green panties.

When she sinks lower onto my lap, I groan. She reaches forward and finishes loosening my tie before slipping it over my head and discarding it. I reach up to unbutton my shirt, but she playfully slaps my hands away and does it herself.

Once my shirt has joined the tie, she starts to undo the straps that fasten her dress. "No," I say to stop her. "Fair is fair. Let me." As I pull on the thin strap, the whole front of the dress falls down to her lap. She is bare to her waist and I suck in a breath at the sight of her. "You are perfect."

She laughs and grinds forward slightly. I reach around to cup her amazing ass in both hands and bend my head down to introduce my mouth to her exposed breasts. When she groans and bucks slowly, I feel an excitement that courses through me at lightning speed, making me rock hard.

I need her. I move my fingers into her hair and gently tug at the strands to pull her head back. Once the long column of her neck is presented, I feather soft kisses from the underside of her jaw to the hollow at the base of her throat.

"Logan..." she purrs and I gently suck at the tender skin at the side of her neck before moving lower to run my tongue in lazy circles around each breast.

Lifting her by her waist, I raise her off my lap and set her down on the couch cushion beside me. She stiffens and her eyes widen in displeasure at first, but when I stand and pull her up in front of me, she relaxes.

Her dress falls to the floor, pooling at her bare feet. I drink in the sight of flushed skin and the small swellings of her breasts, tipped by perfect, rosy nipples, tightened by desire. My eyes move lower, and I reach forward to let the tips of my fingers trace over the small lines of her ribcage and the flat plain of her stomach. I make it all the way to the front of her bright green panties before I start laughing.

"Liv's contribution?" I ask, running my index finger under the waistband.

"Of course," she pants, encouraging me to continue my exploration.

I trace the two, large letters that cover the front of the panties. They read "Go" and I grin. "Is she telling me I have her permission to proceed?"

"Sort of..." Charli admits, but she sounds evasive as she slides her foot nervously across the floor and avoids eye contact.

"Would you care to elaborate?"

When she turns around, I almost choke. The back of the panties are bright red and say "STOP." "She thought this would be a funny way for me to let you know that a certain location is an exit only and off limits," she explains.

Her nervousness suddenly makes more sense. I take her shoulders and turn her back to face me. "You thought I wouldn't ask first before trying something like *that?*"

She shrugs. "This way no asking is required, because you are completely aware it's totally off the table."

Shaking my head, but laughing at her logic, I pull her closer and kiss her. When we break apart, I whisper directly into her ear. "Have I told you before, that you two are completely insane?"

Turning her head to face me, she nips my bottom lip. "You may have mentioned that a time or two, but apparently you like my kind of crazy."

I slide my arms around her. "Apparently, I do."

Reaching down between us, she unfastens my belt and the front of my slacks. Bending over slightly, and giving me a beautiful visual, she yanks hard enough for the pants to fall. I kick them out of the way, along with my socks and shoes. Standing before her in nothing but my black boxer briefs, she has to be aware of how much I want her.

I reach down and pick her up. She wraps her legs around me and I can feel her heat pressed against me. I need to be inside her...now.

I use my large hands to palm Charli's firm, gently rounded ass and pull her tightly against me. I take the first step that will take us to my bedroom when I hear the unmistakable and unwanted trill of my cell phone. I want to ignore it, but I know I can't.

Fuck.

Chapter Twenty-Two: Charli
What's That Banging?

What the hell?

Wearing nothing but a pair of panties, I'm wrapped around a man that I'm absolutely crazy about. I'm close enough to feel exactly how much he wants me too as it presses between my thighs. We are about to go to his bedroom and fulfill all the naughty fantasies that have kept me awake since meeting him when his body tenses and he stops.

That's when I hear the incessant ringing of his cell phone from near the front door. I can tell he is deciding whether or not he should answer it, so I narrow my eyes in warning. "Don't you dare," I say.

Eventually, the noise stops and he relaxes enough to start kissing me again. Just when the heat between us is strong enough to make me hurt with wanting, the damn phone rings again.

Surely he knows better than to answer it? But no, apparently he doesn't. He is actually peeling me off him and setting me back down on his couch.

"Charli, I'm so, so sorry! I've just not been myself lately at work. My shit focus has been noticed and we have an important client right now. The firm is really putting pressure on me to wrap this up… I just have to take it."

With an apologetic look, he turns toward his dining table and goes to retrieve his jacket from the chair. I cross my arms across my bare chest and pinch my lips into a tight line as he fishes the phone out his pocket and answers the call.

"This is Logan."

How can he sound so calm and controlled? I'm still a panting mess. Maybe this isn't doing for him what it's doing for me. I slide my foot out from underneath me and put it forward in an effort to hook the edge of my dress on the floor in front of the couch. Finding success, I slide my leg back toward me, bringing my dress with it.

"Oh… Ummm… No thanks. Really, I can't," I hear him say into the phone.

I quietly stand up, glad his back is to me and slip my dress back up my body. I'm looking for my shoes and purse when his next words hit me hard enough to shove a slicing pain right through my center.

"Thanks, Victoria. I appreciate the offer, and it sounds great, but I can't tonight. Maybe another time?"

The red heat of anger consumes me and there is a painful pressure behind my eardrums that makes me feel like my head might explode any second. *Did he just tell her he'd take her up on her offer another time? And that offer sounds great to him? Is that what he's just said?*

And then it gets even worse.

"No, I'm not doing anything special tonight. I'm just really tired. Have fun. Yeah, you too. See you Monday. Bye."

I had originally intended to leave quietly and calmly. I hadn't wanted to start an argument. I just wanted to tell Logan that he's great, but I need to be with someone who wants to be with me, and that when they are with me, it's only about me.

I had wanted a lot of things.

Instead, I pick up the fancy remote control to his giant flat screen TV and throw it at him. The heavy, satisfying thump of it hitting his shoulder blade, and the following thud of it landing on the hardwood floor, is the result of those "wants" taking a nose-dive off a cliff.

"Ow!" Turning to look back at me, he rubs the red spot blooming on his back.

"What the hell, Charli?"

"Take me home, Logan! Now!"

"Look, I'm sorry I took the call. My job is important and it could have been crucial to the merger. I have a lot of responsibility on me and you need to understand that." He walks toward me, hands held out in front of him.

I put up one hand in the universal sign of "halt". I would have put up both hands, but I'm still trying to hold up the top of my dress. I'm not letting him look at my boobs now! "Your *job* is important, but obviously, I'm not! And besides, you weren't doing anything *special* tonight, right? Well, now you aren't doing ME tonight either, asshole!"

His face pales and I guess he's now realizing how his words had sounded from my end. *Good! Why hadn't he ignored that damn phone? Why hadn't he told Victoria that he has no desire to hang out with her, because he is with me?*

He looks down at the floor. "I'm sorry it sounded so awful, but I was saying all that for you." I snort and he looks up, pleading with his eyes for understanding. "I want to keep you special and away from my work obligations. You shouldn't have to deal with that shit."

I hold my dress even tighter against my body. "Believe me, I'm done with all your shit."

His breathing gets heavier and I see him clenching and unclenching his hands at his sides. "My career is necessary, Charli. I do it because I have to. We can't all be like you and have the luxury of a job that's more like playtime!"

"Fuck you, Logan!" I head for the door, but he catches me right before I manage to pull it open. Spinning me around, he pushes my back against the door and traps me by placing a palm flat on either side of me.

"Stop! You aren't leaving until we fix this!" he demands. *The calm businessman on the phone a few minutes ago has left the building.* In his place is a seething, frustrated male with the body of a god and the ability to fuck up my world nine ways to Sunday. Despite my desire to leave, Logan is determined to make me see his side of things.

"So are you holding me, hostage?" I throw out, squirming against the restraint of his arms.

"If that's what it takes!" He lifts one hand and slams it back hard against the door, causing me to flinch. "You always assume the worst about me, Charli!"

"No, I've just learned to pay attention when someone doesn't appreciate me."

"You think I don't appreciate you?" He chuckles bitterly and although his anger is intense and powerful, it magnifies his glorious perfection.

I'm so mad I could lose my mind, but I'm still in awe of this beautiful man. It's so unbelievably unfair. I want to leave and never come back. I want to stay and never leave.

"Charli, haven't you figured out what you are to me yet?" His voice softens and I can see the fury draining slowly from his muscles. "I'm having a hard time at work because all day long, all I want is to be with you. I can't get you out of my head for more than a few minutes, so I can't get any work done!" He runs a finger along my bare shoulder and I shiver. "I appreciate everything about you."

He cups my chin, and even though I put up a slight resistance, he bends forward and kisses me. My body responds without my permission. I feel the hot invasion of his tongue and the silky firmness of his lips sliding over mine. When he pulls back to stare into my eyes, I'm undone.

"Charli, you are so smart but so damn frustrating. I love that you are following your dream of writing and I'm glad you have a job with people that love you." He places a simple kiss on my forehead. "I love that you are true to yourself and won't take less than you deserve." He runs his fingertips over my eyes to close them and then places a kiss on each eyelid in turn. "I am really and truly sorry that I'm such an incredible asshole and didn't tell Victoria and everyone else I know just how much tonight means to me."

"Logan... Oh, sweet heaven..."

With one hand, he captures both of my wrists and pulls them high above my head. His other hand tugs insistently at my dress until it surrenders to him and I shiver as the cool silk slides down my body. Lowering his head, he kisses and softly ravages every inch of my bare skin. *I can't get enough of this man.*

When he finally releases my hands, I run my fingers through his hair and sensually trace a path across the solid heat of his beautifully muscled back. My breathing has lost its normal rhythm and a tension is coiling deep inside me.

He looks into my eyes with complete victory, and instead of my competitive nature kicking in to fight for dominance, I smile back. I want him too much. It's impossible to stop now.

He stands up and backs away from me, and I want to cry from the loss of contact with his skin. Our separation isn't long as he squats slightly, reaches around with both arms, and hauls me up and over his shoulder like a caveman.

Instead of complaining about his barbaric tactics, I giggle with my face pressed upside down against his back as he carries me off to his bedroom. Stopping at the foot of his king sized bed, he tosses me down onto the pile of blankets that cover his giant mattress.

He must be one of those guys that think making a bed is stupid when you plan on crawling back into it the next night. I can tell he just washed everything since the bedding smells like lavender and a dryer sheet has become tangled in my hair.

The bed dips as he puts one knee down on the bed beside me. Then, he adds the second on my other side, so that he is right above me. Being gentle and taking his time, he whispers sweet, soft kisses over the flushed skin of my stomach and I tighten my abdominal muscles in response. It tickles in that good way that is tortuous.

When he gently sucks at my breast, I arch my back with desire. My hands had been grasping at the sheets on either side of me, but now I use them to dig into his back and pull him in even closer. I feel the definition of the muscles on his shoulder blades and the knobs of his spine and then my breathing becomes so erratic I'm in danger of hyperventilating.

Wanting even more, my hands continue their explorations and they move around to the small gap of space between us, in order to trace the ridges of muscle that create his perfect, wash-

158

board abs. Then I find those deep grooves between his stomach and hips, the ones that make that V that points us all in the right direction, and my path is clear. *I'm so hot I may spontaneously combust.*

Slipping his fingers gently under my panties' lace edge, he skims them down my legs and tosses them to the floor. I'm not half as gentle as I yank his boxers down with Nascar speed and pay no attention at all to where they end up. Now completely naked, we take the time to learn each other completely.

"You're perfect, Charli." He runs his hands from my breasts, down my ribs, and onto my thighs.

I smile. "I have small boobs." I take his hands and guide them to cover each breast.

"Well, I like them just the way they are." He confirms this by removing his hands and placing a gentle kiss on each peak. Then one finger starts at the base of my throat and traces a pattern down to my navel. He raises an eyebrow, questioningly.

"Don't you dare tickle me again, Logan," I warn, so he laughs and moves on.

Deciding to exert a little control, I gently push him over onto his back. Lowering myself down his body until my face is right above a long, silvery scar on his right thigh, I look up at him.

"What happened?" I ask.

"Just kid stuff." He brushes my question off, but I can tell there's more to it.

I run the tip of my tongue along the path of this old injury and he draws in a deep breath. The end of my journey has put me very close to somewhere else I'd like to explore in more depth. I alternately kiss and nibble my way closer and he groans as his hips move involuntarily.

When I reach my destination, he bucks up so fast he almost

pokes me in the eye. I laugh. He scowls. So I laugh harder.

"Are you laughing at him, Charli? That's sort of emasculating, you know." This makes me giggle even harder.

"Well, don't..." I try to stop, but now I'm laughing so hard I end up snorting. "Don't put my eye out with that thing! I'd have to wear an eye patch. I'd look like a pirate. And then I'd have to..."

"Oh, shut the fuck up!" he growls at me, but he's smiling indulgently as he grabs my shoulders and hauls me back up so our faces are only inches apart. "I have never met anyone so weird and unpredictable, or so beautiful and funny." He presses his forehead against mine. "And I've never wanted to know someone, inside and out, they way that I do you." His lips come down on mine and I lose all sense of time.

When we have to pause long enough to breathe, I lay a hand on his chest to stop him from lowering his mouth to mine again and smile. "Where do you keep the condoms, boy scout?"

He shakes his head with forbearance and reaches for his bedside table drawer. "Have I mentioned how weird you are?"

After handling our protection needs, and rolling me back so that I'm resting underneath him, he starts kissing me again. He begins with my now swollen mouth but makes sure he's giving equal attention to every inch of my body.

While worshipping my breasts again, he moves one hand down between my thighs and pushes them apart slightly. He lazily runs a finger down until it stops at that one perfect little place that can tip me over into the abyss. He gently circles and this motion has every muscle in my body tensing with anticipation. I'm almost there when he stops.

What the hell? I frown at him and he laughs at me. I start to complain, but he covers my mouth with his and kisses me deeply.

Using his tongue, he mimics the rhythm he had so recently employed a little lower.

I moan into his mouth and my climax is building, even though his hands aren't touching me anymore. He's right over the top of me, braced on his forearms with our bodies so close they almost touch. Then I feel him and I start to quiver lightly.

"Please, Logan. Now." When he finally slips into place, I feel his heat and gasp in pleasure.

"Are you okay?"

"Don't talk, Logan. Just keep going."

Never let it be said he can't take orders. He thrusts slowly at first, but as I lift up to meet him, he gets the point and increases the pace. My heart is hammering so hard I can feel it against my ribcage, and my throat is starting to hurt from dryness since I can't seem to close my mouth with all the panting and moaning. I see the beads of sweat forming at his hairline, and notice his eyes are closed in concentration. I'm happy to have his full attention.

Our rhythm falls into sync, our breathing is hard and steady, and I feel that building pressure that precipitates a shattering climax.

When it hits me, I feel the spasms rocking me for what feels likes a blissful eternity.

Logan!" I scream out.

The clenching of my body sends him over the edge, and his moment isn't long behind mine. I'm pleased to hear he can get rather loud too when the situation warrants it.

He's still supporting his own weight on his forearms and even in my current euphoria, I know if he collapses on top of me now I'll probably suffocate. He rests his forehead against mine as we stay connected and ride it out. It had definitely been worth the wait.

Our carnal appetites temporarily satisfied, and slick with a thin sheen of perspiration, we both notice something is out of the ordinary at the same time.

"What in the hell is that banging?" I ask, confused. "It sounds like someone is knocking a wall down next door."

Logan starts laughing so hard that he accidentally slips out of me and then rolls over to his back on the bed beside me. I feel the loss of his warm body and wonder why he's laughing, as the whole bed shakes with it.

Then I hear the voice, coming through the wall behind the headboard. It's muffled, but is sounds like, "Keep it down!" I guess we pissed off his neighbor.

"Logan?" I ask softly after we're done laughing.

"Uh huh," he responds, with his eyes closed. I can tell he's exhausted and won't be conscious much longer.

"Tell me about it."

"About what?" His brow furrows in confusion.

I run my finger over the top of his leg. "The scar on your thigh."

He pauses to consider it, then nods and starts to explain. "I was good at baseball, and in high school that goes a long way, so I had a pretty active social life and enjoyed some great times."

"But?" It's so unusual to see his confidence wavering.

"But, before that I had some difficult times. My school was in a very affluent community and almost all the families were very wealthy. I mean, I wasn't dirt poor or anything and I had a good childhood, but sometimes kids can be cruel. So, around eighth grade, I really liked this girl Claire, and I think she liked me too but hung out with some kids that were… well to be nice about it… spoiled rich brats. But this one time, I got invited to a pool party with them and I was so excited, knowing she'd be there."

He pauses again and takes a deep breath before continuing. I lie still and try to offer silent support.

"So everyone wanted to play 'truth or dare' but I was too nervous to choose 'truth,' afraid of what they'd want me to reveal. The 'dares' everyone got were pretty harmless mostly, but mine seemed harder and kept getting worse with each round. We were hanging out in this pool house, I'd never even seen a pool house before, and one of the walls had these huge, sliding glass doors that we'd left open since everyone kept running in and out. When my turn came again, they had Claire stand right in front of those doors while they blindfolded me and spun me around a couple of times. I was dared to just walk around and find her, and she wasn't supposed to move, but I only had one minute or I'd have to tell a truth instead. So I'm trying to hurry, but she had moved and someone closed the doors. They'd also put this heavy iron doorstop thing in my path, so I lost my balance and went through the plate glass doors. We were just kids and I'm sure they thought I would crash into it, not through it. But an ambulance ride and thirty-two stitches later, I'd decided I was tired of being the brunt of their jokes."

"Oh," I say, unsure how to respond. My heart aches for the little boy Logan had been. Once, I'd been made to feel like I wasn't good enough, either.

"It's no big deal, Charli. It was a long time ago," he says. Then he snuggles me tight against his side, kisses me lightly, and drifts off to sleep.

Chapter Twenty-Three: Charli
I Like My Bitches Docile and Complacent

"Well, we've all done the 'walk of shame' I guess, but Charli, is this the 'work of shame?'" Liv looks me over and purses her lips to let me know my unkempt appearance is offensive to her.

"Shut up, Liv," I say pleasantly, unable to be angry at anyone. I am ecstatically, stupidly happy, like, I've had multiple orgasms in the last twelve hours, happy. So, she can say whatever she wants.

"You could have at least washed your hair. It looks like birds have been nesting up there." She pulls a strand toward her and then quickly drops it before wiping her hands on her apron.

I just smile even more and float away to my next table. My customers are great. My job is great. My life is great. Hell, even Liv is great. I think maybe sex with Logan has scrambled my brains.

"So, I take it, he's good in bed?" Liv tries again to have a conversation with me when the evening hits a lull and we both end up at the end of the bar together.

"Uh huh." I know I'm still grinning like an idiot.

She shakes her finger at me and scowls. "Oh, you are unbelievably annoying. If this doesn't wear off soon, I'm quitting... and I'm moving out!"

"Who's moving out?" Liv and I both snap to attention when Kyle slides up next to us. He puts an arm around Liv's shoulder and smiles at me, and I appreciate that he's really making an effort to be friendly again.

"No one is moving anywhere!" I glare hard at Liv, warning her to keep her comments to a PG rating. Kyle doesn't need my sex life details shoved in his face.

"Oh, I was just complaining about Charli's poor hygiene and threatening to move if she doesn't start making more of an effort." Liv pinches the end of her nose and Kyle laughs. "She's damn disgraceful."

"Uh huh." Kyle looks at the knotted hair I haphazardly clipped to the top of my head, my wrinkled bar shirt that might be on its second shift, and the lack of any makeup. "Luckily, Charli always looks good, even when she needs a shower." His sinfully sexy smirk cuts right through me.

Is he still trying to let me know he wants me? Or is he just letting me know that he knows what I've been up to? Either way, I'm ready to change the subject.

"Are we still going shopping Tuesday with Carol?" I direct my question at Liv. She understands and follows my lead. She might be sarcastic, but she isn't cruel.

"Yep. You know how Mom loves to shop. And she said that Momma D is going to try meeting us for lunch if she can get out of work for a bit."

"Awesome! I haven't seen Dana in ages. I hope I find a dress for the gala. I don't have anything formal enough," I say while mentally running through the contents of my closet.

"Don't worry. I have mad shopping skills," Liv reminds me. "We'll both find the right dresses. I just hope we get to enjoy the benefit and don't have to work the whole time."

Kyle slips his arm off of Liv's shoulder, throws his hands up in surrender and starts backing away. "THAT is my cue to leave. I can't stand here and listen to shopping and parties and all that shit. It totally ruins my manly image." He winks and we laugh as he escapes back to his refuge behind the bar.

"You know, the article for the paper will just be a general coverage of the event, and your moms won't expect you to photograph every minute of it, so we'll slip in some fun," I promise Liv, hoping I'm right. *I wonder what Logan is doing that night.*

Liv looks over her shoulder to make sure we're alone and then leans in to whisper, "Are you going to invite Logan?" Once again my best friend has read my mind. It's a little scary.

"Maybe. I'm not sure. It's definitely more in keeping with what he's used to, and it might be nice to show him that I don't always hang out in a bar."

"Charli..." Her aggravation surfaces. "Stop it. You know he doesn't think like that. Why do you keep throwing out these comments?   Logan is nothing like Nick."

"I don't want to talk about Nick," I hiss through my teeth. She knows how I feel about discussing my ex.

"I know. I get it, but you have to stop assuming every guy that has to wear a suit to work is a social climbing asshole. You and Logan are good together, so quit trying to sabotage it."

Is she right? Am I scared and trying to ruin this? I sigh, accepting the wisdom of her advice. "Okay, Liv. I'll behave. I promise."

"Good girl." She pats me on my shoulder and hands me the tray I had discarded on the bar. "That's how I like my bitches, docile and complacent. Now get back to work."

Chapter Twenty-Four: Charli
*Macaroni And Cheese Is Better Than D*ck*

Stuffing another huge spoonful of macaroni and cheese into my mouth, I close my eyes and sigh in contentment. *I love macaroni and cheese. It's so cheesy and so yummy.*

"Is that your 'O' face?" Liv asks me with curiosity and a little revulsion as I spit some of the macaroni back into my bowl.

"What?" I choke out.

Carol reaches over the table to smack her daughter's arm. "Olivia!"

"What? Look at her, Mom." Liv uses her fork to point in my direction. "She acts like macaroni is better than dick."

"Well, I think it is!" We all turn to see that Liv's other mom, Dana, has been able to join us for lunch after all. *Did I mention Liv gets that wicked sense of humor from her Momma D?*

"Dana!" Even Carol has burst out laughing at this point.

Liv and I just smile at each other as Dana puts her arm around Carol and gives her a quick kiss before sitting in the chair next to her. "But it's not nearly as good as you, my love," Dana says and I'm pretty sure Carol is blushing. *I pray I have a love like theirs one day.*

"How was work, Momma D?" Liv asks while sliding a menu over to Dana. This is our first time to try out the new Italian café outside our local mall, but I've decided it needs to be a regular for us. It's good.

"Busy as usual, but I couldn't miss lunch with all my best girls." She smiles toward the waiter and he comes over to take her order. "So did you find dresses for the charity gala?"

I silently watch as Liv tells her all about the dresses we found, the heels we plan on wearing, and how after lunch we're going shopping for the perfect jewelry to complete our looks. Liv and her moms are so close and I love them. I wish my own parents were still here too, but I know I have a lot to be thankful for. My mind drifts as I think of Logan and how important to me he has become.

"You know," Liv says, and I turn to see where the conversation had ended up after I zoned out momentarily. "...since you guys decided Carol would be my birth mom, you could have least chosen an African American sperm donor so I could look like both of you."

"Not this again!" Carol complains.

"Everyone can tell you're my Mom, and I love that we look so much alike. If you had awesome red hair like me instead of blonde, we could be twins."

"No one is going to mistake me as your twin with all these wrinkles," Carol argues, but I can tell she's pleased by the compliment.

"Bullshit. You look great and you know it," Dana tells her.

"But..." Liv continues, "do you know how much hotter I could be with a little more color? No one believes me when I tell them

Momma D is one of my parents."

"We've been over this a hundred times. We worried it would be hard enough for you to explain having two moms and didn't want to add the burden of the prejudices some people feel against bi-racial children," Carol explains.

"And besides, even if you don't look like me," Dana says, "you sure act like me!"

"That's the truth!" I add, getting back into the conversation. Carol is Mother Earth. Liv and Dana are smart assed She-Devils.

I startle as my small crossbody bag starts to jump and hum in my lap. I'd forgotten my phone was still on vibrate from last night. Nothing sucks more than working late and then having your cell phone wake you up too damn early because of a telemarketer, a wrong number, or a friend that forgot you work nights.

I slide the screen to answer. "Hello?"

"Hey." My whole body turns soft and warm just from his voice. I tuck my chin low and hide behind the curtain of my thick hair, hoping my face doesn't betray what this man does to me.

"Hey, Logan. What's up?" *That's it, Charli. Keep it cool. Don't let him know your heart is pounding as you remember exactly what part of him was up a couple of days ago.*

"I was thinking maybe we could meet for lunch today?" he says. "I don't normally have time to leave the office, but a meeting that doesn't involve my client is running over so I thought I would take advantage and see you. Or maybe I could just come over and take advantage *of* you?"

I groan a little and bite on my bottom lip. *Oh, why couldn't I be home right now?* "I would really love that, Logan, but..."

"But?" I can hear the disappointment.

"Today is my shopping trip and lunch with Liv, Carol, and Dana, remember?"

"Oh, that's right. I forgot. Okay, well that sucks." He laughs lightly. "Sorry. I'm being selfish. I hope you're having fun."

"I am, but...it does suck. I want to see you." I cup my hand over the phone so I can whisper and still be heard. "I really am sorry I'm not free right now. Your idea sounds...nice."

I hear a low chuckle. "Nice? I had wanted it to sound naughty."

Oh My God... I can't be thinking things like this while sitting across the table from my best friend and pseudo-moms. "Logan..." I breathe his name out, soft and deep, and this time I hear him groan.

"Our schedules are what really sucks. I might set my alarm for 3:00 a.m. and meet you at your place when you get off work if that's okay. I don't think I can wait for this weekend. I'm hiding behind my desk all day because just thinking of you... and what I want to do to you... is creating evidence enough for someone to file a public indecency claim against me."

I laugh at the thought of him having to hide out. "I'd love to see you tonight, but you would be a zombie at work tomorrow."

"It would be worth it!" he growls at me and I sigh.

"Okay, but, I need to go. Text me later, okay?" I'm going to need to put my phone on the charger twice a day with all the use it's getting now.

"Sure. Charli... I... ummm."

"Yes?"

I feel his hesitation through the line. "Nevermind. Talk to you later."

"Okay. Bye." I continue to hold the phone to my ear, reluctant to end the connection, and his breathing tells me he is facing the same dilemma. "Bye," I whisper one last time before making myself hang up and tucking the phone back into my purse.

When I look up, probably wearing a goofy grin, I encounter three nosy faces staring back at me from across the table.

"So do we get to hear about this new man of yours, Charli?" Dana asks, and from the look of excitement on Carol's face, I know she's been waiting all day to hear details too.

"Sure. Of course. Where do I start?" I pick up my fork and the move the remaining macaroni around the bowl.

"Well," Dana says, "According to our daughter, you're floating around in an orgasm induced euphoria? That seems a good start to me!"

You'd think I'd be used to this kind of candor by now, but I still blush. "Damn, Liv! You don't have to tell them everything!" I look over at the traitor.

"Hey... I share all and I've never lied to my moms." She can't keep a straight face, and Carol and Dana are laughing hysterically at her. I mean, she does tell them almost everything now, but Liv's teenage years had been a series of late night escapes, lies to cover her tracks and even a few minor run-ins with the authorities that luckily were never serious enough to land her with a record.

Ignoring her, I try to explain about Logan. "He's a lawyer and has a great job. He's really good looking too. We've been seeing each other for several weeks now. And..."

"YAWN!" Dana yells over at me.

"Don't say that, Dana! He sounds great, honey." Carol smiles and pats my hand that rests on the table near my water glass. You can always count on Carol to be polite.

"I don't want his resume,' Charli. I want to know how he makes you feel." Dana leans back and crosses her arms over her chest. "I want to know if he's good enough for you. I don't think anyone is good enough for either of you girls actually, but I need to know he at least understands and appreciates that."

I feel the tears start to well up and swallow hard. They always say just the right thing to make me feel loved and protected.

"You know, it's hard sometimes. He works a lot and his career is important, but that's a good thing. I want someone with goals and ambition. And he really is hot, like totally shit hot, but it's more about how I feel when I'm with him. I hate when we're apart, and when he's near it's like I lose control of my own body. I want to be with him and touching him and ..."

I realize the table has gone completely still and quiet. Even Liv isn't say anything. *Well, this is embarrassing.*

"Oh, sweetheart," Carol says smiles and I can see glistening moisture in her eyes. "You've fallen in love."

Oh my God. How had I gone from wanting to spend time with this guy, and really, really wanting to have sex with him, to falling in love? Once before I thought I was in love and had thought my heart was broken when it ended. But it never had, even in that glorious beginning stage, felt close to what I'm feeling now.

I swallow hard and take a deep breath before speaking. "Fuck me," I whisper.

"Naw... You aren't my type." Liv answers, as she raises that one eyebrow at me again. "And Logan seems to be getting the job done anyway."

Chapter Twenty-Five: Charli
Call Security!

I can do this. I'm his girlfriend and this is a totally normal thing for a girlfriend to do. Guys like surprises, right?

I take two more steps toward the glass and metal door, the entrance to the fortress that is Logan's job, otherwise known as Strickland and Burke. Last night had been amazing. Logan had showed up, as promised after my shift ended and had stayed until six this morning. This barely gave him enough time to make it back to his apartment to change for work.

We'd made good use of those hours. Considering how much I'm yawning today, even with dragging out of bed at eleven, I can't begin to imagine how exhausted Logan must be. I knew he wouldn't have time to take a lunch with him, and probably wouldn't have time to leave the office today either, so I'd decided to bring this little surprise to him.

Mentioning several times that he loved the Philly cheesesteaks at the deli near his office, I set my alarm instead of sleeping until early afternoon as I usually do. I put on a nice pair of black slacks, a silvery gray, sleeveless blouse, and even a pair of black heels in an effort to impress. Without much trouble, I found the deli and bought my man his favorite sandwich.

This is a good idea, right?

So now, with the brown paper bag clutched in one hand, and the large cup of coffee I knew he really needed in the other, I bravely stepped into the marbled foyer and headed for the information desk.

The poised and sophisticated receptionist looked up at me and raised her eyebrows in inquiry. *She can't even smile a little, or ask me if I need help?* You must need a degree in bitch to get a job here.

I set the coffee cup down on the high sleek counter, while she watches with disgust, and then clear my throat. "I'm here to see Logan Mitchell."

"Do you have an appointment?" Her nasal voice and mask of boredom make me start to sweat.

Maybe this was a bad idea. "Ummm... no. I'm his... Ummm..."

"Oh my God!" An instantly recognizable, feminine voice carries easily across the open expanse of the building's bottom floor. "What are you doing here?"

With ice in my veins, I turn to see Victoria as she marches with purpose from the bank of elevators. She's heading straight for the reception desk... and me.

The receptionist answers before I can. "She says she's here for Mr. Mitchell. Should I buzz him, Ms. Howell?"

I love how they are now talking to one other like I'm not even here.

"No, Shay. I can take care of her. Thanks." Victoria takes hold of my elbow and starts to steer me away from the front desk, but I jerk out of her grasp.

"I'm just here to see Logan. I'll call his cell. Thanks, anyway."

She slowly shakes her head at me. "Sweetie, I wouldn't do that."

"Oh, really? Why not?" *Why am I even asking her this?* She isn't my friend. I can't stand her and I know the feeling is mutual. She needs to just get out of my way.

"Look, I get it. Really. Logan is *amazing.*" Her voice drops conspiratorially like we both share intimate knowledge of him.

I just glare harder, refusing to show what her word do to me.

"You're cute and young and probably quite the wild little thrill. I can see why a guy would want to take a test drive, but that's all it is. You are a little diversion from a stressful career, but he has big plans and a real future here. That is the most important thing to him." She tilts her head to the side and smiles with pity. "He won't become truly serious about anyone that could jeopardize his potential with this company. Why do you think he's never invited you here before? Why haven't you been at any of our many mixers and office social events? He's fine with you on his dick, but you'd be an embarrassment on his arm."

Hauling my arm back, glad for the extra height my heels have provided, I smack her so hard across her face she stumbles. Her look of shock is almost as satisfying as the deep red imprint I made on her cheek. Almost, but not quite.

"Ms. Howell?" The receptionist has come out from behind her desk and is running toward Victoria as fast as her stilettos will take her.

"I'm fine." Victoria snarls, while waving off the attention.

"I'm calling security!" the receptionist hisses at me, but I don't even acknowledge her. I just throw the brown bag into the trash receptacle near the door and walk out.

Chapter Twenty-Six: Logan
*Will The Smell Of Baby Sh*t Eventually Fade?*

Why me? What in the hell have I done to deserve this?

"Oops! Sorry!" Kelly comes running toward me, jumping over a mountain of toys, sliding momentarily on a little pink quilt, and navigating past two baby bouncers with plastic balls attached to trays, before scooping the chubby bundle off my lap.

I wish she'd been able to remove the awful smell along with the baby, but, unfortunately, it still lingers.

Scott is holding the other baby, Isabella, with his left hand and resting a beer on his knee with his right. He's also laughing at me.

"Oh, did my little Sophia make a poo?" Kelly coos into the girl's neck as she walks briskly toward the hallway that leads to the nursery.

How can she stand to snuggle up to the origin of that vomit-inducing smell? "When do they get old enough to use the toilet like real people?" I ask, with complete seriousness.

After Kelly had asked Scott and I to watch the twins for her, reassuring us it was for just a few minutes, she'd plopped them down, one on each of our laps. She then hurried off to attack the piles of dirty clothes covering their laundry room floor.

I thought Sophia was the cutest thing ever when she looked up at me with those big brown eyes and started cooing and giggling while waving her chubby fists around. She was even more fascinating than the football game I'm actually here to watch tonight. But when she started to turn red, squirm around like a wild animal, and then make explosive noises that vibrated my leg, I'd had enough.

Scott just took a drink of his beer. Apparently fatherhood has trained him to be able to withstand anything.

"So... it's not a big deal that I haven't heard from Charli all day, right?" I ask while staring at the screen with no idea which team was ahead. He probably thinks I'm whipped, and I feel like a total pussy even asking, but I'm getting worried.

Scott makes a dismissive noise in his throat and looks over at me. "Do you really think I know why women do the shit they do?"

"You're married to one of them."

"And your point is?" Scott shakes his head and laughs.

Maybe I need to think about something else. "I finally told Matt and Victoria I'm seeing Charli," I tell him.

Scott frowns. "How did that go over?"

"Matt didn't say anything, which pretty much says it all. I knew he was into her that night and he's pissed that I'm with her now. He'll get over it," I say with more confidence than I feel.

"Maybe. What about Victoria?" he asks with interest.

"She smiled and gave me a hug. She even said she was happy for us."

"Then you should be scared shitless, my friend." He tips his beer in my direction but has to move it quickly when Isabella reaches out to grab it.

"I know." I lean forward and rest my head on my hands and take a deep breath.

"Did Charli ever fully forgive you for fucking up and answering your phone? If so, you are one lucky bastard. If I answered the phone when Kelly was about to give me some...I'd never get sex again."

"I think so. God, I hope so. What the fuck was I thinking?"

"I don't know. I thought I'd taught you better than that." He makes it clear he thinks I'm an idiot. I have to agree.

I sniff near the knee of my pants, inhaling deeply. "Will the smell of baby shit eventually fade? Because I feel like it's burned into my nose."

"I barely smell it," he assures me with a smirk.

"So...about Charli," I begin again.

"I thought you were here to watch the game, Logan."

"I am!"

"You sound desperate. Man up. Girls don't want needy guys." He sets his empty beer bottle down on the small end table and lifts his daughter above him. He lowers the baby long enough to kiss her belly and then raises her up again. This routine is repeated until Isabella is giggling loudly.

"What are you talking about, Scott?" asks Kelly when she comes back into the room with a now clean Sophia.

"Nothing, honey. I love you."

"Uh huh... Logan? What's going on?" Kelly slips the baby she is holding into the bouncer seat and stands right in front of me with one hand on her hip.

"It's no big deal, Kelly. Really. Thanks though," I tell her.

Coming forward, she sits right next to me on the couch. "Are you and Charli having problems? You know you should never have answered that phone."

"Scott!" I glare over at him and he at least has the decency to look guilty.

"She's my wife. I don't keep secrets from her. She doesn't like that and I like sex, remember?"

"Out with it, Logan" Kelly insists.

"I just haven't heard from her all day and I was wondering if I should be worried. It's probably nothing."

"Do you normally talk to her during the day?" she asks.

"Well, yeah. She had to work last night and then I'd stopped by and we..." I clear my throat before continuing. "Well anyway, I'm sure she was tired and slept in later than normal but she usually texts me when she gets up. And I always call her on my lunch hour but she didn't answer."

"You haven't heard from her since you left her this morning?"

"No. Is that bad?"

"Doesn't sound good," she admits. "Maybe you should try calling her again."

Kelly pats my knee and then leaves to finish up the laundry she'd abandoned for the diaper crisis.

Shit. "What should I do?" I ask Scott.

"Don't do anything. Do you remember how you hated it in college when girls blew up your phone?" Scott reminds me. "That was your cue to bolt."

"Shit, you're right. Forget I asked."

"But...women do speak a different language. Half the time I can't even tell when Kelly's pissed at me until she spells it out. I've learned the hard way that it's always better to assume you were a dick and apologize, even if you don't know why."

"Okay, but how in the hell am I supposed to apologize if she won't answer her damn phone?"

Scott gives this some serious thought, and then an idea comes to him. "Don't you have her friend's number? Text her and see if everything's okay."

"You are a genius!" *Why hadn't I thought of this?*

I pull out my phone and scroll through the contacts until I find Liv. I try to sound like I'm not a needy stalker, but just tell her I haven't heard from Charli and want to make sure everything is good.

Her response is almost instantaneous, in full caps, and scares the shit out of me. Not literally of course, I'm not as bad as Sophia, but it certainly makes me jump off the couch and go for my jacket.

"Where are you going? The game isn't even over!" Scott yells at me while standing to bounce a fussy Isabella on his hip.

"I have to go see her," I tell him.

"Look, I know I said to assume you did something wrong and I know from the way you've been acting this week, the sex must be fucking amazing, but that doesn't mean you have to beg for forgiveness while she's at work."

I look directly into his face and try to keep calm. "Liv said I better get my ass over to the bar and fix this immediately or she will end up personally killing Charli to save everyone else from having to deal with her shit. And while I'm sure that's a slight exaggeration, with Liv, you never know."

Chapter Twenty-Seven: Charli
Just Give It To Me, Kyle!

"He's not even here, Kyle." I sound whiny, even to my own ears. "Just give it to me!"

"No, Charli. You know I want to, but it's not right."

"Please..." I cajole as I come close to him. I can smell the leather of his jacket and feel the heat coming from his body as he sighs heavily. He rests his hand on my shoulder and I look up into those sinfully dark eyes. "Please, Kyle?" I try again. I'm feeling very determined to get what I want from him.

"What in the fuck is going on here?"

I jump, so startled by his voice that I fall forward and right into Kyle's strong arms. I'm trying to regain my balance, when I feel myself being forcefully pulled away from Kyle and my back makes contact with a wall of muscle I know all too well.

Logan is here. *Oh shit.*

"Hey! Don't you dare hurt her, asshole!" Kyle says as he takes a step toward Logan and they both tense in preparation.

This is bad. *Shit. Shit. Shit.*

"I would NEVER hurt her! I LOVE her!" Logan booms back at him.

Had Logan just said he loves me? Starting to feel light-headed, I crumple into the low chair behind the bar. This is enough to make the men stop acting like Neanderthals and they both squat down, one on either side of me.

I put out my arms to make them keep their distance. "I'm fine. Don't touch me. Either one of you."

Kyle decides to give us some space and walks away. Logan stays kneeling but moves right in front of me. He waits for me to get my equilibrium back before speaking and I can tell he's furious, but I'm not sure why. *I'm the one with the right to be angry, not him!*

"Why, Charli?" he asks through clenched teeth, but then the anger melts away and he looks like his heart is broken. "I thought we really had something. You said you weren't a cheater."

His whispered accusations tear at my heart. He's confusing me again and not making any sense, but he sounds so hurt. "What are you talking about, Logan? I haven't done anything." My head pounds and I'm afraid I'm going to be sick.

"Maybe not yet, but you were trying weren't you? Look, I know you and Kyle are close. I get it that he's a lot cooler than me but why did you let me think I was important to you if you really just want to be with him?"

I rub my head. I have a serious migraine coming on. It could be from the lack of sleep, but it's probably heavily aided by the liberal shots of tequila I'd downed before work. There's a reason Liv refers to tequila as "to kill ya" and I need to remember that. "Logan, I don't want Kyle. I want you." I speak slowly and carefully. *Why doesn't he know this?*

"But I heard you. When I came into the bar, you were pleading with him to give it to you." His lips curl in disgust and now he looks like he's ready to vomit.

I feel bad for him, but I want to laugh. Of course when I try, my skull starts to crack. "Owww…" I bend forward, close my eyes, and put my hand on Logan's squatting knee. "I wasn't asking for Kyle to screw me, stupid. I was trying to convince him to give me a drink. It's against bar rules, of course, but Ronan isn't here tonight, so I was being a brat and begging for it. He was right to tell me no."

In utter relief, Logan sinks down to the floor. *Is he aware he's sitting behind the bar, on the damp floor, in some really expensive suit pants? And why do I suddenly smell a dirty diaper?*

"Thank God," he says. He lays his head in my lap and I run my fingers through his hair, stroking him like I would a small child.

"But Logan, we need to talk."

"Okay. We'll talk about whatever you want. Just don't scare me like that again. I was serious, Charli. I love you." I suck in my breath and feel the tears threatening to spill over.

"I want to believe you. I really do." He'll never understand how much I want to believe him right now. Once before I'd believed Nick loved me enough, and I'd been so wrong.

"Why don't you? What happened today?"

I want to tell him about Victoria and the awful things she'd said, but I hesitate. I know he has to work with her and his job will become even more stressful if he knows about me hauling off and bitch slapping her.

There's always the possibility she'll tell him, but I doubt it since it won't put her in a flattering light. And, as Liv has been trying to convince me all night, those had been her ugly assumptions, not his. I'd never given him the chance to tell me how he felt. Victoria made me doubt his intentions and I hadn't even trusted him enough to ask for his side.

"I'm sorry. It's just my own insecurity, Logan. If you tell me you love me then I believe you."

He stands and pulls me up to him. Putting his hands on the sides of my face, he leans down to kiss me. The kiss is so full of tender desire and his belief in his love for me that my heart's rhythm outpaces even the horrendous pounding of my head. His tongue is softly exploring my mouth and it feels so good, but I feel so bad right now. *I swear if I have to pull away from him to vomit, I will die of embarrassment.*

"Tequila?" He looks amused now that the pain and shock have been subdued.

"Oh, yeah. Maybe just a little..." He kisses me again and I think I'm more intoxicated by him than I ever was on the tequila. "Ummm, Logan?" I pull away a little and look at him.

"Yes, Chuck?"

Smiling, I tell him, "I love you, too."

"Great!" Liv scolds. "You love her. She loves you. Everybody fucking loves everybody! Now can you please get back to work, Charli? I'm tired of covering all your damn tables!"

We watch as she rushes by. Poor Liv, I'm not in any kind of shape to help her tonight and I'm going to owe her big time. She won't forget it.

"I do need to at least attempt working. If Ronan were here, he'd kill me," I whisper almost directly into his mouth.

He groans softly. "Okay, but I'm so exhausted I'm about to fall asleep standing up. Can I crash upstairs for a couple of hours?"

"Sure." I hand him my key. "Get a nap. You may need it when my shift ends."

"Really?" He raises his eyebrows in doubt.

"Well, maybe after a few cups of coffee, several bottles of water, a dozen aspirin, and a couple hours of sleep. You can just wake me up before you have to leave in the morning for a quickie."

"Deal." He kisses the top of my head and leaves for the apartment stairs.

Chapter Twenty-Eight: Logan
Yes, Sir. Of Course, Sir. No Problem, Sir.

Staring at the documents in front of me, I try to make sense of what I've read for the third time. This merger is important. Victoria and I have worked hard to make sure it's airtight, and I can't afford to miss something crucial because of my personal life. My Olympic sized yawn prompts me to take another large gulp of my black coffee. *At this rate, I'll have stomach ulcers by the end of the weekend.*

I should be worried about my ridiculously short attention span today. I should be worried about messing up this deal. Mostly, I should be worried that I'm not worried at all. I'm happy. I'm happier than I think I've ever been.

Giving in, I lie back in my chair, close my eyes, and think of Charli. I remember the sound of her voice, nervous and hesitant, as she first admitted she loves me. I remember the second time she told me even better. She'd yelled it with full abandon, head thrown back and eyes closed as she moved above me and shattered my soul. Liv didn't seem to enjoy the latter declaration of love nearly as much as I did. She had spent the following five minutes outside Charli's door, screaming a lecture so riddled with unique combinations of profanity, I've decided she may be a genius.

I love Charli. I am in love with Charli.

"Logan?"

I jerk up in my chair and bump my half-full coffee mug. It sloshes onto the papers that litter my desk. "Shit!"

I look around for something to mop up the mess as it soaks through the layers and starts to spread toward the desk's edge. Finding no better solution, I use my T-shirt from the small gym bag under my desk.

Crisis contained, if not completely averted, I finally take a moment to see the cause of my mishap. Standing in the doorway of my office, and looking at me with concern, is my boss. I feel panic starting to surface.

"Mr. Burke, hello. What can I help you with?" I beckon him forward and indicate the chair across from my desk, but he declines with a shake of his head.

"Sorry to disturb you, Logan."

"Oh no sir, not at all. I'm sorry you caught me like that. I just closed my eyes for a second to focus my thoughts and ensure I hadn't missed any loopholes." We both know it's a lie, but he lets it go.

"Logan, I like you. I really do."

I swallow hard. This doesn't sound like a start to anything good. Don't bosses usually tell you how great you are before they let the axe fall? "I'm glad sir."

"You've always stepped up and gone that extra mile when I've needed you. And I need you to again," Mr. Burke says, in a way that allows for no argument.

188

"Okay. Sure. What can I do?"

"Our firm provides legal help to several local charities and humanitarian efforts throughout the year, as you know. It's good for our reputation and it gives us some much need tax breaks."

"It's also good for those causes, sir."

He narrows his eyes slightly. Maybe throwing that out there wasn't a really smart move on my part, but I just couldn't stand here and be so callous about the firm's motives. "Of course. Of course that's the primary reason we do it."

"Yes, sir. Of course," I agree.

"So we're getting special recognition at a fundraising gala tonight. There will be media coverage of this event and we need to be represented well. It was my intention to attend, but we've just learned my wife's mother has been hospitalized and our family will be flying in to spend time with her this weekend. Ordinarily I would ask Matt to take my place, but obviously he will be with us since this is his grandmother." He points in my direction. "I need you to handle this for me."

"Of course. No problem. I'm sorry to hear about your mother-in-law."

"Thank you. I appreciate that."

"Is this something I can take a date to?" I know Charli has to work, but maybe she could beg some time off? I don't think she'd enjoy it and I feel guilty about that, but at least we could spend some time together.

"Actually I already have your date taken care of," he says with a satisfied smile.

"Sir?" *What the hell is he talking about?*

"I've asked Victoria to go. You guys are a great team, she represents our firm well and honestly... you two will look great in the press coverage."

"Oh." I'm not sure what to say about this. It makes complete sense from his point of view since we're both employed by Strickland and Burke. Victoria is a natural at giving interviews and speeches too, but I know Charli won't be thrilled by the idea. She's made it perfectly clear she thinks Victoria is a Grade A bitch.

Surely she'll understand we work together and this is just part of the job? I decide there's no reason to even tell her. We're just now getting past her meltdown at the bar earlier this week and I don't want to upset her again. This is just work and it's no different than when Victoria and I collaborate at the office.

"Okay, sir. That's fine."

"Good. Good." He smiles and claps his hands together like he's accomplished a brilliant merger. "Our company car will pick you up at eight. I appreciate you giving up your weekend time and showing me you know how to be part of the team."

"Sure. No problem." With my recent, mediocre at best, work we both know refusing this event is not an option.

Not wanting anyone else to enter my office unannounced and maybe interrupt a phone conversation, I opt for a text.

> **Logan**: Hey beautiful.
>
> **Charli**: Good morning!
>
> **Logan**: It's afternoon.
>
> **Charli**: Well it's MY morning so don't give me shit ;)
>
> **Logan**: I just found out I have to do a work thing tonight.
>
> **Charli**: Are you still coming by later?
>
> **Logan**: YES!
>
> **Charli**: Did you forget I'm helping out Liv and her moms tonight?
>
> **Logan**: Shit! Sorry. I did.
>
> **Charli**: So you can't come with me?

Logan: I wish I could.

Charli: I want to introduce you to Liv's moms - Carol and Dana

Logan: Sorry. I really am. It's work.

Charli: I know.

Logan: Mad?

Charli: No. I get it.

Logan: How late will you be?

Charli: Until midnight I think?

Logan: 3 hours earlier than when you work the bar! Count me in.

Charli: "In" is exactly how I want you.

Logan: You are KILLING me. How am I supposed to get any work done?!

Charli: Be a good little boy and do your lawyer stuff today!

Logan: And???

Charli: I have big plans for you later tonight and all day tomorrow.

Logan: Hint??

Charli: Don't you like surprises?

Logan: Everyday with you is a surprise...can't wait.

Charli: It will be worth the wait. ;)

Logan: I have to go to meeting now. Sorry.

Charli: I understand.

Logan: I love you, little Chuck.

Charli: I know ;)

Chapter Twenty-Nine: Charli
He Looks Like Sex On A Stick

"You can't see my ass crack can you?" I twist around like a dog chasing its own tail, trying unsuccessfully to see my own butt.

"No. I've already told you this a million times. You look shit hot, and you need to quit worrying. You may not have big tits, but your ass is amazing and the dress is perfect for showing that off." I've probably mentioned this before, but my best friend rocks. You should be jealous.

"I love this dress," I say for the hundredth time. "Like, 'I may have to wear it every day,' love this dress. Think Ronan would be okay with me waiting tables in it?"

"Does Logan need to be jealous of this dress?" Liv asks me mockingly.

She's been making fun of me unmercifully since the night I made my loud declaration of love for Logan and had woken her up. Well actually, it wasn't at night but an early morning and after an earth shattering orgasm. She swears I hit a pitch that made all the stray dogs in the neighborhood howl in agony.

"I just wish he could see me in this dress. A selfie won't do it justice. I'll just have to stay in it until he comes over later tonight to take me out of it." I sigh just thinking of how delicious it will be when he slips it down my shoulders and it drops to the floor.

Oh no, on second thought, he's going to have to carefully help me out of it and then wait for me to hang it up before we get busy. This beautiful masterpiece of a dress had cost me a fortune and I wasn't going to have it end up a wrinkled mess on my floor.

"Thanks for doing my hair, Liv. The updo is perfect." I grab her handheld mirror and turn around so I can see the back of her masterpiece.

"We couldn't have all that hair hiding your back," she says in explanation.

I'm not kidding when I say I love my dress. The under layer is a skintight, silky sheath of nude, the exact shade of my skin. Over that is a delicate black lace, with scalloped edges. It runs straight across from one shoulder to the next, completely encases my arms to the wrists, and covers my front half all the way to the floor. It also has a high slit that exposed my right leg up to mid-thigh. But the thing that makes this dress spectacular is the back. It's completely bare, to right below the small of my back, and it exposes the small dimples at the top of my butt.

I look at myself in the mirror and smile in contentment. I would love for my parents to see me all grown up. And I would love to introduce them to the man I'm in love with.

"Are you done being narcissistic?" Liv comes over and turns her back to me. "Zip me up, hooker."

I oblige, then grabbing her shoulders, I pivot her around so she can get a good look at herself in the mirror beside me. Liv's dress is a deep emerald green with a sweetheart neckline, cap sleeves of soft transparent tulle, a corseted and cinched waist encircled with crystals and a full skirt that bells out and gives her the perfect hourglass silhouette.

"You look amazing, Liv. The men at this thing won't know what hit them."

"Well if they are rich, hot, single and hung like a horse then I'll be the one hitting them... over the head with a club and dragging them home to make them see how perfect their life could be. It's my turn to be in love."

"I agree." *Everyone should experience this feeling.*

Even though I decided Logan wouldn't be getting any selfies and would need to wait for the full effect in person, that doesn't stop us from taking lots of pictures with our phones to post on every social media site we can tomorrow morning.

We put our impromptu cell phone photo shoots on hold a few minutes later, so I can answer a knock and Liv can take a pee break. I open the door to see Kyle standing in the hallway.

"Hey, Kyle! Come on in." I smile and do a little twirl to show off the dress. "It's pretty amazing, right?"

"You're pretty amazing, Charli."

I stop and see his soft expression. *Shit.* We'd finally managed to get back to being friends. I thought he was over me, but now he looks like I've broken his heart all over again. "Thanks," I whisper and try to look away but he puts a finger under my chin and raises my face back up to his.

"Don't do that. You don't have to be embarrassed or feel bad. You didn't really think you were that easy to move on from, did you?"

My sinuses start to ache and I feel the pressure of tears starting to build, but try to blink hard and stop them. It won't help anything for me to cry.

"I know you don't feel the same," he continues. "I can't say I'm happy about it, but I get it. You can't help who you love, any more than I can. I'll be fine... eventually."

I wrap my arms tightly around him and lay my face against his warm chest. I truly love Logan and can't imagine my life without him anymore, but if he'd never walked into the bar that night, would things be different with Kyle? "You know how much I would love it if we felt the same for each other?" I ask him.

"Well, that would definitely make things a little easier, babe." I laugh and he gently takes my shoulders and pushes me back a little. "Let me see you." He walks all the way around me and whistles in appreciation. "Logan is a lucky man. Make sure he knows it, or I will."

"He does. And thanks, for everything."

"Damn, Kyle! Did you make her cry?" Liv comes charging into the room, a tissue held out, ready to fix any damage my emotional display has done to her perfect makeup job.

"Well actually, I came to let you know that your ride is here. Dana sent over a limo to pick you up in style. Can I escort you down?" He proffers both elbows and we link arms, barely managing to turn and squeeze through the single person doorway, and head out for the gala.

The event is being held in the ballroom of a very luxurious downtown hotel and arriving in a limo, dressed like we are, I feel very "Pretty Woman." *Well except for the hooker part of course. And Liv doesn't look anything like Richard Gere but the point is we look good.*

"Girls! You look beautiful!" Within seconds of arriving, Carol has us in a group hug that threatens our perfect appearance. Liv is trying hard to extricate us without hurting her mom's feelings.

"Thanks!" I tell her. "You're stunning, as usual. Where's

Dana?"

"Sorting out a minor disaster with the caterer. Always something! But you know she'll have it under control in no time." She waves off any suggestion, even implied, that there's anything her Dana can't handle. "I know you'll be taking pictures later in the evening, honey, and Charli will be taking notes for the article but for now, please try and have some fun, okay?"

"Good food and wine, lots of eligible men with fat wallets... and no competition from my best friend since she's in love... Yep, I'll have a grand time, Mom." Liv kisses Carol on the cheek affectionately as we say goodbye.

We run by the coat check room to leave Liv's camera equipment safely stashed, until the party gets in full swing, then head off to the bar.

"I notice when you were talking to Carol, you left off the part about being hung like a horse? Did you finally decide to show a little restraint around your poor mom?"

"Hell no. I was just trying to wrap it up quick and avoid a lecture so I could come get a drink. I need some alcohol fortification to deal with a few of the pompous shits that always attend these things and think that cozying up to me will get them in good with one, or both, of the moms."

We laugh and enjoy ordering drinks instead of serving them like we normally do on weekends. Several minutes into a story I'm sharing with her, about Logan of course, I notice her formerly bored and glazed eyes regain focus and sharpen with awareness at something over my right shoulder.

"What?" I try to look in that direction to see what has caught her attention but she shushes me and jerks me back.

"Don't look at him!" she commands without moving her lips or losing her smile.

"What are you talking about?" I'm thoroughly confused now.

"The clouds have parted and angels are singing." Liv has gone all soft and dewy, and I see her shifting to stand with a hand on her hip as she licks her lips.

"Have you lost your mind?" I ask. *What in the hell is going on?*

"Charli, there is a guy standing about three table away that may be a god in human form."

"Really?" I try again to turn and look... and again she jerks me back to face her.

"Be cool! I'm totally striking a pose and looking like I don't even notice him, even though he is absolutely checking me out, so don't ruin it by letting him know I see him!"

I don't think I've ever seen Liv try so hard to get a guy's attention. He really must be amazing and I'm dying to turn around. Maybe if I do it really slowly and...

"Ow! Quit squeezing my shoulder like that, Liv!"

"Then quit trying to look at him, Charli!"

"What does he look like?" I need details!

"Like sex on a stick," she breathes out softly.

I cross my arms in frustration. "Oh, that's very descriptive. Thanks." Liv laughs even though I know it isn't because she finds me funny. She thinks this will make her look more attractive if the hot stranger really is checking her out.

"He's tall with olive toned skin, brown eyes the color of melted chocolate, and really dark hair." She licks her lips. "His face is perfection. Do you know how I would love to photograph him? Or the way the light would hit the angles of that face? And his body...hmmm..."

She seems perfectly serious. *Where is her signature sarcasm?* It's been replaced with actual sincerity and I'm a little speechless.

"There's something else too," she continues, without noticing my mouth hanging open. "What is that? I think it's a scar through his left eyebrow. It actually makes him look even hotter. He looks way too cool for this place."

"Hey!" I seem to have finally found my voice. "We're cool and we're here."

"That's true," she concedes.

"So he's tall, dark and handsome?" I give her an exaggerated wink but she doesn't even notice.

"Definitely. Now I just need to figure a way to meet – FUCK!"

I'd like to tell you that she says this softly and privately, for my ears only, but that's just not my best friend's way. Instead two older women with heavily beaded gowns and silvery blue hair gasp in shock and move away from us as I apologize.

"What happened?" I ask.

"I should have known!" She scowls and takes a large drink from her wine glass.

"What?"

"All the good ones are gay or taken... or both."

"So he's gay?" I ask. Liv's moms certainly have a lot of gay friends and supporters and some of them are definitely hot.

"No. A really beautiful woman just sauntered up, wrapped her skinny bitch arm around him and kissed him."

"Oh. Maybe she's his sister?" I offer this up, still hoping for the best.

Liv shudders. "Well if so, I really don't want him anymore because that kiss involved tongue."

"Ewwww! Let's hope not, then. Sorry." I want to laugh at her. She looks so pissed off over a total stranger!

"So what are the chances she's a prostitute?" she asks, seriously.

Is she really considering that possibility? "Doubtful. Why would he bring her to a $500 a plate fundraiser when he could run her through Jack in the Box and enjoy a little time at a cheap hotel? Especially if she charges by the hour."

"Damn. He probably has bad breath and a small dick anyway, right?"

I pat her shoulder and play along to make her feel better. "Absolutely."

Chapter Thirty: Logan
That Rude Little Waitress

"Logan, stop checking your watch." Her voice is quiet and she's smiling but she's clearly pissed.

"Fine," I mutter, again.

Victoria and I arrived only half an hour ago according to my traitorous watch but I would swear we've been here for hours already. I smile at everyone we meet, say all the right things, laugh at all the stupid jokes and pretend I'm so happy to be representing Strickland and Burke. All I really want to do it run out the door, hail the nearest cab and head over to see Charli.

I console myself with the thought that she's also working, so even if I weren't stuck here, I wouldn't be able to be with her right now. *Just three more hours and I'll see her. I'll be able to hold her. I'll be able to bury myself deep...*

"Logan?" Victoria snaps.

"Huh? I'm sorry, what were you saying?"

"Look... I know what's going on and I get it. But you need to get back to reality before you really mess something up."

I feel my anger starting to creep in at her words. She sure as hell better not be saying what I think she is. "Would you care to explain that comment, Victoria?"

She's alert to the hard edge of my voice but plunges ahead anyway. "It's that rude little waitress. She's going to screw up your career, Logan. Just get laid and get her out of your system. You don't have to *date* her. You're too smart to jeopardize everything over a cheap piece of ass. We both know the type of woman you should be with."

Fucking bitch. "I don't know why you think you have any right to say anything at all about my personal life but just let me tell you something about that waitress." I push my finger hard against her bare shoulder. "She is the most amazing woman I've ever met. I'm completely and hopelessly in love with her."

"Logan," Victoria warns as she looks around at all the people near us that have stopped to listen. "Keep it down."

"I won't keep it down! Trying to keep my relationship quiet has caused most of my problems!"

"Your job..." she whispers.

"Charli is worth more than this job, or any job, could ever be to me. And if you're trying to say that you or anyone like you would be a better choice for me... you're so fucking delusional it's pathetic. You'll never come anywhere close to being what Charli is. I'm the lucky one to have her in my life and I plan on spending every second of every day making sure she knows it."

Victoria's face goes stony pale, except for the deep red crimson spots of color high on her cheeks. She looks like I've slapped her even though I'd somehow managed not to. She is also trembling slightly as she reaches up to smooth her still perfectly styled hair.

"I had no idea you felt like that about her," she says stiffly.

"Well, I do. The really pathetic part is that I've actually defended you to her. I tried telling her she was wrong about you, that your ambition gets you mistaken for being a bitch. But she wasn't wrong, I was. I was so fucking wrong it's unbelievable."

Maybe I should feel a little sorry for her as I watch her breath catch and her eyes widen slightly, but I can't. Several seconds pass before her face relaxes and the smallest of smiles appears. *Has she finally accepted I don't want her?*

"I apologize, Logan. I really do. I should never have said that. It was just my jealousy speaking. You know how I've always felt for you and I'm highly competitive."

She takes a step closer to me and I want to retreat but I hold my ground. We do still have to finish the night and work together regularly so I'll be civil but never again will I have any illusions about us being friends.

"Can you forgive me?" Her voice has gone all soft and feminine, making me nervous.

Surely she doesn't think she still has a chance with me? "Don't ever presume to know me or dare to say a bad thing about Charli in my presence again."

"Never. I promise." She takes that final step to close the distance between us. I just stand perfectly still as she wraps her arms around me and squeezes lightly.

"We've always been so good together, Logan. I want that to continue," she whispers directly into my ear and then lays her head on my shoulder.

Hell no. I can't stand it a minute longer and no matter what it looks like to the people around us, I'm ending this. I reach up and grab hold of her shoulders to push her away but before I can, she twists us both so I'm facing the opposite direction.

And then I see her.

She's dressed in a column of black lace that hugs her perfect body like a second skin and the look on her face stops my heart.

Charli.

Chapter Thirty-One: Charli
Now I Have Bathroom Cooties

"Charli!"

I hear him call my name, but I can't answer. I can't breathe. My heart seizes for a minute and then races at breakneck speed, thundering so hard in my chest I'm sure it must be visible from the outside. My vision is dark around the edges and there is a roaring in my ears. I turn to run.

Logan is coming toward me, fast. People are jumping out of his path and he's gaining on me. Liv is yelling something at me, but I won't turn back. I have to get away. *I can't do this here.*

The damn shoes are slowing me down and he almost catches me, but I make it to the women's bathroom just in time to push the door closed behind me and enjoy the solid thunk of the lock sliding into place.

The heavy pounding of his fist on the thick wooden door starts immediately. I cover both of my ears with my open palms, close my eyes and sink to the floor. My sobs overtake me and I'm choking. The swelling of my nasal passages has made normal breathing impossible. I want to scream at the top of my lungs. I can't. It would take energy I don't possess.

"Damn it, Charli! Let me in!" Logan's tortured voice slashes at my soul, but I refuse to answer him.

I can hear Liv's voice too. She's calling Logan every name in our cursing library and telling him to leave me alone. She's asking me to open the door, but even for my very best friend, I can't. *I can't.*

The heavy door is a formidable barrier but Logan still feels too close. I crawl across the floor and I think the lace of my dress has ripped but I don't stop until I reach the farthest corner. Once there, I pull my knees up to my chest, wrap my arms tightly around my legs and lay my head down on them.

"Charli? Honey?" Carol is begging me to unlock the door.

Instead, I open my small clutch and pull out my cell phone. I dial the familiar number but it takes three tries before I can speak loud enough to be heard. "Kyle?" I croak out his name.

"Charli?" His voice sounds panicked and distantly I feel bad that I'm upsetting him.

"I need you."

"What happened? Where are you, baby?" He is pleading with me now. It's faint, but I detect the sound of his heavy motorcycle boots crunching swiftly across gravel.

"I'm here, at the gala. Can you come and get me?" I whisper, with my eyes closed and my heart dying.

"I'm on my way. Don't move." The last thing I hear is a car's engine roaring to life before we are disconnected. I continue to sit, still and silent.

Some time later, I can't tell if it's been ten minutes or ten hours, I hear Kyle's voice outside the door. "It's me, Charli. You have to open the door. It's a slide bar and I can't get in to you."

Slowly, using the wall for support, I manage to stand up. Vaguely, I register I've removed my shoes, even though I don't remember doing it. When I finally make it over to the door, I whisper through the crack. "Is it just you?"

"Liv's here. And Carol and Dana," Kyle answers.

"What about... What about..." *I don't want to say his name.*

"No, babe. They had security make him leave. Open the door, Charli. Please. You're scaring me."

I reach up, slide the lock and push the door open slightly. Kyle grabs the outside handle and opens it the rest of the way.

"I'm so sorry!" I tell him as he enfolds me in his strong arms and I sob against Kyle's chest. "I didn't mean to scare you. I shouldn't have called you. I didn't know what else to do."

He rests his chin on the top of my head. "Don't be sorry! I'm here for you. It's okay."

I turn my head sideways and see Liv standing there. She has tears streaming down her face. *This can't be right. Liv never cries.*

She walks over, wraps her arms around me, and lays her head against Kyle's chest too. "Don't you ever do that again, hooker. You know better than to lock me out."

"I'm sorry, Liv. I shouldn't have. I just couldn't let him in and he was at the door and he... I just..." My voice sounds raw and strange to my ears.

"Shut the fuck up. You don't have to apologize. Just don't do that shit again."

"Okay."

"And you totally ruined my perfect makeup application." Liv slides a finger across my cheek and comes away with a dark gray smudge. "You have streaks of mascara all the way down to your chin and you look like crap."

I smile weakly. "So do you. Can we go home now?"

206

Kyle kisses the top of my head and then Liv's. "Absolutely," he says. "Let's go."

The three of us walk out together, after Liv retrieves my purse and shoes from the bathroom floor. She tells me she is going to disinfect me when we get home because I'm probably contaminated with public restroom cooties.

We've almost made it to the safety of Kyle's car when I hear his voice in the darkness. *Logan is still here.*

"Charli?" He sounds frantic and I tense as he steps out of the shadows to stand about ten feet in front of us.

"Just leave her alone, asshole. You've done enough," Kyle says and his arm becomes even tighter around me.

"Let me explain. Charli, it's not what it looked like."

"What it looked like?" Liv pulls away from Kyle and steps in front of me to point an accusing finger in Logan's direction. "It looked like you were out tonight with Victoria when you told Charli you had to work. It looked like the bitch had her arms around you and was whispering into your ear. It looked like you were cheating on my best friend."

"NO! I was not cheating. Please listen to me, Charli! I was working." Logan takes a step to the side so I can see him past Liv. "This was a mandatory event and we were chosen to represent the firm. I didn't want to be here. I wanted to be with you! Please talk to me!" He tries again to come closer but Kyle moves me farther away.

"Let me tell you something, Logan..." Kyle stands straighter, pushing his chest forward, and tries to move me behind him.

"Stop," I croak quietly, but they hear me and do as I ask. "Kyle, Liv...please get in the car. I need a minute."

"Are you sure?" Liv asks.

"Yes."

Kyle is harder to convince, but he finally gives in and both of my friends climb into Kyle's car and close the doors behind them. I turn toward Logan. Maybe it's better if we just get this over with.

He takes a deep breath before beginning. "Charli, I love you. I would never..."

"Stop, please," I beg. Thankfully he does as I ask, but when he again tries to come closer, I put my hand up. "Don't!"

Logan's shoulders slump and his hands hang with no purpose. "I was not here on a date with Victoria. Please tell me you believe me?"

"I do. I believe you."

"Oh, thank God!" He smiles and runs a hand through his messy hair. "I was just..."

"But..." I interrupt.

"But, what?"

I take a deep breath and try to explain. "Even if you didn't cheat on me, even if you were here for work... you knew exactly how I'd feel about you coming here with her. You didn't try to explain the situation first. You just came and hoped I'd never know."

"No, I didn't. I just thought..."

I stop him again. "You probably have functions like this from time to time. You probably have other work events and office parties and things like that, but I don't really fit in, right? It's not my scene? You wouldn't want to bore me with your job stuff, right?"

Logan fidgets with his tie and pulls on the hem of his jacket. "Well, yeah I guess I did think you wouldn't like this kind of event but..."

"But the real issue is how it would make you look." I give him a small, hurt smile of understanding.

"What? NO!" His fists clench and he tightens his jaw in denial.

"Yes, Logan. I've never been invited to your office. I've never seen the place you work and I'm supposed to be your girlfriend. I've never met any of your co-workers except when they came into the bar that first night and we know what they thought of me. I only met Scott and Kelly because we ran into them accidentally. I've never met your family. You make me feel like your shameful little secret."

"You aren't. I love you, Charli." I notice the tears forming in his eyes and I'm sorry to be hurting him, but it can't be helped.

"I believe you, but love isn't enough. Our lives don't work together. I think I always knew that. I'm strong and independent and I swore to never again feel like less than someone else. That's exactly how you made me feel tonight." I turn away and open the car door.

He swallows hard. "Please, don't go..." he says softly.

I smile back at him with my heart breaking, but I climb into the front seat of the car, next to Kyle, and close the door behind me. "Please take me home now."

Kyle just nods and starts the engine. After we've backed out of the parking spot and start to pull out of the lot, I notice in the rear view mirror that Logan is still standing right where I left him.

Chapter Thirty-Two: Logan
He Wasn't Kidding... I Stink Like A**

There are thirty-six grooves in the wainscoting on the wall behind my dining table. The leg of the chair closest to the kitchen has a deep scratch in it and I have no idea how it got there. I really need to clean my front door around the doorknob. It's disgusting. *How did it get so dirty in just that one spot?*

I raise my head up off the couch, just enough to pour more of the tequila down my throat. It's a good thing this isn't the bottle with the worm. I might choke on it since I can't make the effort required to sit all the way up.

My cell phone starts to vibrate and I watch it jump and twitch on the coffee table. *It's not Charli, so what's the point?*

I've been awake for fifty-two hours now. You'd think between the exhaustion, the liquor and my lack of activity, I would've fallen into a coma many hours... hell, *days* ago. But I can't.

Every time I close my eyes, I see her. I see her standing there, so small and hurt but so sure of herself as she tells me the best thing in my life is over. If I close my eyes, I can hear her voice -

raw and raspy - because I have broken her heart. I've made her believe that I don't see how amazing she is and that instead, I want to hide her from my world like she's some kind of embarrassment.

I am every creative, derogatory name Liv has concocted for me and worse. I lift the bottle again and I'm shocked to see it's empty. *Shit. When had that happened?*

I finished the bourbon that first night and I can't even remember what else I've been drinking since then. I think this is the last bottle of alcohol in the house. *I should get more.* I can't even imagine the effort it would take to get off my couch.

Then the pounding starts. I think at first it's just my head. Lord knows I deserve the mother of all hangovers after this weekend, but it's something else. Someone is at my door.

"Damn it, Logan. You won't answer your phone. You won't answer the door. We're coming in!" It's Scott's voice and I remember that I gave him an emergency key awhile back. Maybe I should be mad he's about to invade my home without permission but I'm just glad the banging will stop without me having to haul my ass over to the door.

Hey, maybe I can convince him to make a run to the liquor store for me? He's supposed to be my friend, right? But I know it's wishful thinking.

I stare up at the ceiling above my couch, my hand still wrapped around the neck of the empty bottle, and wait for the lecture. From my peripheral vision, I can tell Matt is with him. *Great, it's a fucking intervention.*

"Done feeling sorry for yourself?" Scott asks with disgust as he looms above me.

"Not yet. But thanks for asking." I roll away from him to face the back of the couch but he grabs my shoulder to roll me back.

"You're lucky it's me asking and not Kelly. I can't tell you how hard it was to convince her she should stay home and leave this to me."

"Should I thank you for that?" I ask sarcastically.

"Hell yes, you should!"

"Well, thanks. You can go now." I wait but he and Matt just continue to stand there, side by side with arms crossed, as they stare at me.

"You obviously cared for this girl, but..." Matt tries to chime in and help.

"Cared for her?" I laugh despondently. "I love her, Matt." I know he's having a hard time really understanding this.

"I'm sorry," he says, "I'm sorry that it didn't work out if you really do love her."

"If? What part of 'I LOVE HER' don't you understand?" I scream back. *Fuck. I shouldn't have done that.* There's a jack-hammer in my skull now.

"Logan, don't take it out on Matt. We're here because we're your friends," Scott says.

"I know." I close my eyes briefly and run my hand through my hair. They don't deserve my anger. I'm mad at myself, not them.

"What are you going to do now?" Matt asks.

"I don't know, man. I really don't."

Scott lowers himself down onto the edge of my coffee table. It's a good thing it's a big solid chunk of wood because he'd bust something less substantial. Marriage must be agreeing with him. I'm sure getting to marry the woman you love is a great feeling. *Apparently I won't be so lucky.*

"Did you cheat on her?" Scott asks this quietly and without judgment.

"NO!" I yell back at him but regret it when again my head throbs.

"Did she cheat on you?" Matt asks this time. There might even be a little glint of satisfaction in his eyes and as hard as I've tried to stay friends with him, if he says one negative thing about Charli, I'll kill him.

I had in the past explained to Scott my suspicions about Matt's interest in Charli, but he's convinced that Matt's real issue is being jealous of me. I told Scott his idea is crazy. *Why would a guy from a wealthy, powerful family, that's always been handed everything easily, be jealous of a poor kid that had to work for everything he wanted?*

"No, Matt. Charli isn't like that. She didn't mess around while we were together, but... right now? Who knows what she's doing with that fucking bartender."

"The bartender? The old one with the crew cut?" Matt asks with too much interest.

"No, I'm talking about the younger one. He's one of those badass guys that can wear a leather jacket without looking like a douchebag. And he's crazy about her." I put my forearm over my eyes to block out the lamp light Scott had just reached over and turned on.

Matt nudges my elbow. "You think she's hooking up with this bartender?"

"I have no idea. They're good friends and have a lot in common. Didn't I just tell you he is crazy about her? She won't return my calls or texts. Liv is threatening to shoot me, and that bitch is wicked good with a gun. I fucked up the best thing I've ever had. And now, I've probably given that long-haired, ripped jeans wearing, rock star of a bartender the perfect way to convince her he was the right choice all along." They let me go on and on about

213

everything until my angry words dry up and I can't think of another single thing to say.

"So are you going to just give up on her?" Scott asks without accusation.

"I don't know." It hurts to even toy with that idea but I'm beginning to worry she's made that decision for us.

Scott lets out a heavy breath. "Why don't you take a few days off and..."

"What?" Matt interrupts Scott's suggestion. "He's working on that merger and..."

"Matt, don't be an asshole. Do you really want him dealing with that in his current state of mind? As his friend, you should see that he needs to get away. If you want to put the firm first, then what happens when he fucks up the whole deal because he doesn't have his head screwed on straight right now."

Matt reconsiders. "Maybe you're right."

"Logan?" I know Scott has my best interests at heart, but I kind of wish he'd just leave and let me get back to my silent misery. "Maybe you should go see your folks."

I scoff at this suggestion immediately. "Why would I do that?"

"Get away from all this shit. Go hang out with your parents and Jenna. How long has it been?"

"Too long," I admit. *Maybe it isn't such a bad idea.*

"Do it. Tell them hello for me and give little Jenna a hug. Give yourself some new scenery and some time to think about where you should go from here."

I look at my phone. The battery is nearly dead and it's lying in a sticky glass ring on the coffee table. Besides taking a piss and grabbing a new bottle from above my refrigerator, I have been completely worthless all weekend. Something has to give.

"Okay," I decide.

Scott pushes my arm and it falls away from my eyes. "And before you pack up and head out, take a shower. You stink."

"Fuck you," I tell him, and he grins.

"Do we need to hide the sharp objects before we leave?" Matt asks in a joking tone.

I shoot him the finger and he laughs. "Fuck you too."

"Great! You're back to your charming self. We can leave knowing our job here is done," Scott says as he gets up and gives my poor coffee table a break.

"You can also leave that key I gave you on your way out," I tell him.

"Hell no. I might have to come cheer your worthless ass up again in the future." Scott waves the key in my direction and blows me a kiss.

"Just leave, assholes"

When they let themselves out, I look again at my silent cell phone. I reach for it and when I do, I get a whiff of myself. *He wasn't kidding. I stink like ass.*

I dial my parent's house and wait impatiently until the familiar voice answers. "Mom? I think I'd like to come down for a couple of days."

Chapter Thirty-Three: Charli
Indecent Proposal

"Traitor!" I set my tray down on the bar next to Liv's.

"I'm not a traitor. I just think you should at least talk to him." Liv sighs and reaches for her order of drinks. "I've never seen you so miserable and it's damn depressing to be around. I'm not saying kiss and make up, but clear the air so you can move on."

I narrow my eyes. "Since when are you an advocate for a level head and rational behavior, Liv?" Staring at my friend, I wonder how much Logan is paying her. I know she likes him, but she's supposed to be on my side.

"I'm just an advocate for getting the real Charli back. I'm tired of your sad ass dragging around our apartment and the bar. It sucks."

She has a point. I've tried to get back to my life before Logan but I see him everywhere. My room is so tainted by his memory that I've had to start sleeping on our couch at night. I try to open my laptop and write but all I can do is remember how he encouraged me and made me promise to dedicate time each day to making my dream a reality. I go to work and I watch table four just in case he shows up again but if he did I don't think I could have stayed. *How had he so completely insinuated himself into every aspect of my world?*

"You're right. I'm a post-breakup crazy woman. I've had my cry and eaten my weight in mint chocolate chip ice cream, so it's time to prove I'm that girl I've always claimed to be." I paste a smile on my face, determined to fake it until it feels real.

Liv smiles and gives me a thumbs up before leaving to deliver her drink order.

"Hey, beautiful. How are you?" Kyle breezes behind me and flips my ponytail as he passes.

"I'm great!" My enthusiasm and smile make him pause. He turns back toward me with a mix of hope and skepticism.

"Really?" he asks.

"Really. Well, maybe not great exactly... but I'm okay. And I have you to thank for a lot of that. What would I do without you, Kyle?"

"You'll never have to find out." He smiles and I realize it's the first time he's relaxed since saving me from my embarrassing meltdown at the gala. My problems have been affecting my friends. I won't let it happen anymore.

"I do need something now if you're up for it?" I wink at him.

"Anything."

"I need a whiskey sour and a Jack and Coke for the couple at the pool table. I think it's their first date. Look how cute they are." We both look toward the giggling young woman with strawberry blonde hair and the tall, awkward guy standing near her.

He laughs. "Coming right up!"

"What the hell?" Kyle and I both turn back to the bar and see Liv has returned. She's staring toward the bar's entrance with a look of disgust.

Striding across the bar, like he owns the place, is Matt. The three of us stand perfectly still and wait for an explanation. Within seconds, he's crossed the distance and leans one elbow on the edge of the bar as he smiles wide enough that I can see his molars.

"Hey, Chuck. What's up?" Matt asks, looking at me as though we are the only two people in the room.

Even his voice gets on my very last nerve! Liv and Kyle both come up to flank me but I motion them away. "I've got this, guys. Thanks, but can you give us a minute?" They reluctantly leave, with assurances they aren't far if I need them.

"What do you want, Matt?" I try to remain distant and keep all emotion out of my voice.

"World Domination? A good cup of coffee? The list is endless," he says with a smirk.

Does he think he's funny? He's not. I sigh in exasperation, "Just get to the point, please. I have work to do."

"Of course you do." He looks around the bar in amusement. I doubt he considers my job to be of any real importance. Looking back at me, he reaches an arm out and places his hand lightly on my shoulder. "And just how are you doing?"

My skin crawls with the contact as I shrug his hand off. I have no idea what prompted his visit but I want him to say what he needs to say and leave. *Is he here on Logan's behalf? Does Logan even know he's here?*

"I'm fine," I say slowly, barely moving my mouth.

"Good. I'm glad to hear it. I was worried when Logan told me about what happened." I stand in silence, unwilling to acknowledge anything about Logan to this arrogant, condescending man. "Even though we all knew it wouldn't work out in the long term..." he adjusts his tie and examines his nails, "I can certainly understand the impulse to try something new for a while."

"Try something new?" *How dare he come here and say this shit to me!*

"But he says you were worth the effort so I just thought I'd stop by and see if you were willing to go out with me? I think we'd be good together."

I guess I should be angry. Maybe he deserves a good bitch slap like the one I handed out to Victoria but all I can do is laugh. I laugh hard. It's the first time I've laughed since Logan and I broke up and Matt isn't happy about my response.

"Are you seriously standing here thinking I would EVER waste one minute of my life in your company by choice?" I feel like holding my side, I'm laughing so hard. "I might have been wrong about Logan, made the mistake of thinking we had a chance, but even if you were truly, madly, deeply in love with me... I couldn't love someone so self-absorbed. You ridiculed me the first night we met. You have Logan convinced that you are his friend and would be there for him if he needed you but as soon as you find out we've broken up, you come here to hit on me? Why in hell would I give you a chance after I've had someone like Logan?"

"You think Logan's better than me?" he spits out.

"Oh, I *know* he is, Matt."

"He comes from nothing and will never have all that I have. And you? You think a low class little waitress can do better than someone like me? You're lucky I even made the offer!"

"I'm just lucky I saw through you from the start and never bought into Logan's misguided belief in you," I throw back.

Matt is turning an alarming shade of purplish red and erratically jerking his hand through his hair, completely ruining the perfection he normally maintains. "You think Logan is so great?

You think he's better than me but he's the one that didn't waste any time before moving on. You're walking around nursing a broken heart over a guy that never gave a shit about you! And now I see why." He straightens his jacket and tie before smoothing his hair back into place. "I can't blame him for not even waiting two days before taking off. I hope he and Victoria are having a great time out of town."

Turning quickly, he leaves the bar without a backward glance. All I can do is watch him. Suddenly I don't feel like laughing anymore.

I'd believed Logan really loved me, even if we hadn't been able to make the relationship work. I want him to find happiness but my heart rips at how quickly he's been able to move on. I do still hurt and I can't imagine a future where the thought of him won't hurt. *And of all the people in the world for him to move on with, did it have to be her?* That hurts most of all.

Chapter Thirty-Four: Logan
Are You Gay?

Sweet Jesus, this is awful. I feel like throwing up, or at least gagging, but I know how sensitive she is. She would act like everything was fine but it would hurt her feelings and she'd done this just for me.

"So?" She asks expectantly, with that big smile that everyone says I inherited.

"Mmmmm, yeah, they're great. Thanks, Mom. You shouldn't have." *Oh, she really shouldn't have!*

"Well, I know they're your favorite, honey." Walking to where I'm standing near the breakfast bar, she reaches up and ruffles my hair with affection before heading toward the living room.

The minute I'm sure she is far enough away, I spit the partially chewed, but thankfully not yet swallowed, chocolate chip cookie into a paper towel. I then ball it up tightly and bury it in the bottom of the trashcan. *What does she put in these things? Dirt?*

I love my mom. She is a wonderful person and an amazing

mother but the woman can't cook for shit. She's a pro with a frozen pizza, canned soup, grilled cheese sandwiches or a big bowl of cereal. Anything requiring her to combine ingredients in correct proportions or use the stove and oven for more than re-heating is impossible. She can't even master boxed macaroni and cheese. Dad, Jenna and I have an endless supply of jokes about how the cheese sauce becomes thin as water or so thick you can use it as wallpaper paste.

I slump down onto the same avocado green stool I'd sat on while eating cereal every morning of my life, until leaving for college, and enjoy being alone for a while. It's been hard to pretend everything is okay when I'm dying inside.

Scott was right to suggest I come home, though. It hadn't been easy convincing Mr. Burke I needed to leave so close to the completion of the merger but it was worth the trouble. I've been here two days now and while I still feel like someone has dug my heart out of my chest with a rusty spoon, I can at least get off the couch and ignore the liquor cabinet.

Well, most of the time. *Is it weird that I still feel the urge to replace what I've taken out of the vodka bottle with water like I did in high school?*

"Shit! Did Mom make cookies again?" Jenna breezes in, turns up her cute little nose in disgust, and makes a gagging noise.

"Watch that mouth, squirt." I completely agree with her, but I'm still her big brother.

She grabs a diet soda and comes to sit on the stool next to me. "Whatever."

"So... how's school?" I ask. *What else do I say to a teenage girl?*

"Really? You come home for an unexpected visit, mope around like you're on your period, and even drink Dad's vodka, but you want to ask me about school?"

Jenna is seventeen, so cute I feel my blood pressure rising from the male attention she receives every time we're in public, and smart as a whip. I shouldn't be surprised she's observed so much. "Yes. I want to ask you about school, smartass. How's it going?"

"Fine. Perfect. Couldn't be better. Thanks for asking. Now... what's her name?"

I groan and give up. Liv would adore my little sister. They are remarkably similar in directness. Thinking of Liv makes me think of Charli, and thinking of Charli is a never-ending torture.

"Charli," I tell her, knowing she won't give up until she finds out anyway.

She looks toward me with excitement. "So... you're gay now?"

"What? No! Charli is a girl."

"Oh, okay. Cause if Charli is a dude, I'm fine with that. I'd actually be really cool with having a gay older brother. All my friends think gay guys make the best friends so if you were gay that would be so awesome and we could..."

"I'm not gay, Jenna!" Sometimes it's hard to stop her stream of conscious bullshit.

Jenna narrows one eye and tilts her head as she looks at me with doubt. "If you say so..."

I sigh with exasperation. "Her name is Charlotte. She just goes by Charli."

"Oh, well that's cute. I like it. So what happened?" She takes a drink from her can and swivels the stool in my direction.

"It's complicated."

"I'm sure I can keep up." She rolls her eyes at me.

Are all teenagers this annoying? Surely I hadn't been. Is it a teenage girl thing? "Charli seems to think our lives are incompat-

223

ible," I try to explain, hoping this will satisfy her curiosity.

"Why? Is she a rich bitch socialite like that Victoria person that works with you?"

I start laughing. Again, her observations are brutally honest and right on target. "Actually, Charli is under the delusion that I think she isn't good enough for me." I tell her this, very matter of fact, but it hurts to even say it. I never once believed she wasn't good enough for me. Quite the opposite, actually.

"Damn, why would anyone think that? You're a dorky lawyer and your life is boring."

"Thanks a lot." *Nothing like family to make you feel even worse about yourself.*

Jenna shrugs and looks apologetic. "Sorry. Tell me about her."

"She's beautiful and so smart. She's writing a book, she loves animals, she can race go-karts like she was raised on a track, she waits tables in a great little bar, has amazing friends that love her, she truly cares about people, eats like a toddler and is cool as shit." Charli is all of this, and more. I can't even explain who she really is and how she makes me feel.

"Hmmmm... sounds like she is way cooler than you."

"She is," I admit and I smile at my little sister, wishing more than anything I could introduce her to the amazing woman I fell in love with.

"Then why don't you go home and fix it?"

"Sounds good, squirt, but it's a lot harder than it sounds." I reach over and steal a drink of her soda, instantly regretting it. I forgot it was diet and it tastes like shit. Maybe not as bad as Mom's cookies...

Jenna pulls the can back to her and grins at my face of disgust. "Did you cheat on her? Or did she cheat on you?"

"Well, no..." Although I think she doubts my fidelity after seeing me at the benefit with Victoria.

"Did you hit her? Or steal from her?"

"Of course not!" *Where does the kid come up with this stuff?*

Jenna stares at me intently. "Do you love her?"

"Yes!" There is absolutely no hesitation on my part because it's so true.

"Then go home and fix it, dumbass."

My sister might be the smartest person on the planet.

Chapter Thirty-Five: Logan
Open Heart Surgery

I'm a pussy. How long will I sit in my damn truck before I get the nerve to walk into that bar and demand she talk to me?

In actuality, I may end up having to beg her to listen to me. Charli isn't the type to deal well with demands and I'm pretty sure I'm high on her list of people she's actively avoiding anyway.

I had tried texting and calling her almost continuously after that nightmare evening but all I got was her voicemail and ignored messages. *Jenna was right, though. I have to make Charli see how much I love her and how much I want her to be in my life.*

I'm proud of who Charli is and want to show her off to everyone I know. I want her to understand that in our relationship, I was the one that didn't deserve her and not the other way around.

It's 2:15 a.m. The bar is closed and they should be doing clean up so she won't have any customers. All I have to do is enter from the back, ask her to step out with me for a few minutes, explain what happened that night and make her believe me.

Sure. Piece of cake.

It's 2:30 a.m. If I don't get my stalling, cowardly ass in there now, it's going to be too late and she and Liv will have gone up to the apartment. Shit.

I finally manage to get out of the truck and make my way to the backdoor. I know they keep it unlocked during clean up so they can haul all the trash bags out to the dumpster. I also know Kyle and Ronan are usually close by, on guard for drunks hanging out around back, and I need to be careful as I enter without invitation. *That's all I need is to get shot for trespassing.*

I push the door open a little and look in. It's well-lit inside so I can see pretty clearly... but what I see knocks the wind of me.

Kyle has his back to the end of the bar and Charli is snuggled up against his chest with her arms wrapped tightly around him. He kisses the top of her head and whispers something. Then she smiles. It's the real smile, the crooked one that shows off her dimples. *My smile.*

I back up, with my eyes closed against the horror I'm witnessing, until I feel the door behind me. Letting myself out as quietly as I can, I practically sprint back to the refuge of my truck. I only thought I hurt before.

I was wrong. That had been pain with heavy anesthesia. This is open heart surgery without even the relief of an aspirin.

I jerk the cab door open, ignoring the grinding squeak of protest from my poor, abused truck, and jump in. I'm ready to leave this parking lot and never return. My hand fumbles the key into the ignition and I'm about to escape when, thanks to my rolled down window, I hear my name being yelled. It's so tempting to pretend I don't hear it, but instead I kill the engine and wait.

"Logan?" Liv has come out to drop a garbage bag into the

dumpster and she walks over to the truck. Leaning on the door, she peers inside at me in confusion. "What are you doing here?"

"I'm wondering the same thing."

"She's really pissed at you."

"I get that."

"You shouldn't have gone with Victoria. Or at least, you should have told Charli about it instead of keeping it secret," Liv says, telling me something I already know.

"I get that too."

"Do you love her?" She seems genuinely curious, instead of angry with me, so I decide to answer her. It seems every woman I know is going to interrogate me about my feelings for Charli.

"Yes, Liv. I do." I sigh and drop my hands from the steering wheel. I look down at where the landed in my lap.

"Good."

"Really?" I jerk my head up to look directly at Liv. "Because it doesn't feel too good right now."

"That's good too. You really hurt her, Logan. Normally that would sign your death warrant with me but I think you're the one for her so I'm willing to give you a second chance, with conditions, of course!" Liv points a finger at me. "You ever hurt her like this again, they'll never find your body."

I laugh, without humor. "Well thanks a lot for the second chance, Liv, but it's not really up to you. It's up to Charli. And right now it looks like she's moved on and doesn't have plans of giving me any kind of chance."

Liv tilts her head and smiles. "Looks can be deceiving. Come to my show."

"What?" *What in the hell is she talking about? We're talking about Charli giving me another chance and now we're talking about some show?*

"Next week is my show. I have several photos in the exhibit, one of them is the Ophelia, and I want you to come." She pulls a folded piece of paper out of her apron pocket and hands it to me. "You helped me with it and it would mean a lot to me."

I would love to see her exhibit. I would really love to see the Ophelia. But I just don't know if I can. "Maybe. I'll try."

"Just come, Logan." Liv has no problem making demands. She turns around and walks back into the bar.

I unfold the glossy paper and find it's a flyer promoting the art exhibit. It shows the date and time, lists the artists with work in the show, and promises you'll see things that change your perception of our world. *Charli changed my perception of the world.*

Chapter Thirty-Six: Charli
Who Would Bring Babies To A Bar?

"I think you need to get laid."

"Shut up, Liv."

"Well, when Logan was giving it to you regularly, you were in a much better mood." Liv uses the mirror on the wall near our door to adjust a bobby pin that is holding up one side of her hair.

I glare at her and she ignores me. "Shut up, Liv."

"Are your batteries dead?" She pulls her lipstick out of her pocket and adds a fresh coat.

"I'm going to kill you if you don't shut up." I tie on my work apron and don't even bother to check my appearance.

She turns to smile at me, an image of perfection. "Kyle will do you, but that could get complicated."

I walk out of our apartment, slam the door behind me and start down the stairs. I contemplate all the ways I could end my misery. *Maybe a little poison in her drink, during our break?* I could slip into her room after our shift and slide her pillow over her face. It would take her by complete surprise since her sleep is like death.

I'm entering the bar when I hear her tromping down the back stairs to join me for work. She's laughing. She thinks she's funny. *It's her funeral.*

"Kyle, how attached are you to Liv?" He's walking out of Ronan's office and smiling at me.

He comes to my side and puts his arm casually over my shoulder. Looking past me, he's watching Liv coming to join us. He takes my question into consideration and waits a full minute before answering. "Well, she's absolutely gorgeous and I'll miss looking at her. How are you thinking of killing her today?"

"At the moment, just as expediently as I can, but if she keeps up her shit, I will make sure it's also very painful." Liv is now right beside me and I stick my tongue out at her. She laughs at me.

"You going to be there, Kyle?" Liv asks though it's like she's confirming what she knows instead of looking for an answer.

"Wouldn't miss it, babe," he promises and Liv smiles.

I may occasionally want to kill Liv but I'm so happy for her right now. In two days, she will present her photos at the Mormont Gallery. Howard and Bethany Mormont, owners of the art gallery, are very wealthy, very educated and very impressed with themselves. They love to discover new talent and once a year they hold an exhibit to showcase new and upcoming artist in our area. Liv was asked to provide a themed series of photographs for the main hall and she's been working on it for months. This could open all sorts of doors for her and really launch her career.

"What in the hell?" The last time Liv had uttered those words at work, Matt had showed up with his indecent proposal. *If that little shit is here again, I might decide to kill him tonight instead of offing my best friend.*

Kyle looks toward the entrance with confusion. "Do they think this is a daycare?"

His question makes no sense, so I look in the direction they are both staring. Instead of seeing Matt, I see Kelly and Scott. I also see their twins, Isabella, and Sophia. The baby girls are strapped to their parents in those strange baby packs that always remind me of mother kangaroos. Who brings babies into a bar?

The new arrivals notice me, standing with my mouth open in stunned silence, and head over. Kelly is waving her arms around and smiling, looking thrilled to be here even though she has a baby attached to her chest. Scott, sporting baby number two, looks like he'd rather be anywhere else in the world and is avoiding all eye contact.

"Charli!" Kelly runs toward me and manages to give me a weird one armed side hug, being careful not to squish poor little Isabella. *Or is it Sophia? I can't really tell.*

"Kelly, hi. What are you doing here?" I'm so confused.

"We came to talk some sense into you."

Shit. They're here for Logan. I don't want to talk about Logan. "And you decided to bring the babies? To the bar?" My pitch rises a little on the last question and I worry it sounds like an accusation but Kelly takes it in stride and continues.

"Well, we didn't have a babysitter! Scott offered to come alone but no way was I getting left behind again. He gets to have all the fun. He also offered to stay home with the girls so I could come but I wasn't about to do this all by myself. And I really think he thought I wasn't capable of..."

Liv decides she's had enough. "So, you come to a bar...with babies?" Scott winces.

"Yep! You must be Liv!" Kelly extends a hand and Liv shakes it hesitantly. "I'm so glad to meet you. I've heard a lot about you.

Charli and Logan both adore you and I know I will too. But right now, I'm on a mission!" Kelly turns to me.

"Look… Kelly, I appreciate that you've come here… with babies… to try and convince me to work it out with Logan, but it just isn't going to happen."

"Why not? He loves you and we think you love him too. You two need to talk and fix this. Tell her, Scott." Kelly lightly slaps Scott's arm with the back of her hand.

He doesn't look thrilled with the sudden attention thrust upon him but he speaks up anyway. "Charli, I've never seen Logan like this. He screwed up and he knows it but he misses you."

"Well he didn't miss me for long did he?" My voice goes hard and acidic.

Kelly looks to Scott with confusion but he shrugs in ignorance. Then he looks to me. "What do you mean, Charli?"

Had Logan kept this from his friend? "He and Victoria went out of town last week. It didn't take him long to find someone else to spend his time with. In fact, it seems pretty clear to me they must have been spending time together before we even broke up." I'm not trying to bad mouth Logan to Scott, but he should know what kind of friend he's here defending and trying to help.

"What?" Kelly turns to Scott in anger. "Did you know about this? How could you keep this from me? I thought he didn't even like that bitch? You told me that he…"

"Kelly!" Scott interrupts his wife. "He did NOT go out of town with Victoria last week! Why do you think he did, Charli?"

"Matt came in and told me they left town. He also tried to convince me to go out with him now that Logan and I are done." I'm shocked and a little angry when Scott starts to laugh. *Does he find this funny?*

"That fucking piece of shit. I know he can be an ass some-times but I had no idea he could..."

"What are you talking about?" I demand. I'm confused, pissed and tired of talking about Logan. I need him to spill what he knows and just leave me in peace to nurse my wounds so I can move on.

Scott puts a hand on my shoulder. "Charli... Logan and Victoria were both out of town last week..."

"But you just said..." Kelly is jumping around in agitation and I begin to wonder if the baby is going to be jostled until she spits up. *Ronan won't be happy about baby puke in his bar.*

"I said..." Scott continues, "he didn't go out of town WITH her... but they were both out of town. Logan went to spend a few days with his folks. Victoria had to go out of town to complete the negotiations for the merger. They were on opposites sides of the country and definitely not together."

I feel like the iron bands encircling my heart since that awful night just loosened a bit. Not a lot, but just enough I can breathe easier. He still hurt me. I'm still upset. But at least I don't feel completely betrayed.

"Thank you, both of you. Logan is lucky to have you two as friends. I hope he knows that. And I appreciate what you're try-ing to do but it doesn't change anything. Sometimes love just isn't enough."

"Who in the hell would bring babies into MY bar?" *Well... Ronan has just noticed us.*

Chapter Thirty-Seven: Logan
I Really Need A Drink

She is relentless! Does she ever take no for an answer?

I slide my phone into my desk drawer and decide I'll answer her later. I need to catch up on my work since I skipped out a couple of days last week to see my family. Throwing myself back into my career is probably the best way to move on anyway.

I can hear the skittering hum of my phone vibrating in the drawer. *Damn. She's still texting me.*

Giving up, I pull the phone back out and read what Liv has texted this time. It's her insistence that I attend her show, just as the previous hundred or so texts had been. Now she's really laying on the guilt.

I really would like to be there for her. I'm dying to see the end result of the photo shoot at the park. That day was the first time I'd kissed Charli. Dressed in her Ophelia costume, wet and shivering but so fucking beautiful that I remember doubting she was real, I had wanted her more than I'd wanted anything else in my life. The feel of her cold arms wrapped tightly around me and the soft chill of her lips against mine had sent my brain into overtime, dreaming up all the ways I could warm her. Later, I'd learned that my imagination was nothing compared to the reality.

The thought of seeing Charli again is thrilling and terrifying. I want her to need me in that all-consuming way that I need her. I want her to love me and trust me. I want her to fight for us and believe in us. *I want her to feel like I do.*

And I'd really thought she had. *How had one evening's miscommunication become our downfall?* I made a mistake and I'd apologized for it. If that was all it took for her to jump ship then she didn't want us to work out nearly enough.

When my phone rings it startles me. Liv has been texting non-stop but hasn't actually tried calling me. Looking at the screen, I realize it's Scott, not Liv.

"Hey, everything okay?" I ask. *He never calls me at work.*

"Look, man. I need to tell you something."

His voice sounds hesitant and now I'm really starting to worry. *Are Kelly and the girls okay?* "Of course. What's up?" I ask.

"It's about Matt," he says and now I'm confused instead of worried.

"What about Matt?"

He hesitates before speaking. "He went to see Charli."

"What the fuck?" *Why would Matt go see Charli? He knows how I feel about interference. I don't need him trying to fix my shit.*

"Actually...he asked her out..." Scott says, but surely I heard him wrong.

"He... He did what?" I feel my head throbbing and a heat creeping up my neck. My eyes are aching and I know my blood pressure must be through the roof.

"He stopped by the bar after you left to see your folks, asked her out and even insinuated you had left town with Victoria."

I stand up so abruptly my chair shoots out behind me and crashes into my file cabinet. I pace around the room, clenching my fist, trying to convince myself that murdering that piece of shit is a bad idea.

"How do you know this?" I can't imagine Matt telling on himself, especially to Scott, knowing he would tell me.

"Well..." Scott clears his throat and tries to stall, but I'm in no mood.

"Tell me what you did."

"Well, Kelly had this idea..." he starts.

I groan and manage to sit back down at my desk. Kelly always thinks she can fix everything. I should have known she'd try something.

"You know she has your best interests at heart. She cares about you and wants to see you happy," Scott adds hurriedly in defense of his wife.

"I know she does, Scott. Just please explain everything."

"Okay. Well, so...we loaded up the girls and went over to the bar and..."

"Wait a minute. You took Sophia and Isabella to a bar?"

"It's not like we were there to buy them a drink and party, dumbass! We didn't have a babysitter!" He's defending himself but I know he thinks it was ridiculous too.

"So a guy and his wife walk into a bar with a couple of babies... That sounds like the beginning of a really bad joke," I say, but he isn't amused.

"Do you want to hear this or not?"

"Fine! Yes. Tell me all the gory details."

"Kelly just wanted to see if she could talk to Charli and tell her how miserable you are," he says and I cringe. *My friends are making me sound like a pathetic loser.* "And she might have been successful if it weren't for Matt's visit last week. I did, of course, tell Charli the truth but I think it was too late. I'm really sorry, Logan."

"It's okay," I tell him. What else can I say? He and Kelly had wanted to fix things, not cause more problems.

I hang up with Scott and think about how to deal with Matt. I also think about Charli. After the shit she got on the night we met, my not acknowledging her on the phone to Victoria, my mistake of not telling her about the gala and now Matt going to her job to hit on her... maybe she's better off without me in her life.

It's time I have a talk with my good friend Matt. I walk out of my office and I must be radiating anger because everyone in the hallway takes a step back without saying a word. I walk directly to Matt's assistant's desk and stare at her until she notices me.

"Mr. Mitchell...uh...can I help you?" Her eyes are open wide and she's pushed back in her chair as far as she can get.

"Is he in there, Rebecca?"

"Yes, but he's on an important..."

Not giving her time to finish, I open the door and walk in. Matt is leaning forward on his desk, talking into his phone. When he sees me in the doorway, he smiles and beckons me in. He also indicates the chair across from him but I choose to stand. I never smile or relax my stance and he starts to realize we have a problem.

"Listen, I'll call you back," he says into the receiver before setting it back down. "Logan, is something wrong?"

"You could say that."

He steeples his fingers in front of him and narrows his eyes. "Can I help with anything?"

"I doubt it. I'm pissed at myself for not realizing earlier what an asshole you are."

He stands up and comes around the desk. Directly in front of me, with his arms crossed over his chest, he is glaring as if he is the one that's been wronged. "What the hell are you talking about?"

"I'm not scared of you, Matt. I never have been. You can throw your weight around and use your name to intimidate people in this office but no one respects you and now, neither do I. I'm done letting a few nice gestures in our past make me believe you have anything decent inside you."

"Nice gestures? Are you fucking kidding me? I got you this job. You'd be nothing without me!"

The sad part is I think he believes what he's saying. "You're wrong. You got me an opportunity and I took it. Through my own abilities, I earned this position. That's something you can't say. But right now, I couldn't care less about that. Right now, I want to know why you went to see Charli."

At my words, he starts to smile. "That's what this is about? You want to throw away our friendship over a cheap piece of ass?"

It takes me all of two seconds to have my hand wrapped around his throat and his body pushed up hard against the wall. "You fucking piece of shit," I snarl quietly. There's no need to alert anyone else near his office before I'm done with him.

"Logan..." he chokes out while trying desperately to pull my hand away.

"The only reason you can still speak is because you aren't worth going to jail over." Matt's eyes bug and he believes me. I give one quick hard squeeze before releasing him and he sags with relief.

"How dare you," he spits out with a hard glare.

"I'd dare anything where Charli is concerned."

Matt sneers. "The two of you deserve each other. You're both low class."

That's when I hit him. I hit him hard.

He doesn't hit back. Wiping the thin trickle of blood off his mouth with the back of his hand, he looks me eye to eye.

Then we both turn as his door is pushed open and Victoria rushes in. "What the hell, Matt? Your assistant isn't at her desk and everyone says Logan is pissed. Did you tell him about Charli coming here and..."? Then she notices me and her mouth snaps shut.

"Would you care to explain that comment?" I ask coldly.

"I didn't know you were in here. I'll just come back." Victoria starts to back out of Matt's office.

I walk around behind her and close the door. "No, I think you need to stay." She tries to put as much distance between us as she can.

"Go ahead, Victoria...talk your way out of this one," Matt tells her with a bitter laugh. "She hit you and now he has hit me. I think it's over."

"Somebody better explain this to me. NOW!" I yell and slam my fist down on the desk. Victoria goes very pale and starts to tremble.

"Logan, I'm your friend and I was only trying to do what's best for you," she says.

"Try again," I tell her.

"She will ruin your career!"

I close my eyes and rub the bridge of my nose. I feel a massive migraine coming on. "What the fuck happened?"

"She came by the office a few days before the gala..." she stutters.

"Charli? She came where? Here to the office?" I ask. *If she'd come to my office how had I not known about it? Reception should have called me immediately.*

"Yes. She was bringing you lunch, a surprise obviously, and I saw her before you were called."

"What in the hell did you do, Victoria?" My rage is simmering so near the surface, I have to clench my fists to try and contain it.

"I convinced her that her visit wouldn't be appreciated." Victoria sits down on the edge of Matt's desk, smoothing down her skirt. I told her you'd be embarrassed for someone like her to show up on your job and that you have ambitions that can't include someone like her."

I realize this must have been on the day Charli freaked out and refused to talk to me all afternoon. Hell, she'd even gotten drunk.

Why hadn't she told me about what had happened? But I know why. My little Chuck is too strong and self-sufficient to admit someone else's words had made her feel worthless.

"You deserve to be hit as much as Matt," I tell her this calmly and directly.

I haven't hit anyone since I got in that one fight in high school. Now today I punched Matt in the face and want to hit a woman, even though I was raised to never do such a thing. My words to her are the unadorned truth and she believes me. She also laughs, though I can't figure out why.

"She beat you to it," she explains.

"What?"

"Your little wai... I mean, Charli, she beat you to it. She slapped me and she's very strong for such a little thing." I think there's a note of admiration in her voice.

I truly smile for the first time since losing her. I can picture her defending herself, not at all afraid and letting everyone know she can take care of herself.

My little Chuck is one tough cookie. Except, she isn't my Chuck anymore.

"I will never forgive either of you." I leave Matt's office and return to mine. I sit behind my desk, unsure what to do with this new knowledge.

Does it really change anything? It certainly makes me more aware of how badly it must have hurt her to see me with Victoria. It's probably similar to what I'd experienced when seeing her with Kyle at the bar.

I decide that I've had enough. I'll make some lame excuse but I'm leaving work. I can't take anyone else explaining how they'd managed to help me fuck up my relationship with Charli.

I really need a drink. It's a damn shame I can't go to the bar I like best.

Before heading out, I grab my cell phone and send Liv another text.

>**Logan:** I'LL BE THERE
>
>**Liv:** Of course you will be. Quit texting me in all caps.
>It denotes yelling and that's rude. ;)

Fucking Liv.

Chapter Thirty-Eight: Charli
Love Isn't Enough

"Oh, Liv, I love it. I love them all, but this one..."

I stare at the Ophelia print. It's framed with a simple, white mat and presented under a soft spotlight. It doesn't look at all like me and I find it hard to believe I was the model. The current of the stream around the ethereal figure looks like flowing satin and blends seamlessly into the layers of the dress. The soft focus and rich colors of the background draw the eye to the muted girl that has given up her life over her mistaken belief in love. It's tragic and heartbreaking and beautiful.

"It's my favorite too," she whispers with a proud smile.

We raise our champagne glasses in a toast to the lost girl.

"You rock, Liv and this show is amazing," Kyle says as he slides up between us, throws an arm over both of our shoulders and pulls us into a quick hug.

"Thanks, but you're about to spill my champagne so chill with the hugging shit." He just laughs at Liv's reprimand and hugs us again anyway.

Then Ronan joins us. "I just saw that crazy couple that brought the babies into my bar. Did you invite them?" He sounds like he thinks the idea of actually wanting them to attend and risking another baby invasion must be a mistake.

"Yep. They're cool... but did they bring those kids?" Even Liv looks upset as she asks this. "Maybe I should have put 'adults only' on their invitation?"

"It's just them," Ronan says and Liv is obviously relieved. I laugh.

"Thanks for coming tonight. All of you." She might be sarcastic and sometimes difficult but Liv really does care and this event means a lot to her.

"We wouldn't have missed this for anything," Kyle tells her. "Hell, Ronan even closed the bar tonight. And we know he never closes on a weekend."

He'll never admit he chose Liv over his bar but we all know. "What else was I supposed to do when my whole staff is here?" he asks gruffly. "Speaking of the bar, Kyle I need you take care of it next week."

"Really?" Kyle is trying to keep cool but I can tell he's surprised and thrilled by this new responsibility. "What's going on? You never take vacations."

Ronan actually smiles. "I'm going to see my daughter. Kinleigh is graduating from high school and she even got a scholarship to business school." She's his only child, and he may not say much about her but when he does it's obvious how important she is to him.

Kyle slaps him on the back. "Congrats, man! That's awesome! Your bar will be in good hands."

"It better be," Ronan grumbles.

Liv looks down at her watch. She then encourages Ronan

and Kyle to join her at the bar for another drink. I start to follow but she stops me. "Just wait here. I'll be back in a minute. I want to talk to you."

What on earth does she want to talk about? "Is everything okay, Liv?"

"Everything will be fine. Just wait here."

"Okay, sure." I take another small sip from my glass and turn to look at the photograph.

A few minutes later I feel the presence of someone coming up behind me. At first I assume it's Liv, back to talk with me about God only knows what, but I quickly realize that's not the case.

I smell sunshine and the warm, crisp scent of outdoors. My body tingles with that particular tension I only experience near one person.

Logan.

Keeping my eyes fixed on the photograph, I wait for him to make the first move. He's so close now that I imagine I can feel the warmth he radiates reaching out for me. His soft sigh tickles at my memories and I close my eyes as the pain knots up my insides.

"Charli?" His whisper is so faint I wonder if he really spoke or if my need to hear his voice again has conjured it out of thin air.

Turning around, I slowly open my eyes and a salty dampness has made a path down my face. I don't want to cry in front of him but I don't know how to prevent it. Through the wet blur, I can sense he's about to lose it too. His usually full and beautiful lips are compressed into a thin, tight line with no color as he fights for control.

"Charli." I watch his words form this time, and know he has spoken, but the broken ragged sound isn't his normal voice at all.

"What do you want, Logan?" *I want to sob. I want to scream at him. I want to run into his arms. I want to run far away.*

"I want... I need for you to listen to me. Please."

"I don't think this is a good idea." I look down at my feet, fighting my desire to stare at him and soak in every detail I've been deprived of recently.

"Please," he implores with a pain that matches my own.

"Fine." *I don't want to hear this!* But I can't make my legs walk away. Some traitorous part of me has decided I have to hear this.

"I spoke with Victoria."

Her name punctures me so unexpectedly that I inhale quickly, the breath catching, and I feel faint. I look up at him, angry at myself for still caring so much. "I don't want to hear about you and her!"

He tries to come closer, as though he wants to wrap his arms around me in comfort, but I back away so fast I end up pressed against the wall. With painful understanding, he stops, steps back and slides his hands into his pockets.

"Charli... I'm so sorry. Just listen. She's nothing to me and she never was. I should have told you immediately about having to go to the fundraiser with her. I knew you wouldn't like it and I was trying to prevent you getting upset for your own sake but for selfish reasons too. I didn't want to fight about it. I was worried about my job and felt I had to do it but I was an idiot for not sharing my reasons with you."

He pulls one hand out of his pocket and runs it through his hair in frustration before continuing. "I just found out about what happened between the two of you at my office." He pauses and there's the smallest lift at the corners of his mouth. "I would have loved for you to surprise me with lunch but honestly, I really was avoiding bringing you to work."

This admission hurts more than I thought it would. Some part of me still hoped he didn't think of me as unworthy of him. "Well, it's a good thing we're done then." I try to smile at him but I just can't.

"No! It's not a good thing at all! It's the worst thing I've ever gone through in my entire life, Charli. You don't get it! I didn't think I should be with someone better or more suitable...I was embarrassed for you to be around my co-workers and friends because they should be better! They wouldn't appreciate how incredible you are. I was trying to protect you but also I worried that you might think I was like that too. I'm not good enough for you and I didn't want you to figure it out!"

I can hear what he's saying, but it's not sinking in. "What are you talking about, Logan? You all have six-figure salaries, work in a fancy downtown office and believe the world is yours for the taking. I know that to you guys, I'm just a low paid nobody, but I'm not. I'm proud of where I come from and the life I've made. I don't need all those material trappings and I will never again be with someone that can't understand that."

"I do understand that! And that isn't how I see you at all. I see a beautiful woman that lost her parents too young but instead of becoming bitter and hard appreciates every precious second of the life she still has. I see someone who has friends that love her enough to die for her if necessary. I see your amazing talent and passion and the drive that pushes you to realize your dreams. I see a woman that captures everyone's attention and doesn't even realize it. I see you."

My tears have become real sobs as I continue to lean back against the wall. He is saying all the right things but I don't think any of it really matters. It doesn't change anything. "Logan...I just..."

"Charli, please give me another chance. I'll never be as cool as you, most of my friend's suck, my job is boring and I'm just going through the motions… but I love you. When you're with me, I love my life."

"Logan," I take a deep breath and die a little on the inside, "I love you too. I love that's how you see me but I hate that you see yourself like that. You're smart and successful. Scott and Kelly are wonderful and I know they love you, so you do have some great friends. I've heard you talk about your parents and little sister and they sound amazing. But… we want different things out of life. I'm not saying it's a bad thing to be focused on your career because I am certainly focused on mine, even if it hasn't really happened yet. I don't want a life filled with elegant dinner parties, work-related social functions and always trying to fit in with people I mostly don't like. I would suffocate and complain and cause problems…and you would end up resenting me for it."

"No. I don't have to do that shit… or if I do, you don't have to go!"

I finally manage a real smile, even though my heart is in shreds. "You do have to do that shit. And me not going with you to share that part of your dreams would mean too much of our lives spent apart. Find someone else. Find someone that can stand by your side and want what you want."

He risks coming closer and this time I let him. Encouraged he takes me into his arms and I melt into his warm embrace. I know this is the last time I will feel his body against mine and the agony is so deep it tempts me to throw better judgment aside and give in. But I know if we put this off, it will eventually kill us.

"Please baby, don't say that. I want you." His voice is muffled as he speaks into my hair.

"I know, but we don't always get what we want."

I press my palms against his chest and push him away. He resists at first, but then finally believes I'm serious. He stands there with his face completely blank. Without another word, he turns and walks away.

Closing my eyes against the onslaught of pain, I think about the times Logan and I have shared. He showed me what it feels like to really love and be loved.

Once, a couple of years ago, I had thought I'd found love. Nicholas was intelligent and witty. He worked for his father and it was understood he would one day inherit the business. He even had aspirations for eventually turning toward politics and I'd been so impressed by all the good things he said he would do if he gained office. He loved to buy me extravagant gifts and took me on weekend trips to beautiful locations, but never home to meet his family. I made excuses because he told me he loved me and I'd believed him.

While working on my first story for the newspaper, I'd seen the mockup of the weekend society page. There, in full color, was a story about Nick's recent engagement to a young woman from an influential and wealthy family. I stared at the article for hours. Their smiling faces, the words of approval quoted from both sets of parents and the details of the elaborate wedding planned for the following summer had mesmerized me. Nick had big dreams and he'd made the decision needed to guarantee them.

When I'd confronted him, he'd explained how truly sorry he was. He swore he really did love me, but surely I understood what was expected of him? His parents had made it clear that to marry someone like me would hurt his political dreams. I'd told him that it sounded like antiquated horseshit, to which he shook his head in confirmation that he'd made the right decision. He had an obligation to his family and himself to marry the kind of girl that would further the things he knew he deserved in life.

At the time, I had thought my heart was broken. What I'd felt for Nick was absolutely nothing, a mere shadow, in comparison to how I feel about Logan.

I believe Logan when he says he loves me. I believe him that he didn't cheat on me. I also believe, that in time, he'll choose someone very different than me to share his life and if I don't find a way to let him go now, that eventuality will be more than I can survive.

Some time later, I have no idea how long, Liv finds me, still leaning against the wall near the Ophelia, trying to remember how to breathe.

Chapter Thirty-Nine: Charli
Down The Rabbit Hole

"Holy shit, Batman!"

My voice carries through our apartment and Liv runs into my room. "You're done? You're really done?"

I grab her hands, pull her up to join me on my bed, and then we start jumping like we did as kids when Donnie Spencer finally gave me my first real kiss. It had been in the seventh grade, in the back of the library during study period and it had been magical. *Well, magical might be an overstatement but he was good kisser for a thirteen-year-old boy with braces.*

"I did it, Liv. I can't believe I did it!"

"Well, I knew you had it in you." She gives me a quick hug, then pushes me away. "Now let me off this bed before you mess up my hair. I have a date tonight."

I stop immediately and bug my eyes at her. "Why didn't you tell me? Who is it? I know I've been completely wrapped up in finishing my book but I would remember if she'd told me about meeting someone.

She gets down off the bed and uses my vanity mirror to repair the damage to her hair. "You don't know him."

She's being evasive but I'm determined to find out what's up. "Who is it, Liv?" She doesn't answer, just smiles before turning toward my door.

I follow her out of my room and into hers. I have to throw my hand out to prevent her from closing the door in my face.

"A friend of Scott and Kelly," she says quickly before disappearing into her closet.

I didn't realize she still spoke with Scott and Kelly. Does she also talk with Logan? I decide I don't want to know. It's been four months since we'd finalized our goodbye at Liv's photography exhibit and while I still think of him more than I should, I'm finally managing to enjoy some parts of my life again. I don't need to step backward.

I sit down on the edge of her bed. "So, what's this guy like?" I need for her to believe I'm fine with this. I want her to meet someone special, and yes it's very scary that this date has a connection to my past, but I'll find a way to deal with it if she really likes him.

"I have no idea," she says when emerging with a pair of aqua blue, peek-a-boo toe pumps. "It's a blind date. I've never met him."

I gawk at her, unsure what to even say to this news. Liv never agrees to blind dates. She is super picky about guys. Many ask her out, so she's never had to rely on someone else's suggestions. "Okay. That's a new one..."

"Yeah, I know." She looks a little aggravated. "But Kelly insists he's great and I'll just love him. I haven't found the right one on my own so I'm trying to keep an open mind."

"Good for you!"

"There's just this one thing," she says as she slips into the shoes and starts rummaging in her purse for her lipstick.

"What?" I'm really curious now.

"He has five kids."

Surely I didn't hear that right. "He has..."

"Yeah. You heard me, hooker. The dude has five kids."

"Ummmm..."

She throws me a look. "Shut up, Charli."

"I'm not saying anything!" I'm trying not to giggle.

With a sigh, she points a finger at me. "I can hear what you're thinking."

I'm actually too surprised to think anything yet. "Five? Five kids? And he's raising them?" I ask.

"Apparently. I don't know the full story yet but they all live with him. Kelly is going to babysit so we can go on this damn date."

"Five?" It still isn't computing.

She holds up all of her fingers on her right hand and waves it in front of me. "Five. Like you have five fingers on each hand. Like five little piggies went to market. Get it?"

"I get it. I think." But I'm not sure I do. *Five?* She exhales loudly and crosses her arms. I'm still trying not to laugh. "How old is this guy? I mean, if he has five kids already?" I'm doing the math in my head. We're not teenagers anymore or anything but we are still at the start of our twenties and I can't picture her with some guy in his forties. *Especially not one with five kids!*

"He's only thirty. He got married really young, started a family immediately and the kids are really close together in age. The last time resulted in twins. That's how Kelly knows him. He's in her twin support group or something."

"Okay. Twins. Young twins. And...five kids." I keep saying

this, thinking it will make me actually believe it.

"Look, I like kids. I really do. I even want kids someday, as long as that someday is far, far away. Five is really freaking me out, though. But, Kelly can be really persuasive and well, who knows?" she says.

"Five?"

"Shut up, Charli!"

Five. Now I'm laughing so hard at the thought of Liv playing with this guy's FIVE kids when they try to hang out that I'm clutching my stomach and rolling around on her bed. This won't upset her since she never makes the damn thing anyway.

"Don't you have something better to be doing?" she asks grumpily.

"Nope. Because I finished my book!" I sit up and flash her my cheesiest smile. Liv, I finished my book!"

"Yes, and we celebrated that by jumping on your bed so why are you on mine now? Get out and let me finish getting ready."

She looks over at the clock, and then a sly smile briefly flits across her face before turning to me. "You need to take a copy of the book to Dana and Carol. You promised them they could read it when you were done."

"I know but I can just email it to them."

"NO!"

I jump when she screams this at me. *What's her problem?* "Why not?"

Dana is more tech savvy than Carol but both women use email regularly. I send them things all the time and so does Liv.

"Ummmm..." She taps her fingernail on the dresser for a few seconds and then smiles. "It's way too long. They won't want to read so much on the computer screen."

"I assumed they'd read it on their iPad. I know they have

one. Carol told me it was better for the environment. She'll be pissed at me for wasting so much paper to print her a copy."

Liv is acting really strange. Well, stranger than normal, anyway. "No. She specifically told me that for your book she wanted a hard copy to save forever."

"Then I'll give her a real book once they've been printed. I've already worked out the deal with the publisher."

"They don't want to wait that long. Quit being lazy and take them a damn copy, Charli!"

"Okay! Fine." I stand up and give her a salute. "Whatever you want, Sergeant!"

She looks so relieved that I wonder if maybe she doesn't want me here when her date shows up. *I'm not THAT embarrassing!*

I had hit print on my laptop before we started our celebratory jumping and when I get back to my room, there is a thick stack of warm papers filling the printer's tray. *I can't believe I finally finished it.* I know it will get another professional edit and have to be formatted for print and electronic sales but my part is done and I'm overwhelmed by this amazing feeling of pride.

Putting the book, *my book*, into a large accordion file folder, I secure it with an oversized rubber band and grab my purse and jacket. Heading out the door, I run into Kyle.

"Hey!" I smile at him and wait to see why he was coming up to our apartment. It's our day off and I assume he just wants to hang out. *Maybe he can ride with me over to the Garrett Foundation offices?*

"Hey, beautiful. What do you have there?" He points to my bulky folder.

"My book!" I give him a big smile and he hugs me warmly.

"You finished it? That's great. I'm so proud of you!"

I have the best friends. "Thanks! I'm proud of me too. What are you up to, today? Liv has a date," he raises his eyebrows at this, but I go on, "and I'm taking the book to Carol and Dana. Want to go with me?"

"Oh... ummm..." He slides the toe of his boot against the doorframe and I start to worry. He never acts nervous. Something must be up.

"Kyle?"

He looks up at me and takes a deep breath. "Don't laugh okay?"

"Okay." *What the hell? Is everyone going crazy today?*

"I wondered if you could help me with something?"

"Sure. Anything," I tell him.

He looks away from me and explains. "Look, I didn't finish high school. Some stuff happened and... Well anyway, I want to get my GED and maybe take some classes at the junior college."

"Oh my God! Kyle!" I throw my arms around him and squeeze. "I think that's a wonderful idea."

"Thanks, Charli. I wasn't a bad student actually. I made really good grades but I just wasn't able to finish for personal reasons. I thought maybe you could help me go over the math before I take the test... just to make sure I really remember it?"

"Absolutely. I'll do anything I can to help. What made you decide to do this? If you don't, mind me asking?"

"Ronan, actually," he says with a laugh.

"Really? Ronan suggested it?"

"Well, it was more my idea after he left me in charge of the bar. Remember when he left for his daughter's graduation a few months ago?" I nod my head. It had been strange for Ronan to be gone but Kyle had done a great job keeping everything running smoothly. "I liked it, Charli. It was interesting and more of a challenge than I thought it would be. Ronan has been showing me

256

about the ordering and inventory and payroll and everything. I'd really like to get a business degree and maybe open my own bar one day."

I give him a quick hug. "I think that's a perfect plan."

"Thanks." *Is badass Kyle actually blushing?* "I'm about to go down to Ronan's office and use his computer for an online prep thing I found. Just ran up here to ask you about the help.

"Sure. I understand. Come by later this evening and we will celebrate. I'll even spring for pizza." I raise one eyebrow and bump his shoulder.

"Thank God. I have big plans and I can't afford to feed you," he teases before heading down the back stairs to get to work on his new future.

It only takes me about fifteen minutes to get to the building that houses the Garrett Foundation. It's unassuming and plain but very large and there's always the hum of activity when you enter the main doors. What started out as a small charity, under the caring hand of Dana's father, has grown into a thriving foundation that funds multiple causes. The foundation is known for never squandering the money they raise but instead always putting it to good use all over the world. I'd love for my parents to see what they had helped to grow.

Dana and Carol expect hard work and dedication from their employees. Some volunteer and some earn a modest income for their full-time participation but everyone here seems to enjoy what they do.

Walking through the endless rows of desks with casually dressed staff, I spot Dana pacing near a row of windows, gesturing emphatically as she talks into her phone. When she looks up and notices me, the pacing stops and a huge smile splits her face.

"Hold on a sec," she says into the phone as she reaches out to hugs me. "Liv called and said you were bringing over the book! Carol and I are so excited!"

"Thanks!" I start to hand the folder to her but she steps back.

"Can you go up to my office and leave it on my desk? I really need to finish this call. It won't take me long. Carol is around here somewhere, so I'll find her and we'll meet you there in five minutes. Don't rush off! We want to talk with you."

"Oh, okay." I wonder if they just want to congratulate me on finishing or if there's something else. *Please don't let them ask me about Liv's date!* I'm not sure I can keep a straight face when telling them he has FIVE kids. *Five!*

I take the elevator up, smile at Dana's assistant and motion to her that I'm going into the office. She always looks so busy but she smiles back and waves me in.

Setting my heavy bundle down on the top of the desk, I wander around the room and lovingly look over the many snapshots of Liv and I growing up. There are even a few pieces of childish artwork we'd made in elementary school tacked to the side of the file cabinet. Dana likes to act tough but she's just as sentimental as Carol.

My back is to the door when I hear it opening. I turn expectantly but my smile freezes when I see the person entering. Suddenly my legs don't seem able to support me. I slowly lower myself onto the small loveseat adjacent to the desk and hold my breath. *Logan.*

He's entered Dana's office like he belongs here. His hair is a couple inches longer than I've ever seen it... and does he have a beard? *He grew a beard?*

Logan is wearing jeans. His untucked, dark gray shirt has the top button undone and he has a pencil stuck behind his ear and a pen in his mouth. Looking down, concentrating on a load of folders and legal pads he's carrying, he hasn't noticed me.

He deposits his burden on the corner of the desk and still not facing me, he starts to speak. It's somewhat unintelligible, thanks to the pen between his teeth. "So I just got off the phone with the legal department at the transportation office and I swear they..." He stops cold when he looks over and sees that it isn't Dana in her office. The pen falls from his mouth and hits the floor in front of him.

"Logan?" I feel like Alice in Wonderland. I've fallen down that damn rabbit hole and nothing is as it should be.

"Charli," he breathes out my name like a whispered prayer and I shiver at what it still does to me.

"What are you doing here?" I ask. Him being here, and looking like he does, makes no sense at all.

"Oh, I work here now," He says this like it should be perfectly clear, like this is totally logical instead of completely insane.

"You volunteer here? What about your real job?"

He smiles and shifts to sit on the corner of the desk. "This is my real job now."

"Since when? How? Why? What the hell, Logan..." *If he really works here, then why hadn't anyone told me?*

"I left Strickland and Burke a couple of months ago. It started when Liv asked me to help Dana with some legal issues. I figured out pretty fast that I loved being here and dreaded it every time I had to leave and go back to the firm. So, I talked with Dana and she hired me to handle all their legalities." He shrugs his shoulder with nonchalance. "With a charity this large it's more than a full-time job. She also helped me by getting my student loans taken care of through government programs in exchange for volunteer work and legal aid for those who can't afford it. This allowed me to be able to accept the more modest income the foundation can

259

afford to pay."

I start to panic. "Is this my fault? Did you do this because I made you think your career wasn't worthwhile or something to be proud of?" I stand up and start to pace. "Oh my God... Logan, you worked so hard and dreamed of being partner one day! Did I mess that up for you?"

His chuckle is lighthearted and real. The little laugh lines have returned and he looks...happy. "No, this isn't your fault. Well, maybe a little."

My stomach begins to hurt. *What have I done? His family must hate me!* "I'm sorry! I never meant to..." I say.

"Charli, listen to me. It isn't your fault in the way you think." He gets off the desk and grabs my shoulders to stop my pacing. "I didn't leave my job because you didn't like it. I left my job because I discovered I didn't like it. I wanted so badly to have a career that would make everyone impressed, instead of feel sorry for me. I grew up and went to school with kids that had a lot and we didn't. I wanted to give my parents and sister everything they'd never been able to afford. I didn't want my future children to feel like they missed out on anything. But I wasn't really paying attention. My family just wants me to be happy." He pauses to smile with the wonder of it. "They don't care about being wealthy and never did. And those other kids might've had a lot of stuff but I had love and a great home life. I've finally figured out what's really important. By using my education to help those who really know poverty and need, my parents are prouder of me than they ever were at my previous employer. I've never felt better about any decision I've made. This makes me happy." He puts his finger under my chin and raises my face toward his. "So, thank you, Charli."

I believe him. He wears the contentment much more comfortably than he'd ever worn those expensive suits. And I'm so happy for him and proud of him. *Oh, shit. Am I crying in front of this man again?*

"Don't cry, baby" He wraps his arms around me. I'd really believed that I would never feel him near me again. I'd also believed I was getting over him. *I was so wrong.*

My tears escalate and now I'm congested, red-faced, and my vision is blurred. *Shit. I'm doing the ugly cry.* I try to hide my face with my hands, but he pulls them away and wipes my face with the hem of his shirt.

"Why didn't anyone tell me?" I manage to choke this out between sobs and I'm relatively sure he understood the question.

"Because I asked them not to."

I start to pull away. *He didn't want me to know. He's over me and didn't want to see me anymore, and now I've caused this big scene. Shit.* "I'll just go," I whisper.

He takes both of my hands and pulls me over to the small sofa. Sitting down, he then pulls me onto his lap. "Please don't. I've missed you so much."

"Then why didn't you let me know you were here? Why didn't you tell me that you'd done all this?" I look down and twist my fingers together in my lap.

He sighs and leans forward until his head is resting on top of mine. "Because I was afraid. I was afraid that you'd never believe this decision was what I really wanted. I was afraid that you'd feel like you pushed me into this, that you'd worry I'd end up resenting you. And I was so damn afraid that you'd tell me you didn't want me anymore, no matter how my life had changed."

I raise my head and our eyes meet. I give him his favorite smile and then dive into the most amazing kiss we've ever shared. It goes on until we have to pull away to breathe again.

"Since that first night at the bar, I think I knew that for me, it's you. Only you. Always and forever... you," he whispers.

"I love you, Logan."

"I love you, Charli."

Epilogue: Liv

The Speech

"So apparently I'm supposed to stand up here and talk to you people at this thing?"

I'm standing up on the small stage near the back of the bar, wearing a floral print dress in shades of deep coral and forest green. I'm also totally rocking a pair of fucking amazing, pale apricot heels with an ankle strap. Because let's face it, all heels deserve an ankle strap. I look shit hot.

Okay, Charli looks pretty damn hot too. Apparently being engaged is a good look for her. Plus, I did her hair and makeup, so I deserve a little of the credit.

I look around at our friends and co-workers, at my moms, several people from the foundation and Logan's family. I just met his parents and sister tonight and Charli has warned me repeatedly to keep my mouth in check. I might need to avoid them since Ronan has provided copious amounts of alcohol for this engagement party.

So, let the speech begin!

"I'm the maid of honor and I've been informed a speech is required." Charli has looked a little worried since I stepped up and grabbed the mic, but Logan is taking it all in stride with a look of amused acceptance. He's pissed me off a few times but I've decided he's a keeper. Charli has decided the same and I'm glad they're in love and all that shit. I'm going to miss living with my best friend so badly, I'm avoiding thinking about it. I'm sure as hell not going to miss all the noise they make every night. I've had to invest in really good noise canceling headphones. I think they should have to reimburse me for them. They weren't cheap!

"So, I've lived with Charli most of our lives, and now I pass that torch on to our dear Logan. It won't be easy. They've been together for almost a year now and I still don't think he really gets what he's in for... but it's the burden you bear when you love our girl like we do. They may go broke trying to keep her supplied in chicken nuggets because that skinny bitch eats all day long. It's totally unfair. They might get kicked out of their apartment after she tries to bring home every stray animal she comes across. Stay strong, Logan."

I raise my glass in his direction and he laughs.

"He might bore her to death with his talk of litigation and legal loopholes. Let's be honest, he knows how to be a snooze fest... but they'll get through it all because they love each other. They have that rare love that forgives the faults, sees past the mistakes and sets an example for us all."

I look toward Charli and she is crying like a baby. *Damn it. Now I want to tear up too. That is not allowed in public!*

"Stop blubbering, Charli!" I yell over to her, "It will ruin all my hard work and make you look like shit!" This has the desired effect and she starts to laugh. "So raise your glass... to Logan and

Charli!"

I take a nice long drink and enjoy the burn as it goes down. I'm so happy for them, but I'd be lying if I said I wasn't a little jealous.

After I step down, and hand the microphone over to Scott so he can say a few words, I feel Charli clamp onto me like a vice grip. "I love you, Olivia. Thanks for that awesome speech. You rock."

"I do but so do you. I know Logan is the one and you'll be disgustingly happy together." I hug her back fiercely.

We stand together, listening to Scott's speech. It's funny and sweet but not quite as awesome as mine, of course.

I'm kidding. He nailed it, especially with his stories about Logan and the dirty diaper.

Speaking of diapers, everyone was more than a little relieved when he and Kelly found a sitter tonight. Ronan's poor ticker couldn't have stood another baby invasion in his bar.

Toasting complete, Logan comes over to give me a hug. "You're one of a kind, Liv."

"You're not so bad yourself." I lightly push his shoulder.

"Hey, Scott said Kelly is looking for you."

I groan and start to panic. *Is it rude for the maid of honor to leave early?*

"What's wrong?" he asks. "I thought you liked Kelly?"

"I do! But she's determined to find me a man and her blind dates suck!"

"Oh...is she still setting you up?" I can tell he wants to laugh.

"She's trying but after fertile Freddie and the five kids, Stinky Sam with the breath that makes you lose your appetite and Timothy with the..." I shudder with revulsion. "Nevermind, I'm just not ready to talk about Timothy yet."

"I get it. I'll ask Scott to have her lay off."

"Thanks. I think I just want to concentrate on my work for now, anyway. Since the show, my business has really picked up."

"That's great! Oh, that reminds me, I'd almost forgotten...do you shoot weddings?"

"Logan, you already know I'm going to shoot your wedding, even though I'm having to get some help since I have those maid of honor duties."

"Yeah, of course. I know you're doing ours but do you shoot engagements and weddings and stuff for others?"

"Sometimes. Why?" I ask.

"I have this friend, actually he's one of my groomsmen and should be here tonight, but he's running late. Anyway, he just got engaged. I was telling him about your work the other night and they'd love to meet you. We went to school together in my hometown, but he just moved here recently to open a new restaurant so I'm excited to hang out with him more often."

"Sure. What's his name?"

"Zachary Reynolds but he goes by Zac. His fiancé is Sabrina and I think you'll really like her." Logan grins at me. "She is a 'no bullshit' kind of girl."

"Then I like her already," I assure him.

"Great. I'll bring them over when they finally get here." He gives me a quick peck on the cheek and heads off to find Charli.

I wander off toward the bar to get another drink. *It's a party after all.* When I slide around behind the bar, a perk of working here, I see Kyle with his nose buried in a book. Again.

"You know it's okay to take a break once in a while, Kyle." I lean on the bar and raise one eyebrow. "You made a 4.0 in your first semester and Charli says this one is on track to be just as good."

He smiles at me but just shakes his head and goes back to reading, so I refill my glass and lean on the bar. It's nice to let it do the work of holding up these heavy tits for a change. I look around the room, pleased that Ronan offered the use of his precious bar and happy that Logan and Charli have so many great friends and family to attend. When my glass is all the way to my lips and I feel the amber liquid heading my way, I jerk involuntarily and spill it on the front of my dress and the top of the bar.

What the hell is he doing here?

Coming Next
Liv's Story: "The Fall"

I pull my best friend out of her chair and drag her off to the ladies' room. Logan furrows his brow but keeps his seat. He's used to me dragging Charli away when I need her. They've been married for a couple months now but she's been my best friend for my whole life.

"What's wrong, Liv?" she asks as soon as the door swings shut behind us.

"Charli, be honest with me. Is it wrong to be at a wedding, and want to fuck the groom?"

Acknowledgements

I want to thank my husband – Donnie. He is the stud muffin to my cupcake. To my oldest son, Shawn, you've made me so extremely proud of the man you've become and your support during this crazy adventure has been unwavering and more appreciated that you know. Tyler, my baby...how can I ever repay you for the countless hours of work as you formatted this novel, designed our website and navigated this entire scary "self-publish" idea we jumped into? This would never have happened without you.

Cupcakes & Kisses;
Karen

Calvin, you think I'm a complete nerd and love me anyway. I love you more. Kayla, my first baby, I can't believe you are all grown up and such an amazing woman. Steven, you became my son in a non-conventional way... but I know you were meant to be mine and I love you more than you can ever know. Hannah, you are the baby and the miracle that blessed all of our lives. I also have to thank Karen's boys, my "pseudo-sons," for all their invaluable help. I love them like they are mine... and they kind of are.

Love & Laughter;
Stacey

Thanks to **Amber Byford, DeAnna Ben**, and **Carol West**... aka "The Book Girls." We adore you and can't thank you enough for your help! The road trips, book signings, and epic adventures are unforgettable. (The sheets, D!!!) **Kristina Fisher**, you were such an awesome beta reader. You were blunt and honest but gentle and we loved that we could trust you for an honest opinion. **Tyler**, thanks again for the awesome formatting and help making this possible. **Donward**, forgive us for ever doubting your mad editing skills... you are totes amazeballs and we love you! **Jennifer Alexander** and **Kristin Mayer**, you guys were so great about answering all of our many questions quickly and never made us feel dumb for asking. Thank you to **Laura Hampton** with Swoon Worthy Books and iScream for the edits, our first professional review, and your amazing encouragement. **Kelly Elliott**, you rock. Even though you are so successful and so busy, you made time to meet with us and even bought us lunch!! You helped us figure out this whole writing thing. You were even willing to invest your personal time by reading our book and giving us advice (show not tell!) Thank you from the bottom of our hearts.

-Stacey & Karen

About The Authors

Once upon a time, these two hookers became best friends...

Stacey Brandon and Karen Bell both live in the same small Texas town on the Gulf Coast, are happily married and the proud Moms of awesome kids. Stacey owns and runs a photography studio and Karen designs and sews her own children's clothing line. They met over fifteen years ago when they decided to turn one large professional space into a single home for both businesses.

Well, that's all the boring facts expected to be included in an "about the author" page, right? The reality is so much more fun. Stacey and Karen and their families spend holidays together, travel together... and generally turn every situation into some-thing crazy and chaotic. They are both fluent in English, Sarcasm and Profanity and have decided the irrefutable proof of their best friend status is how often people assume they are "together" when in public. The poor husbands are good sports about it... and might even encourage this misconception at times for sheer entertainment value.

When Karen battled cancer... and kicked its ass... in 2014, they learned to value every day and quit worrying about what others think. Do what you love! Karen is happy to take advantage of the situation though. She loves to remind everyone she "had the CANCER, dammit!" and now she can always and forever claim the last brownie ;)

www.ingramcontent.com/pod-product-compliance
Lightning Source LLC
Chambersburg PA
CBHW020246180626
46810CB00006B/2387